The King's Executioner
By
Donna Fletcher

The King's Executioner

Cover art
Kim Killion Group

Ebook Design
A Thirsty Mind

Visit Donna's Web site
www.donnafletcher.com
http://www.facebook.com/donna.fletcher.author

Chapter One

Blyth sat in the gathering chamber, worries weighing heavily on her. She was not sorry for what she had done nor did she regret her decision, though it had broken her heart to send her daughter, Anin, away. What choice had she? She could not let Anin wed King Talon. It would not do. It would not do at all, especially if the King ever discovered the truth.

How could he though, since she was the only one who knew the secret.

Blyth shook her head. It would do her no good to dwell on it. It was here and now that mattered and she would see her daughter protected even if it meant her losing her own life.

She stood and walked around the large, stone encased fire pit in the center of the room, its smoke swirling up and out of the hole in the roof. The sun would rise soon. Those assigned to the feasting house were probably already busy preparing the morn repast. She pressed her hand to her middle as it protested the thought of food. She had eaten but a mouthful since sending her daughter away seven days ago and she had little flesh to waste away. She had always been thin and taller than most women and though her long, dark hair was now sprinkled liberally with gray, it still shined from the extra care she had always given it.

Blyth pushed the sleeve of her shift up to her shoulder to look thoughtfully at the arm bands that covered her arms. Body drawings were a source of pride to the various Pict tribes, each drawing representing something important. How many body drawings one wore depended on your tribe. The Lammok, Blyth's

3

tribe, only wore intricate arm bands. Each band signified the level of skill achieved with weapons. Blyth recalled her first drawing with fondness and pain. More bands followed through the years until both arms were nearly covered from shoulder to elbow. The men of her husband's tribe received their first body drawing with their first hunt and kill. More followed and for various reasons.

A shiver ran through Blyth when she recalled seeing some of the King's personal guard. Their upper bodies were covered with drawings, but it was said that no body drawings were like those of the King's executioner...Paine.

It was believed that Paine's body drawings magically appeared on him each time someone suffered at his hands or died by his battle-axe, fate having decreed that his evil be displayed for all to see. No one knew where he came from or if Paine was his true name.

The only thing she and others in Girthrig knew was that Paine was coming for Blyth.

"Do you want to lose your head, woman?"

Blyth jumped and her slim hand flew to her chest, her husband having nearly scared the life from her. She turned and watched him approach, tall, slender, though firm in body and hair that had turned more white than gray and with a scowl he did not often wear.

Cathbad gave his wife no time to answer. "You will stop this madness. You say you do not want Anin being dictated to by a husband? When have I ever dictated to you?"

"You are not King Talon. He dictates," Blyth said her tongue sharp.

"He is King, of course he dictates," Cathbad argued, shaking his head. "This nonsense ends now. When the executioner arrives, you will tell him what he wants to know."

"Or what?" Blyth asked, glaring at her husband. "You can do no worse to me than what the executioner will do."

Cathbad's dark eyes grew wide with anger and he turned, running his fingers roughly through his long hair while taking several steps away from his wife before turning once again and throwing his hands up. "You are a stubborn woman, but a good wife and I do not want to lose you. I had no choice but to agree to this union. No one denies King Talon. Besides, there is no place for Anin to hide. The executioner has never failed the King. He will force you to confess. "

Blyth took determined steps toward her husband, stopping to stand near face to face with him. "He can try."

Cathbad grabbed his wife by the shoulders. "He will make you suffer."

Blyth rested her brow upon her husband's. "I would suffer anything for my daughter."

Cathbad eased his wife away, then cupped her face in his hands. She was a beautiful woman and had only grown more beautiful with age, but worry had left lines and wrinkles that he had never seen before and he easily felt and understood her pain. But when the King commanded, his people listened. There was no other way.

"You cannot stop this union, Blyth," he said, hoping to make her see reason.

A lone horn sounded throughout the village as morn dawned without the sun and a second horn sounded soon afterwards, letting all know that someone approached.

Cathbad took his wife's hand. "The executioner has arrived."

"You will do nothing that will bring you harm. I will have your word on that," Blyth said, squeezing her husband's hand.

5

"You are already tearing my heart in two. What difference would more pain matter?"

"If you lift a hand to protect me, it will not only be you who suffers but our sons as well."

"Then remember that and tell the executioner what he wants to know." Cathbad did not give his wife a chance to respond, he hurried her outside and down the few wood steps to see that their people had lined both sides of the lone path to the feasting house in anticipation and curiosity of the executioner's arrival.

Heads turned and necks stretched when out of the morn's mist stepped a large, black wolf. His gait was slow and cautious and his fiery orange eyes roamed over each and every one there. His mouth was drawn back to show his sharp fangs, and a continuous low growl rumbled from him as he walked down the path.

As frightening as the wolf was, he was not half as frightening as the warrior who followed behind him. Not a sound, not even the slightest gasp was heard when the executioner came into view.

Never had Blyth seen a man the size of the executioner. He appeared a giant, standing a good head over the tallest man and a mantle hung on his broad shoulders, its hood draped over his bent head, leaving most of his face shrouded in mystery. Though the chill of harvest time had settled over the land, he wore no shirt under his dark tunic that barely covered his lower body. Smooth, dark hides were strapped to his muscled legs and foot coverings with leather ties.

He stopped a moment and threw back his hood, his cloak falling away from his arms.

Abundant and strange body drawings covered his thick-muscled arms and neck and one could only wonder as to the drawings that lay beneath his garments. His dark hair was cropped short around the sides and back, the remainder short but not shorn. If none of that caused one to gasp, his fine features and bold green eyes did, and Blyth's first thought was...how could one so pleasing to look upon be so cruel?

She continued staring along with her fellow tribesmen and the closer he came the more she saw and the more frightened she grew. His green eyes were empty. They held no warmth or coldness. There was nothing there. Nothing at all. And she could not help but notice that there were no lines or wrinkles around his eyes or mouth which meant he never smiled or frowned.

Could it be true? Could the executioner have no heart?

She lowered her glance, not wanting to gaze upon him a moment longer and she could not keep a gasp from slipping from her lips as her eyes fell on the battle-axe he held at his side. The double edged weapon appeared as if it was recently sharpened in anticipation of his next execution.

Cathbad heard his wife's sharp gasp and quickly wrapped his arm around her. He was relieved that he had sent his four sons away on what they believed were important matters. He wanted them gone when the executioner arrived, for he knew they would not stand idle and watch their mother suffer. He could not as well, and this day might bring both he and his wife's deaths.

The executioner did not stop when he reached the couple. He walked up the steps and as he passed Cathbad, said, "I will speak to your wife alone."

Cathbad kept his voice firm as he spoke. "I will—"

"Do as I say," the executioner ordered and opened the door and turned, casting a look at Blyth.

She whispered reassuring words to her husband as she struggled to free herself of his firm grasp. On trembling legs, she walked over to the door and slipped past the executioner without dare glancing at him.

"Bog, guard!" the executioner commanded and the wolf took a stance in front of the door as soon as it closed shut.

Blyth went to the fire pit and stretched her chilled hands out to the flames, hoping the heat would warm them and stop the shivers that had her trembling, though no doubt it was more fear than chills that had her body quivering.

After several silent moments, she managed to ask, "May I get you food or drink?" And before she lost the courage, she turned to face him. She stumbled back when she almost collided with him, he stood so close to her.

"Sit," he ordered and took her arm and hurried her to a bench at one of the tables, forcing her to do as he said.

"Why did you send your daughter away?" he asked.

Blyth had not expected that question, though the strength of his tone left no doubt that he would have an answer. "Anin would not make King Talon a good wife."

"That is not for you to decide."

"I am her mother and know her best, and the King would not be happy with her."

"The King does not seek happiness, merely a wife."

"How sad for him."

The executioner stared at her for a moment before he demanded, "Where is your daughter?"

"I do not know. Do what you will to me, but the answer will remain the same. I do not know."

He placed his battle-axe on the table and swung one leg over the bench a short distance from her.

Blyth sat frozen, too fearful to move. He was much more intimidating sitting so close to her, his muscles thicker and his eyes so barren that it seemed there was no life in him at all. She turned her eyes away only to

8

have her glance fall on his hand that rested on the table near the handle of his battle-axe. His hand was large and no doubt strong from swinging his weapon with enough force to chop off heads or to inflict endless suffering.

Blyth struggled to regain her wits and to delay or, dare she hope, prevent any torture. "Let me tell you why Anin would not suit King Talon." When he nodded, she wondered that perhaps her words would not be wasted. A foolish thought, since he was here to carry out the King's command and nothing she said would change that.

"King Talon needs a strong wife, a woman who will stand by his side with courage and fight beside him if necessary. A woman who will give him many strong sons."

"Like the four brave sons you gave your husband. Are you not from the Lammok Tribe of women warriors? Does your daughter not have your warrior heart?"

Blyth shook her head slowly. "Anin is gentle and kind, though strong in her own way. She is no warrior."

"The King will see her kept safe."

"And will he discard her as he did his other two wives when she fails to bear him a child?"

"Take care with your words, woman, or you will soon have no tongue."

"Forgive me," Blyth said quickly realizing she had gone too far. There may be talk that it was not his wives, but the King himself who could father no child, but no one dare say or imply it.

The executioner rose off the bench, grabbing his battle-axe as he stood.

Blyth flinched, for she thought he meant to bring it down on her, but she felt nothing.

"Outside," he ordered sharply.

"Please," Blyth said, "whatever you intend to do to me, do it here where my husband does not have to be witness to it."

He pointed to the door. "I will not tell you again."

Blyth walked slowly to the door, every step laborious, fearful of the suffering to come and not only her own. Her heart weighed heavily with worry for her husband and her people. It was good she did not know where Anin was, for if she had known, she would have confessed much too easily to the executioner. She trusted her daughter would know where to seek shelter and be kept safe.

The black wolf moved to the executioner's side as soon as he walked out the door.

Blyth saw the look of relief on her husband's face when he saw that she was unharmed and he was quick to stretch his hand out to her. She did not wait to see if the executioner would stop her, she hurried to her husband's side, taking firm hold of his hand.

The executioner walked over to stand in front of them both, though he looked to Cathbad as he spoke. "The tribes in the south are restless. You are Overlord of the Western Region. Will you be ready to stand with your King if necessary?"

Cathbad understood that his wife's refusal to obey the King had placed his allegiance in jeopardy, so he was quick to reassure. "I, my sons, and my tribe will fight to the death for King Talon,"

"He will be pleased to hear that and now I go and collect your daughter Anin and take her to King Talon to become his wife."

"Thank goodness you came to your senses," Cathbad said to his wife.

Blyth stared in surprise at the executioner and shook her head confused. "I could not tell him what I do not know."

"You told me everything I needed to know or you would not be standing here unharmed beside your husband." With a quick step, he was beside her and whispered in her ear, "I will learn your secret and may mercy be with you if I must return here."

Blyth felt her breath lock in her chest, her limbs grow weak, and just before she dropped into a dead faint, she saw the executioner and his wolf fade into the mist.

Chapter Two

Anin was too tired to go any further and with light soon fading to darkness, it was better she sought shelter. She had hoped to reach her mother's people, the Lammok, before it turned dark, but her gait had slowed, her legs finally protesting the days of endless walking. She hoped she had enough strength to secure herself a safe spot to sleep. If she began her journey when the sun rose, she would reach the Lammok village by the time the sun was high in the sky.

She surveyed the area with a keen eye. The forest could be welcoming, but when the light faded it could turn dangerous and being alone made her all the more vulnerable. Of course asking the forest creatures for safe passage always helped and since her journey thus far had been without incident, she believed they were looking after her.

With a tilt of her head and turning slowly, she finally found what she was looking for, a tree that would cradle her safely until the sun rose once again. She went hunting for the vine that clung tenaciously to certain trees and, once found and gratitude given, she cut a long piece with the small dagger she kept in a sheath on the belt at her waist.

It was not difficult for her to throw the vine over the lowest branch that was too high for her to reach and use both ends to work her way up the tree and settle herself in the crook of two thick branches after curling up the vine so that she could use it to get down on the morrow.

The leaves were just beginning to turn so they were still plentiful on the branches and hid her well. No one would know she was there and with a gentle hand pressed against the rough bark she asked the tree spirit to keep her safe.

Before it grew too dark, she peered past the branches to take one last glance over the surrounding area and to make sure she was alone. She smiled when she spotted a nearby stream, pleased that she would be able to wash up and look presentable when she arrived at her mother's village.

Her green, soft wool cloak served as an excellent blanket and juniper berries in the pouch at her waist would sustain her until morn. She had collected them along the way during the day so she would be prepared if she did not reach her mother's people by night. Once she arrived at the Lammok village, she would be fed well by her mother's two sisters.

A lone howl had her pulling her cloak tighter around her and had her wishing she was home tucked safely in her sleeping pallet. She missed her mum and da terribly and even her four brothers who could torment at times and be much too protective at other times. But she loved each and every one of them.

She had always thought that one day she would join with a man of her tribe or a neighboring tribe and live a good life with him and with her family nearby. She never imagined or desired to go to the center of the Pict Kingdom—Pictland—home of the ruling High King and away from all that was familiar to her.

When word arrived that King Talon had chosen her to be his wife, it had been received with mixed feelings by all. Her father had seemed proud that she had been chosen to be Queen to King Talon. Her mother had been shocked and insisted no such union would take place. Her four brothers, Forgan, Reid, Turcan and Hance thought it splendid, seeing the benefits it would bring them having their sister as Queen.

After a fairly short time, it was apparent to all that no amount of talking with her mother would change her mind. She insisted that Anin would not wed a man who would dictate to her. That Anin's life was hers to choose. While she had never seen her da dictate to her mum, she was aware that some tribes gave their women little freedom while in other tribes the men and women were equal and still other tribes, like her mum's tribe the Lammok, the women were warriors and allowed no one to dictate to them.

Her father had come to her and asked her to help him make her mother see that the decision was final and no amount of arguing would change it. Anin's mum refused to listen to her. It had not helped that her mum had known that Anin was not pleased with the King's edict. After all, her mum had promised her that she could wed a man of her own choosing, the way of the Lammok Tribe. Anin wished that could be so, but when the King commanded his people obeyed. When her mum insisted that she leave and seek shelter someplace safe, Anin knew what she must do.

She would go to Lammok village and wait there for the executioner, accepting her fate, for he was not a foolish man and would surely track her there. She wished the King had sent someone else to collect her. The executioner was known to instill fear on sight and she was already apprehensive enough with the prospect of being King Talon's wife.

The executioner was one of the King's most trusted warriors and could chop off a person's head with little effort or reason and the King would praise him for it, or so she heard. Though, she told herself that she had no worry as long as she went willingly with the executioner. What truly should concern her was wedding the King. But then, it was in fate's hands and fate would have her way. She always did.

Fatigue took hold and soon Anin fell into a deep sleep not waking until well after the sun had risen and to a disturbing sound. She shook herself fully awake as silently as she could, not wanting to alert anyone or anything to her presence.

The sound came again and she realized what it was. It was splashing water. Someone or something was in the stream. She carefully leaned forward to take a look, fearful of what she would see.

Her hand flew to her mouth to stop the gasp that rushed past her lips. A man, completely naked, stood in the stream, the water hugging his legs past his ankles. He was made of solid muscles that rippled over wide shoulders and ran down along his back to grip at a taut backside. The muscles continued down his long legs and while it was quite amazing to gaze upon such a sculpted body, it was his body drawings that utterly mesmerized. With the exception of his face, they appeared to cover his entire body. Never had she seen such drawings. They curved and arched and turned with his every movement. It was almost as if they were weapons ready to strike at anyone who dared to touch him.

He turned, and she quickly slapped her other hand over the one already covering her mouth. Symbols covered the front of him as well and she was not quite sure where to settle her eyes first or was it her curiosity that had her glance settling between his legs? While symbols circled and spread out around his manhood, it was not covered with any. He was quite a size for not being ready for coupling and she was surprised at the sudden thought as to how large he would grow when ready to join with a woman.

The women of her mum's tribe were warrior women who expected their men to be as strong as them and when the women gathered together they would often talk of a man's coupling abilities. So, Anin was well informed of what she should expect from a man and what she should give in return.

It was odd that she should have that thought now and quickly looked up at his face, and her eyes turned wide. Never had she seen a man with such startlingly fine features and such bold green eyes. He ran his fingers through his dark wet hair, cut short at the top and sheared at the sides. He swiped the beads of water roughly off his body and walked toward the tree she sat in. She eased her hands off her mouth and sat completely still. Hopefully, he would slip his garments on and leave or else she would be stuck there until he did.

It was when he stopped beneath the tree and reached for his garments on the ground that fear squeezed at her insides and a chill settled over her. A black wolf sat at the trunk of the tree, a battle-axe lying next to him.

"The King has sent me for you."

The executioner had found her.

"When I finish getting into my garments, I will get you down from the tree."

Startled, she quickly pressed herself against the tree, whether for protection or to hide she did not know. Neither, however, would serve any purpose. There was no hiding from him and his powerful size made her think that he could simply shake the tree and dislodge her.

He was there to collect her and that was what he would do. Had she not been waiting for this moment when she would meet her fate? She sat gathering her courage and wondering when he had arrived. And how had he found her? No one knew where she was going. Looking down at the black wolf staring up at her, she got her answer. The animal surely had tracked her.

Since he seemed not at all bothered by his nakedness, she wondered if he was from the Drust Tribe to the north. They were the fiercest of the Pict tribes and the ones who covered themselves completely with body drawings. They wore little to no clothing particularly when they went into battle and were victorious more often than not. With the journey to Pictland taking a good six or more days, perhaps she would find out.

Anin pressed her hand against the tree, asking for courage to face her fate. She felt a tingle run along her arm and pleased that the tree spirit had answered, she called out, "I can get down myself just have the wolf move."

"Did you not hear me? I will get you down."

A shiver ran through Anin, his strong tone a command that was meant to be obeyed. Why she did not do as he said, she did not know. Or was it the thought of being caught in arms that brought endless suffering too frightening a thought?

"I am ready. Drop down and I will catch you."

Anin grabbed onto one of the branches and leaned over, sticking her head past the leaves to look at him. She was met by bold green eyes glaring back at her. She hurried to speak before she lost her courage. "You cannot mean that."

Paine had long ago stopped feeling. It was what made it possible for him to torture and kill without regret. That was why he did not understand the sudden catch in his chest when he stared at the soft blue eyes wide with surprise that glared at him.

He nearly snarled at her when he said, "I always mean what I say."

Anin persisted. "I can climb down."

"You will drop down."

"You might not catch me."

"Stop talking nonsense and drop down out of there right now," he ordered sharply.

"And if you fail to catch me what then will you tell the King?" she argued.

17

"How did you get up there?" he asked annoyed at being questioned. No one ever questioned him. They simply obeyed or suffered for it.

Anin was quick to get the curled vine and show it to him.

"And how would that help you to get down?"

"I will show you," she said, not wanting to drop down into his arms. She wrapped the vine around a branch and let the rest fall to the ground. Before she could take firm hold of the vine and lower herself, he scaled the tree with the help of the vine, slipped his arm around her waist, yanked her against his hard chest and lowered them both down.

"Listen well, Anin," he said, not letting her go once their feet touched the ground. "You will do what I say when I say it and without question. Do you understand?" She stared at him as if from a distance, her hand resting against his chest. Even through his tunic, he could feel her warmth and gentleness. The top of her head had barely reached his chin when he had taken hold of her and his arm had gone a good ways around her waist, she was so slim. And her breasts felt ample crushed against his chest. He grew annoyed at his thoughts and gave her a shake when he should have given himself one. "Do you hear me?"

She jumped as if startled and quickly nodded.

"You will follow my every command?"

She nodded again.

He let her go, grabbed his battle-axe, and said, "Stay close."

She obeyed without question and fell in step behind him while her thoughts drifted back to when she was young. One day her oldest brother Forgan had suffered a bad wound to his leg while practicing with a spear. One of the wise women had been tending him when Anin entered the room. She walked over to him and with concern placed her small hand on his arm to comfort him and tell him all would be well. As soon as she touched him, she started crying and telling him how sorry she was that he was in such terrible pain and how he should not worry that Da would not be angry with him if he shed tears. She had felt his awful pain and his worries and had spoken them aloud.

Her mum had grabbed her arm, squeezing it hard, and rushed her out of the room and told her never to do that again. She had not even known what she had done, but her mum had been so angry with her that she had given her word on it. It was years before another such incident happened again, but that time she wisely remained silent. It took a few more such incidents for her to realize that there were times when she touched people she could feel their pain, worry, or joy. She dared not speak a word about it. She was much too fearful of what people would think.

Meeka, the wise woman, had tried, through the years, to speak to her about the incident with her brother, but Anin would say nothing. She had wished that whatever it was it would go away, until finally she realized it was part of her and she would never be rid of it. So, she found a way to cope with it and discovered that at times it not only benefited her, but others as well.

Never, though, had she felt what she did when her hand came to rest on the executioner.

The memory of it had her steps faltering. She did not want to think on it and never did she want to feel it again.

Emptiness. Nothingness. Hollow.

It was as if he was dead and still walked amongst the living. What caused a man to feel nothing, care for nothing? Had he made so many suffer and taken so many lives that life meant nothing to him anymore? She would be wise to remember that such a man was dangerous and she would be wise to never touch him again.

Chapter Three

After feeling as if she was running and could not take another step, Anin stopped and called out, "You need to slow your pace; I cannot keep up with you."

He stopped, turned, and walked over to her.

"Your name is Paine, is it not, at least that is what my mum told me," she said through heavy breaths. She did not want to continue to think of him as the executioner and calling him by his name would help with that.

"My name does not matter. What matters is getting you to the King and if you think slowing us down so that your mother's tribe can help you escape me, it is a foolish thought. I will slay anyone who attempts to take you from me."

Anin believed him. "I know I have no choice but to go with you and I have no choice but to wed the King. And my mother's tribe does not even know I am here."

"Then why do they follow us?"

Anin quickly glanced around, but saw no one. That meant nothing, though, since Lammok warriors were good at blending with the forest.

"There are two and they have followed us since shortly after you left your nest in the tree."

Anin shook her head. "No one knew I was coming here."

"Your mother knew."

"Did you harm my mum?" Anin said, anger making it sound more like a shout. She had thought his wolf had tracked her and that he had never bothered with her mum.

"It was not necessary. When we spoke she told me where you went without knowing it herself."

"You would have harmed her?" She did not know why she asked, she knew his answer.

"I harm if I have cause to harm. You would do well to remember that."

"You would harm me, the King's future wife?"

"No, but I would harm anyone who tries to take you from me, including family or friend."

An icy chill settled over her. She would never want to see another suffer because of her. She quickly shouted, "He knows you are here. Show yourselves."

Paine glanced around as he said, "Bog, guard!"

The wolf took a stance in front of Anin, bared his teeth and growled in warning.

Anin was surprised to see her mum's two sisters, Socha and Cara step from behind bushes on opposite sides of the path. The only body drawings the Lammok wore were arm bands that dominated both arms, the more bands the more skilled the warrior. Socha was one of the very few Lammok warriors whose shoulder was covered with a band. It signified the highest skilled warriors in the tribe. The bands also announced them as Lammok warriors. They were both tall and regal in stature. Long, soft dark hair was the mark of the Lammok women and it was worn intricately braided and secured to the back of the head when they went into battle so it would not hinder them. They wore it that way now.

Surprised at seeing them and shocked that they appeared ready for battle, Anin said, "How did you know I was here?"

Socha, the oldest of the three sisters stepped forward. "Blyth sent word of what was happening and suspected you might come our way. She asked that we watch out for you. We see that we were too late, unless you tell us otherwise."

Leave it to Socha to be the wise one. She always gave thought and sought a solution to a situation if there was time and Anin was relieved until Cara spoke up.

"Why should she be forced to wed the King? The only thing he wants from her is for her to breed as many sons as possible. He could care less for her."

"Watch your tongue," Paine warned sharply. "You speak of the King."

Socha shook her head at her sister and kept her voice calm when she looked to Paine and spoke. "We have great respect for the King. His uniting of the tribes saved many lives."

"And caused too many to start blending. Anin should be a full bred Lammok like her mum."

"Silence your mouth, Cara, for you speak unwisely. Lammok women choose their husbands, whether they be from the Lammok Tribe or not. It is might and courage we look for in a man and Blyth found it in Cathbad of the Girthrig Tribe, and they have done well together."

"Yes, Blyth has done well because she found a mate her equal. Anin is no match for the King."

"Cara!" Socha snapped and sent an angry glance at her sister.

Cara ignored it. "I speak the truth whether you want to hear it or not. Blyth is right not wanting Anin to wed the King. He is of superior strength and courage while Anin," —Cara looked to Anin— "you will never match your mum's strength never mind the King's. He will discard you without care or thought as he did to his last two wives."

Anin had always thought her mum's people did not feel her worthy of being a Lammok, but this was the first time anyone spoke of it to her. She went to speak, but Paine spoke before she could.

"You better hope she has the strength to go with me and wed the King, for if you try to stop me from taking her I will slay the both of you and leave your bodies in pieces for the forest creatures to feast upon. And from what I know of your burial ritual—you must die whole—that would mean once dead you could never move beyond."

Cara's dark eyes widened in fury and she went to take a step forward.

"I go with Paine willingly," Anin shouted. "I will be King Talon's wife."

Cara looked as if she snarled when she turned to the executioner and said, "Were you given that name because of all the pain you bring people?"

Paine stepped toward her. "I took that name so people would know what to expect when they meet me. Shall I show you?"

Anin hurried to say, "We have a long journey ahead of us. We must be leaving. Stay well, Aunt Socha and Cara, worry not about me, and please let Mum know I made this choice willingly so that she does not do anything foolish."

"Stay well," Socha said.

"Stay strong," Cara said, though with little faith, and the two sisters disappeared into the forest.

Without a word to her, Paine began walking and she obediently fell in step behind him, Bog trailing behind her. Hearing Cara, the youngest of her mum's sisters say openly what Anin had felt for some time weighed heavily upon her. It also made her wonder if her mum thought the same of her. Was that why she had sent her away? Did she believe her daughter too weak to wed the King? Was she disappointed that she had not grown as tall and strong as a Lammok woman or that she was not nearly as skilled with a weapon as they were even though she had tried desperately to be as accomplished as her mum.

Perhaps becoming the King's wife would show her mum that she did not lack strength or courage. She only hoped it would be so.

The day wore on and so did their steps. They had not stopped once to rest or take nourishment and if they continued this endless pace, Anin was sure that she would simply collapse. She was about to call out to Paine and let him know that she needed to rest when he suddenly stopped.

She sighed with relief.

"You have no more than a few moments."

Anin walked to a tree, sat, and rested her back against the tree trunk, wishing she could remain there much longer than only a few moments. Her glance went to Paine as she ate the last of the juniper berries she had in her pouch. He stood with his back to her, looking out across the stretch of rocky land they were about to cross. She was not familiar with this area, for they had left Lammok land some time ago and there was never any need for her to travel this way.

Paine turned and Anin was surprised when he walked over to her and sat to rest against a tree not far from her. He closed his eyes and that pleased Anin, since it meant they would sit and rest a while longer.

His battle-axe remained in his hand, though it rested at his side ready to strike if necessary. The twin edges of the blade appeared well tended and terribly sharp. Though, it would be the strength of the blow that would bring a lingering or swift death, and the thick muscles in his arms were proof that he could easily deliver a swift death.

Bog suddenly appeared and stretched out in front of them. Never had she thought a wolf could be tamed, but Bog obeyed Paine's every command. They were a strange pair, wolf and executioner, and she wondered how they came to be.

Paine opened his eyes to see Anin staring at him and she did not look away when his eyes met hers. He was once again captured by the soft blue color of her eyes. There was gentleness to them and deep warmth that invited. She had lovely features, creamy skin, and a body that would be pleasing to touch.

He felt himself stir and hurried to stand and turn his back on her. She was the King's intended and he had no right to think such thoughts. What troubled him even more was that he even had such thoughts about her. He took a woman when he felt the need, but rarely did a particular woman stir him.

He turned to face her and felt it again as he looked upon her. His body stirred, his manhood beginning to swell and once again he turned away from her, silently cursing himself.

This would not do. He would get her to the King and be done with it. He heard her struggle to her feet, but he would not turn and help her. He would not touch her. He would not think about her.

"Bog, watch," he commanded and the wolf took off.

"Where does he go?" Anin asked curious.

"To do what he is told as should you," Paine snapped and started walking.

It was going to be a long journey with him ordering her about. Anin once again followed behind him relieved the brief rest had helped some. She was also relieved that Paine continued to temper his pace.

As the day wore on, the sky grew increasingly cloudy and a chill filled the air. Travel was slower than before due to the rocky terrain. She had almost fallen twice and each time she had cried out, Paine had turned and admonished her to watch her step. The third time she righted herself quickly and kept herself from crying out. She would not have him reproach her again.

Suddenly a lone, mournful howl filled the air and Anin followed Paine's lead and stopped along with him. It seemed as if he waited for something, and then it came again, another mournful howl.

Anin was shocked when Paine grabbed her and flung her over his shoulder and took off running. Her insides tightened with worry. Something was wrong, terribly wrong for him to do this. His grip felt like a metal shackle, he held her so tightly and his speed was far faster than she thought possible, especially with her as an added burden.

She raised her head, her body tensed, and she bit back the scream on her lips. Nearly naked warriors, body drawings covering their entire bodies were rushing toward them. They were Drust warriors. But what were Drust doing this far south? She jumped when they began to scream like evil banshees.

"How many?" Paine shouted.

A quick count had her saying, "Six Drust warriors." She gasped. "And they draw their bows."

Paine ran faster and the arrows fell short of reaching them.

He stopped suddenly and dropped her off him and as she scrambled to her feet she realized why. He had made it to the edge of the woods. They would have cover here. He grabbed her arm and hurried her over to a large tree and hoisted her up to the lowest branch.

"Grab on," he ordered.

Anin struggled to do as he said but the branch was not easy to reach. She felt his hand at her bottom and with one hard shove she was up on the branch.

"Go higher and hide." With that he moved away from the tree and raised his battle-axe ready to fight.

27

Anin made her way to a higher branch, finding a spot where she could watch what went on below without being seen. How could one man defeat six warriors and Drust warriors at that? They were one of the fiercest warriors. Again she wondered what they were doing in this area, and why they were attacking them.

Her eyes turned wide when she watched Paine knock two arrows out of the air with his battle-axe and what followed next astounded her. With swift and precise blows of his weapon, two Drust warriors fell. Paine grabbed one of the fallen warrior's spears. Four warriors descended on him and she feared for his life. Suddenly, out of nowhere Bog appeared, taking one warrior down, his fangs buried in the back of the warrior's neck. In quick succession, Paine downed two more warriors, one with his weapon and the other with the spear while the last warrior went for Bog, spear in hand. Bog was faster. He launched himself at the warrior, his mouth closing around the wrist that held the spear. The warrior delivered a hard blow to Bog's side, but the animal refused to let go of him. Before he could deliver another stinging blow, Paine brought his axe down on the warrior.

Paine stepped around the fallen warriors and over to the tree, resting his battle-axe against the side. "Hurry and drop down," he called up.

Anin hurried to the lower branch and looked down.

He held out his arms. "We have no time to waste. There could be more warriors on the way. Trust me. I will catch you."

Anin had no choice. She took a deep breath, closed her eyes, and stepped off the branch.

"You can open your eyes now."

Anin did, his green eyes staring back at her and his strong arms tight around her.

28

"You are safe with me. I will always be there to protect you and catch you when needed."

A flutter settled deep inside her and without thinking she rested her hand to his chest and said, "That is truly kind of you."

He stared at her a moment before saying, "I am not kind. I do what the King commands." He placed her down on the ground and hastily grabbed his battle-axe. "We must go and keep a fast pace."

Anin had many questions on her mind, but she knew now was not the time to ask them. Besides, something else troubled her. Something she could not speak with him about. Though, she asked with concern as he hurried her away, "Is Bog well?"

"He has suffered worse. He will be fine."

She looked at the wolf that had once again taken a position behind her and said, "You are a brave one."

His response was a low growl.

The pace that Paine set was far faster than she expected, but then the prospect of more Drust warriors attacking them kept her going without complaint. She thought or perhaps hoped there would be no time to think, but she was wrong. She could not stop her thoughts from drifting to what she had felt when she had foolishly rested her hand to his chest.

The emptiness was still there, only now there was a stirring of sorts. It was faint, but it was there. She had felt it. She had also felt it in herself and she feared what it might mean.

29

Chapter Four

Paine watched Anin drop to the ground exhausted. She sat there for a few moments, staring at the stream a few feet away. She had to be aching to drink from it. He certainly was after the difficult pace they had kept. Bog was already drinking himself full.

He warned himself to let her be, she would make her way to the stream given time. She was stronger than she looked and stronger than what some thought of her. She might not have her mother's height or warrior's body, but she had strength none the less. She would have never survived the day if she had not been strong. Besides, it was not for him to worry about. His task was to deliver her safely to King Talon.

Her soft groan sent a twist to his middle that annoyed him. He had cared nothing for those the King had sent him after. Not so this woman. When she had dropped down out of the tree into his arms, his body had stirred once again, though more strongly this time. He had wanted to let her go and yet he had not wanted to let her go. He did not know why he had spoken the words he had to her. They seemed to have flowed from his lips of their own accord. It had been her calling him kind that had returned him to his senses.

He watched her stumble for a few moments as she tried in vain to get to her feet. Finally, he could take no more. He walked over to her and had her up in his arms before her legs gave way beneath her again. He carried her over to the stream and placed her by the edge so that she could scoop up handfuls of water.

He remained near her side, cupping his large hands and eagerly quenching his own thirst and saw that she did the same, though at a much slower pace. When she finished, she dropped on her back on the ground.

"I am too tired to move and too tired to eat, yet I am hungry," she said a yawn following.

"We have not finished walking for the day." He stood and snatched his battle-axe off the ground.

She raised herself up on her elbows and turned a disheartened glance on him. "That cannot be so. Dusk will settle soon, then darkness."

"It is only a short distance from here...a dwelling that will shelter us from the chilled night."

Anin groaned and struggled to sit up. She struggled even more, trying to get to her feet. Her body had had enough, especially her legs. They had no strength left to them. Still, she fought against her body's munity and continued to try and stand.

Paine could watch her for only so long before he once again scooped her up into his arms. "You had better grow stronger if you are to be Queen." He could not believe the ache in his chest that he felt when he saw the hurt his words had caused her.

Annoyance. Annoyance at her had caused the ache, nothing more.

No anger filled her response, simply truth. "I am who I am and if the King finds me lacking, then he need not take me as his queen."

Paine was quick to warn her. "I would be careful of what you say to the King. He is accustomed to his commands being obeyed without question, and he is not a patient man."

At the moment, Anin cared nothing for the King. All she could think on was that her head was growing too heavy to keep erect. She could not keep it from falling of its own accord onto Paine's chest, and she sighed with relief as her eyes fluttered closed once her head was cushioned upon it. She did not want to think about the King, about nearly losing her life today, or how comfortable it felt in Paine's arms. She simply wanted to sleep.

Paine was aware sleep had claimed her as soon as her body turned limp. It was not long before he entered the lone hut, the cold fire pit being the only thing there besides cobwebs. Though the night air was chilled, he could not chance smoke from a fire being seen, so the pit would remain cold tonight.

He rested his battle-axe against the wall, then latched the door with the wooden toggle. Bog would be busy hunting to appease his hunger and rest nearby for the night, while keeping alert to any danger. He glanced around, trying to find a comfortable spot for Anin to sleep. There was only cold earth to lay her upon.

His own body began to protest the long day as did his stomach. He had planned to hunt once they stopped for the day, the unexpected attack having changed his plans. Now it was too late to hunt and he was too tired.

On the morn, he would catch fish from the stream and they would eat. For now...he moved his weapon closer to the corner where he lowered himself down to settle for the night. He was about to place Anin beside him when she shivered in his arms and cuddled closer against him, seeking warmth.

He stared at her face as lovely in sleep as when she was awake. He had also noticed that she always appeared pleasant, seldom wore a frown, and was not quick to anger. He wondered how she would fare with the King. He was a powerful man who respected strength, though demanded obedience. His word was not to be challenged and while he wanted a strong woman to be his Queen, there were few women who had the strength to meet his demands or cope with his unpredictable temperament.

With a soft sigh Anin moved, as if settling herself against him for the long night ahead. Instinctively, his arms grew tighter around her and he was annoyed to feel another ache grab at his chest and a stirring disturb his loins. It troubled him to feel this way...to feel at all. Both were obstacles he did not need nor did he want, and he would let nothing stand in his way of completing his task.

Without the slightest hesitation, he placed Anin on the ground beside him. She was the King's intended and he would see her delivered safely to him and be done with it. How many times had he reminded himself of that today? Once was far too many. He rested his head back against the wall and closed his eyes, knowing he would drift in and out of sleep while remaining alert to the slightest sound or movement. And as soon as light rose in the sky, they would be on their way.

Thoughts would not let him rest. The attack today concerned him. He was aware there were those from the various tribes who had not agreed with uniting under one King and continued to cause problems. After the Unification Ceremony, a joyful occasion for most, not one tribe dared to attack the King's executioner when they came across him or when he arrived to carry out the King's command.

So what had happened to change that today? Had it been because he had had the King's intended with him? Was someone trying to prevent this union? If so, were there others he needed to be concerned about? This attack did not bode well for the King and the sooner he delivered Anin to him the better.

Something drifted Paine out of his light sleep. He sat there a moment, his back still resting against the wall, and listened for any sounds. Not hearing any, he opened his eyes and saw that Anin had rolled close and was snuggled up against his side for warmth, not that he could blame her. The earth floor had a chill that ran through you after being on it a while.

He was about to move her, then thought she would only roll back again, so he left her as she was. Besides, they both could use the warmth.

He drifted back to sleep and it seemed like only moments later something stirred him from it again. His body felt heated and as he opened his eyes, he realized why. He was aroused. He looked down and saw that Anin's hand was tucked between his legs, covering his manhood. He stared at the way she intimately cupped him, as if she was laying claim to him. The thought fueled his arousal and he silently cursed himself.

Most hastily, he took her hand and moved it off him. As soon as he let go of it, she moved it back to where it had been, though this time she tucked her fingers tighter between his legs and settled the palm of her hand firmly over his manhood that was growing increasingly harder and warmer.

He tightened his lips and released a low groan. Again, it felt as if she was refusing to release her claim on him, and it troubled him that her innocent gesture could arouse him so easily. He took her hand and this time he tucked it firmly between her chest and where she lay against his side. Of course, it did not help that his hand grazed her breast. It was plump, though not too large, enough to fill his hand. Of course, it only added to his now aching arousal. It would be a long night.

He was never more pleased to see the dawn, though it was a gray one. He hurried to his feet and left Anin sleeping while he went to catch enough fish to provide sustenance for the long day ahead. He left Bog guarding the door.

Something tickled Anin's nose and her eyes hurried open when she realized it was the scent of fish cooking. Her stomach rumbled as she licked her dry lips almost tasting the delicious fare. She sat up hastily and winced at the soreness in her body, the cold, hard earth she had slept on not having helped. She got to her feet, stretching away any aches that persisted and intent on settling the rumblings in her stomach. Her hands made quick work of dusting the dirt off her garments. She dropped her head forward and ran her fingers through her dark hair to get any dirt out of it, then tossed her head back and ran her fingers through her hair again. She took pride in her hair, it being the one thing so much like her mum's.

Anin smiled, seeing the two fish speared on a stick and roasting over the fire when she walked out of the small dwelling.

"I was about to wake you. The fish is ready and once we are done, we need to be on our way," Paine said and looked up as he handed her one of the sticks. Her cheeks were tinged a soft red and her slim lips looked as if they had been kissed by the dawn's dew. He almost reached out to tuck the wisp of her long, dark hair that fell over one eye behind her ear, but stopped himself.

Anin took the stick most gratefully and sighed aloud when, careful not to burn her fingers, she picked off a piece of white meat and hurried it into her mouth. "This is delicious," she said, savoring the flavor.

"Fill yourself as much as you can, for we will not be eating again until this evening," he said, forcing his attention off her and onto the fish.

Anin was careful not to take bone with the meat and careful not to mention that she could pick berries along the way to appease any hunger, since she did not think he would approve. She sneaked a peek at him through bites. He was a fine looking man with a solid body, a sign of strength. His body drawings fascinated her. They were well-crafted and it made her wonder if the tale that the drawings simply appeared were true or was it that an exceptionally skilled drawing master had done such artful work.

You could tell from body drawings what tribe a person was from and learn something about them upon meeting, the body drawings speaking before words were exchanged. But Paine's drawings were different and told her nothing whereas her lack of body drawings spoke loudly. Her skills were few. She could not even prepare fish as near as well as Paine and by now she should at least have had a few body drawings, but she had none. Paine had not remarked about it, which was why she made no mention of his.

She continued feasting on the fish, intending to pick off every last morsel. In between bites, she asked the question that had been on her mind since yesterday. "Why did the Drust want to kill us?"

"A band of outcasts, trying to stir up trouble," he said.

Anin shook her head. "I do not believe so. It is known since the Unification Ceremony that anyone who dared to harm the King's executioner would suffer for it. No one objected, since you do deeds no one else wishes to do. So why would the Drust break the King's edict?"

"There are those who continue to object to the uniting of the tribes and will continue to cause trouble."

Anin finished the last of the fish and brushed her hands of the small specks left. She did not voice her thoughts, for he would not receive them well. She could not stop from wondering if it was not the uniting of the tribes the Drust objected to, but King Talon.

Paine sent Bog to follow Anin when she went to see to her care. She was not gone long and went straight to the stream when she returned to wash her face and hands. The meal looked to have revived her strength. He only hoped their journey this day would not be as grueling or as challenging as yesterday, though the pace would remain strong. He wanted to get her safely to the King as fast as possible.

Anin followed behind Paine, and Bog trailed behind her just as they had done yesterday. Though now and again, he would disappear only to return and take up his post behind her. She was glad she heard no howl when he was gone, for she realized his howl warned Paine of impending danger.

By mid-day they reached open land that stretched as far as one could see. The hilly, desolate area could leave them vulnerable, though it would also be more difficult for anyone to follow them without being seen.

Anin was overjoyed when Paine slowed the pace and it took her a moment to gather the courage to walk alongside him. The size of him alone intimidated, not to mention the double-sided battle-axe that was his constant companion. And though he, by no means, wore out his tongue, she was tired of the silence and hoped to share at least a few words with him.

"Why did the King send you to collect me and not more warriors?" she asked as they walked.

Paine had wondered the same himself. Why had the King not sent a contingent of warriors along with him to make certain his future wife was delivered safely to him? His task should have been complete upon finding out Anin's whereabouts. After that, the King's personal guards should have escorted her to Pictland.

"You appear to wonder the same yourself," she said.

How could she be so observant when he had not changed his expression? He never allowed anything to show on his face. He had been that way for years and would continue to remain so for years to come. "It is not your concern."

"I am not concerned, I but wonder."

"Then do not wonder and do not question the King." Paine increased the pace, moving several steps ahead of her.

"I am not questioning the King," she said, rushing to catch up to him. Her foot caught on something and she flew forward before she could stop herself. Instinctively, she called out to him in alarm. "Paine!"

He turned, his arm snaking around her waist, and caught her just before she hit the ground. He bent over her as he eased her up. He was about to ask if she was injured, but the words never reached his lips. They locked in his throat as he felt his middle tighten.

Anin grabbed onto his arm as soon as his other arm went around her and that's when she felt it...the punch to his stomach, the soar of his heart, and the thought that he wanted to kiss her. What made it worse and confused her all the more was that she would not mind if he did.

She wisely and quickly let her hand fall off him. Whatever was the matter with her? He was the King's executioner and she was to wed the King. Nothing could ever be between them, for the King would make them both suffer terribly for it. And she did not want anything to do with the executioner. His life was nothing but suffering and death.

Paine hastily set her steady on her feet, and snapped, "Stop talking and watch where you walk." He turned and stalked off annoyed with the feelings she had released in him. He wanted none of it. He would not have it. She was the King's intended and he would never dishonor the King.

He hurried his steps, wanting to be done with this task as quickly as possible and wanting to keep as far away from Anin as possible. As soon as he delivered her to the King, he intended to find himself a willing woman to rid himself of this persisting need and be done with that as well.

The land was rough, rocks and stones marring a good portion of it, making travel difficult. He heard Anin stumble and let out a gasp now and again, but she did not call out to him and he did not glance back at her. Though it did disturb him that she struggled so and that he should care, annoyed him all the more.

Finally, he could take it no more and he stopped abruptly and turned. "Can you not walk without faltering?"

"Can you not slow your pace some? You walk as if you wish to be rid of me. If for some reason I offend you, then please return me to my father and he will gladly see me delivered safely to the King."

"Hold on to that strength you showed your mother's sisters, and now show me, and this journey will go quicker for us both."

Strength. He saw strength in her, not many did, and she smiled. "It is my feet that lack strength today, being jabbed much too often by stones."

He wished she would not smile. She was much too beautiful when she smiled. Annoyed at his thought, he responded gruffly, "Watch where you walk and avoid the larger stones."

Her soft laughter drifted along the chilled air and wrapped around him like a warm blanket and once again his body stirred.

"My efforts to avoid them have been pitiful while the stones themselves have been victorious."

The one side of his mouth turned up slightly of its own accord, shocking him. Had a smile tried to surface? He had not smiled since—he could not remember when. Yet, her humorous remark coupled with her gentle laughter had touched something inside him that had him responding without giving thought to it.

His annoyance at himself grew and he tempered his tone. "I will go more slowly, though I want to make certain we reach woodland before darkness falls." He turned and walked off, leaving Anin to follow.

She did, her steps more cautious, though it did not seem to matter. The stones continued to prick at her already sore feet. She would not complain. He was right. They needed to reach the forest before darkness settled over the land. They would be safer there or would they?

Chapter Five

Anin sat on the ground, Bog her only companion, too tired to move. Paine had gone off to hunt for supper as soon as they had found a spot to stop for the night after walking a good distance into the forest. While she was hungry, she was more tired and her feet ached terribly. She did not want to move. All she wanted was to stretch out on the ground and sleep, but her feet needed tending and her stomach needed filling.

She reached down and carefully slipped her shoe off and winced as she did.

Bog turned his head, staring at her, his orange eyes intimidating.

"There is nothing wrong, except that my feet hurt," she said and held her foot up to show him.

The wolf seemed mollified and turned around to sit not far from her.

She winced again when she looked at the bottom of her foot. Skin had worn off in spots and there was some bleeding. She feared looking at her other foot, for it pained her more than this one. They needed to heal and there was no time to let them. She would have to do what she could.

She wondered if a stream ran nearby. Cool water and some mud would help with the pain.

Bog stood suddenly and took off just as suddenly.

Fear froze her. Had Bog sensed someone near? An animal perhaps? She did not know which was worse the Drust or a wild animal. Whichever it was, it would be wiser for her to be on her feet. She winced again when she finally got to her feet. The pain seemed worse, but then she had seen how badly her feet had suffered, so how could they not feel worse?

With a hand on the dagger at her waist, she listened for a sound that someone approached. She wished she had her mother's skill with a weapon, but no matter how much she had practiced, skill eluded her. Weapons were never as comfortable in her hands as they were in her mother's. She felt uneasy holding a weapon, any weapon, and oddly enough she always felt that the weapon felt just as uncomfortable in her hand.

A scream echoed through the forest. Bog had gotten someone. She almost sighed with relief until she heard a noise that had her turning her head. A Drust warrior burst out from behind a bush and ran toward her with a spear held high. A sudden thought had her scooping a good size rock off the ground and throwing it at him. It knocked the spear from his hand, but did not stop him from charging at her.

Anin drew her dagger from its sheath and stood ready to fight. She begged the forest spirits for help and in the next moment the impact of his body against hers sent her flying through the air. He was on top of her as soon as she hit the ground. He tried to snatch the dagger from her hand and she fought back with as much strength as she could. It wasn't enough.

He quickly gripped her wrist and was turning the dagger point down toward her chest. She circled her free hand tightly around his wrist and used all her strength to keep the dagger from plunging into her chest.

She felt it then—hatred. It poured out of him into her. She gasped for breath, the intensity of it suffocating her. *Dead.* He wanted her dead.

He suddenly stopped fighting with her and stared at her as if too shocked to do anything. She felt his hatred turn to such fear that she shivered. He released her suddenly, stood, and stumbled back away from her, his eyes wider than the fullest moon.

He opened his mouth to speak when he was abruptly yanked from behind and tossed away from her. She watched with horror as the executioner's battle-axe came down upon the startled warrior's neck.

Anin turned her head away as she sat up only to see Bog standing beside her blood marring the fur around his mouth. She pressed her hand to her roiling stomach as she closed her eyes.

"Where is your courage?"

Anin's eyes flew open and she turned to face Paine staring down at her, the battle-axe in his hand dripping blood. She shut her eyes again at the sight of it. It could not be the blood that disturbed her, for on occasion she had helped the healer of the tribe. Never, though, had she helped with the wounded warriors. Her mother had forbid it.

"Anin!"

Her eyes shot open and she looked at Paine. A scowl darkened his fine features and she almost scooted away from him. "I did the best I could."

"Your best is seeing victory, anything else will not do. How many times must I remind you that you will need strength to deal with the King?"

"As often as I remind you that I can be no more than who I already am. We should leave, more Drust may follow." She winced, a pain shooting through her one foot as she moved to stand.

"Stay as you are!" Paine ordered and dropped down on his haunches, laying his battle-axe on the ground beside him. His glance went to her feet and he grabbed one ankle, raising her foot. His eyes narrowed. "This is foolishness. You should have told me your feet pained you."

She stared at him, confused by his sincere touch. After all, she was the King's intended. She was even more confused by how gently he held her ankle. His touch seemed almost caring, his large hand warm and comforting and yet his eyes showed annoyance. "Would you have stopped?"

"I would have decided that after looking at your feet." He slowly released her ankle, his fingers lingering along her soft skin even after placing her foot on the ground. When he realized what he was doing, he let his hand fall away. "Your feet need tending." He stood and turned away from her.

"Is there a stream or loch nearby? The cool water and packing my feet in mud should help some."

"Only some?" he asked, turning back around. "I do not see how you will be able to walk on them tomorrow."

"I must, for we need to keep our distance from the Drust," she said, recalling what she had felt when she touched the warrior. She had not known such deep hatred could exist. She thought of telling Paine about it, but she worried that he would think her foolish or perhaps grow as angry at her as her mother had once done. For now, it would be her secret, though secrets came with a heavy burden and she did not know how long she would be able to carry it.

"No more Drust will come—yet—if at all," he said. "They were either a rogue group of warriors disenchanted with the Unification of the Tribes or a group sent on a mission. Once the warriors do not return, it will be known that the mission failed and another troop dispersed and that will take time. By then we will be on Pictland land and word will be sent to the King and he will dispatch his personal guards to escort us the remainder of the way."

44

And her time with the executioner would be done. A shiver ran through her, though she did not know why.

She went to stand.

"Did I not tell you to stay as you are?" he snapped. "You do not listen well, a fault you need to correct."

"I am sure by the time you present me to the King, you will have helped me to correct it," she said with a pleasant smile.

He leaned down, bringing his face so close to hers that their noses almost touched. "For your sake I hope that is so."

She yelped when he scooped her up in his arms and she warned herself not to touch him. She had no choice when he bent down to grab his battle-axe. She wrapped her arms around his neck, her hand landing against his warm skin.

The feeling rushed over her before she could drop her hand away. She felt the thump of his heart grow ever stronger and felt warmth spreading throughout him, growing more heated with each step he took. The darkness that she had first felt in him was still there, but it was not as profound as before and she thought it odd that she actually felt safe with him. Though, she could not forget that no matter what, he was still the King's executioner.

She was surprised to see Bog walking beside them with her shoe in his mouth. Never would she have thought that a wolf could be tamed. Wolves were wild, free creatures and traveled in packs. Was Paine Bog's pack?

He once again left her on her own when he placed her at the water's edge, a wise choice he told himself, since he had been familiar enough with her for one day.

"I need to hunt so we may eat," Paine said, stepping away from her. Bog will protect you as he did the last time, and I will be close by."

Fear stirred in her, but she dared not show it. He had warned her too often about remaining strong as did so many others and she was tired of hearing it. Though, perhaps it was the truth she was tired of hearing.

She gave him a nod and turned, tugging at her shift to pull it up far enough so that the hem would not get wet as she slipped her feet into the rushing water. She shivered from the chill and the sting, then sighed with relief.

She jumped when Paine suddenly crouched down beside her. "I will let nothing happen to you."

One look in his green eyes made her realize he would do anything to keep her safe. The thought touched something inside her, and she had an overwhelming urge to reach out and lay her hand on him. She gripped the folds of her tunic to keep from doing so and could not stop the shiver that ran through her.

He yanked his tightly rolled up cloak that he had secured over his shoulder and back with leather ties and unwrapped it to drape across her shoulders. "It will not bode well for me if I deliver you to the King ill." He stood and walked off.

She stared after him. He confused her. One moment he seemed to care and the next...she turned away. It was not for her to think upon. Why then could she not chase him from her thoughts?

A chill ran through her, her feet having been in the cold water long enough. She quickly packed mud around the bottoms and sides of both feet. She would leave it on until the morrow, hoping it would help heal her wounds enough for her to walk without great pain.

She was pleased to see that Bog had drank from the stream and the water had washed the blood away from his mouth. He once again positioned himself in front of her, his ears and eyes alert. She wished to do her share in helping to protect them on their journey and so was her way, she asked the forest spirits for their protection and help and gave her gratitude in return.

Her eyes were growing heavy by the time Paine returned with a rabbit, cleaned and on a stick, ready to cook. He was quick to start a fire and set the meat to cooking. As tired as she was, she was much hungrier and had no intentions of falling asleep and missing the meal. She had to keep herself awake and the only way she could do that was to talk.

She went to speak and lost her voice. Paine had raised his head and her eyes had caught with his bold green ones and her stomach fluttered. She held his gaze or was it that he had captured hers. All she knew was that she could not look away and she did not want to look away. There was something there in his eyes, something that enticed, something she wanted to explore.

He turned away sharply and she shook her head as if chasing off a daze that had settled over her. When her wits finally returned, she managed to speak to him without a problem, but then his eyes were no longer focused on her. A different question then she meant to ask came out of her mouth. "Why did you become an executioner?"

He tilted his head to the side and gave a simple answer. "The King needed one."

"You would do anything the King asks of you?"

"He is the King."

"So you obey regardless of what the command may be?"

"It is not my place to agree or disagree," he said. "You are to be Queen. You need to guard your words and stand by the King."

"I do have my own thoughts on things and—"

"And it will be the King's decision if he wishes to hear them or not."

The idea that she would not be able to share her thoughts with her husband disturbed her and had her asking, "Do you expect the same of your wife?"

"I am not wed." He turned his head away once again.

"When you do wed will you expect the same of her?"

His head snapped back around. "It matters not about what other men expect from their wives. It matters what the King expects from his Queen."

"Obedience?" she asked.

"King Talon respects strength and courage and, aye, some obedience is necessary when married to the King."

"Then I would prefer to wed a common man."

"That choice is yours no more," he reminded curtly, though he could not say why his own words annoyed him.

"You are right. Fate has decided for me." Not wanting to dwell on what could not be changed, she asked, "You never answered my question. When you wed, will you expect obedience from your wife?"

"You are right. I did not answer your question."

And it was clear that he had no intentions of doing so. Instead, she asked a different question. "How did you ever befriend a wolf?"

"Do you always ask so many questions?"

"Do you always avoid answering questions?"

"Whenever possible," he said.

"It is strange to see a wolf obey your commands," —she smiled— "and even stranger to see him carry my shoe in his mouth." Had Paine's mouth turned up slightly? She could not be sure, but she liked to think it did. She liked to think that he was capable of smiling.

"I found him about two years ago when he was a tiny pup and barely alive. He was curled up against his

48

mother's dead body. I scooped him up, saw that he was fed, and he's been with me ever since."

"What happened to his pack?"

"They were slaughtered by hunters. I came upon their bodies not long after finding him. I think with her last breath, his mother got him to safety. If I had not found him, he would not have survived."

"You are his pack now," Anin said her smile turning gentle.

As if Bog understood what she said, he got up and walked over by Paine and stretched out beside him to show her that she was right...they were a pack.

Paine confirmed it as well as he scratched behind Bog's ear. "I suppose that is true. We have only each other."

"You have no family? What of your tribe?"

"We are all Picts."

"Aye, we are Picts, but there are still tribes. What of yours?" Anin asked even more curious about him now.

"Enough talk. It is time to eat."

They ate in silence and Anin did not mind. The meat was too delicious, and she was too hungry to waste time on talk. Once done, and before she grew too tired, she eased herself to her feet. Paine was getting to his feet when she stretched her hand out and said, "Stay, I need a moment of privacy."

"Your feet?"

She took a tentative step, then another and while there was some discomfit, there was no harsh pain. "Much better."

Paine nodded and ordered. "Do not go far." He then turned to Bog. "Go and protect."

Though she would have preferred to keep his warm cloak for the night, it would not be fair. He would need it to keep the chill away. She dropped it beside him as she passed by and said, "You will need this."

Bog followed beside Anin as she walked into the dark woods. She did as Paine had said and did not go far, but then she had not planned on going more than a few steps. The forest could be unpredictable at night, though she did feel safe with Bog by her side.

When she returned, she went to the stream and scrubbed her hands in the cold water before taking a drink. Bog also took the time to take a drink. After she used the edge of her cloak to dry her hands and mouth, she returned to the fire and held her chilled hands out to it when she sat.

Paine was just stepping out of the woods as she stretched out on the ground, staying close to the fire's heat. He walked past her to the stream and when he returned, he stretched out on the opposite side of the fire.

Bog walked off, disappearing into the woods.

"Where does he go?" Anin asked.

"To hunt and explore."

"You do not share your food with him?"

"If necessary, though I do not want him to depend on me for food. He must be able to survive on his own if something should happen to me. He will return well before the sun rises or he will alert me if we are in danger."

"Then I shall sleep well," she said, curling her legs up and crossing her arms tight to her chest to keep warm.

Paine lay on his side and watched through the flames as her eyes drifted closed. She was nothing like he expected her to be, but then he had not given much thought to her until he had met her. When King Talon had told him that the future Queen was the daughter of a Lammok warrior, he had expected to see a young woman who resembled Anin's mum or her aunts. He had been surprised to see that she was smaller in size, slim, and soft to the touch.

He grew aroused, recalling how she had felt when he had so innocently touched her and wondered how it would feel to touch her intimately. He hastily rolled on his other side, away from her, his thoughts having grown him harder. He had no right to think of her in such a way. He was being disloyal to the King and that would not do. He would keep his mind on the mission and deliver her as quickly as possible to the King and be done with it.

He heard her stir and instinctively turned to see if anything was wrong. She had curled up tighter and was shivering. Though the fire provided warmth, the ground was cold as was the night air and being she was so slim, the cold would seep into her and chill her much faster than him.

Another of her shivers brought him to his feet and he walked around the fire and placed his warm wool cloak over her, taking extra care not to touch her. She smiled gently, but it was the soft moan that had him returning quickly to where he lay on the other side of the fire...away from her.

Once again, he turned his back to her and hoped that sleep would claim him quickly, for thoughts of her continued to plague him and kept him aroused.

If he was not careful it would be him on the executioner's block, for the King would have his head if he ever dared touch the future Queen.

Chapter Six

"Let me see your feet," Paine ordered as Anin dried her clean feet with the ends of her cloak.

"Have a look along with me," she offered, crossing her legs to see the bottoms clearly. She smiled. "They look much improved."

"For now, but once you start walking..." Paine had his doubts even though her feet did look better. "I do not want this journey to take any longer than it has to. Not knowing if that was a rogue group of Drust warriors or that more may be on the way, makes it important to keep a good pace." Besides, he wanted to be rid of her, for his own peace of mind.

"I will do fine," she said with an encouraging smile.

He wanted to believe her, so he let it be, though he warned, "You will tell me if your feet begin to pain you."

"I do not think I will be able to keep that from you."

Her soft tinkle of laughter drifted over him, settling around him like a friendly embrace and he found it comforting. *Comforting?* He was in no need of comforting and he certainly did not bring comfort to others. Far from it, he brought suffering and death.

Annoyed at his growing attraction to the future Queen, he turned away from her and with a sharp tone, ordered, "Keep up!"

"Are you always so pleasant in the morn?" she asked, slipping on her shoes.

"More questions again?" he grumbled.

She stood and dusted herself off. "It is not a difficult one to answer and you should think how it would be for your poor wife, when you wed, to wake to such a grumpy husband."

He swung the ties that secured his rolled up dark cloak over his head and chest and grabbed his double-sided battle-axe off the ground. "I will not wed."

"Why?" she asked and not wanting to miss hearing his answer, she hurried to stay close behind him as he walked off. Bog trailed behind her without being told.

"I would advise that you do not annoy the King with your endless questions."

"Again you find a way not to answer me."

"A clear answer in itself," he said.

"We have many days of travel ahead of us. I would like to think that not all of it will be spent in silence. Or perhaps you spend so much time alone that talking with someone is uncomfortable to you?"

He shook his head. "Another question."

"One that will get an answer?" she asked hopeful.

"I am not alone, I have Bog."

"And does Bog have much to say?"

"Is that another question I hear?" he asked glad that she could not see the unexpected smile it brought to his face.

"Perhaps Bog would answer me," she suggested her own smile growing.

"At least, he does not pester me with questions."

"By chance can I get one question answered?" She once again sounded hopeful.

"It would depend on the question."

Anin thought on it. It would not do to repeat a question he had already refused to answer and it would seem he did not care to answer questions about himself. So, she asked one that he would possibly find acceptable to respond to. "Do you think the King will find me to his liking?"

He would be a fool not to. He kept the sudden thought to himself and answered more curtly than intended. "It matters not. A marriage bargain has been agreed upon and duty must be done."

"It might help if you tell me about his two previous wives."

"That is not for me to say."

"Can you tell me if he at least favored them?"

"The King treated them well."

"Did anyone ever hear him say to either of them '*tuahna*'?"

Tuahna was not a word spoken without great care. It evoked the deepest strongest feelings in another for someone. Many were fearful of using it, for it was said that it bound people together for all time and beyond. Paine had heard his da say it to his mum once and it had filled him with joy. He had hoped one day to care deeply enough for a woman to say it to her. But fate had other plans for him.

"I do not think the King would say that to any wife. He weds so that his wife will give him many sons and through them he will always live, always rule, always be King."

Anin kept silent. Paine made it clear how it would be wed to the King. It would be no more than a duty and the thought troubled her. How would it feel when she touched him? Would there be nothing there? Would she feel that he thought it no more than a chore to be with her? She could tell herself over and over again, that there was nothing she could do that fate had decided this for her. But she wished—oh how she wished—that she could have decided for herself.

"No more questions?" he asked when he grew annoyed at the stretch of silence that followed his remark and grew even more annoyed at himself for letting it disturb him.

"There is no more to ask," she said, suddenly feeling the burden of her future heavily upon her.

Paine felt compelled to ask, "Had you hoped that one day someone would feel so strongly for you that you would hear that word spoken to you?"

"Is that a question?" she asked, a spat of soft laughter following.

He smiled again, though this time he chased it away, feeling foolish. So, his response was more surly than intended. "It is. Answer it or not, it is up to you."

She was growing used to him, his gruff manner not disturbing her. Besides, he was talking with her and that she enjoyed. "A foolish thought I know. And what of you? Did you ever hope to hear it?"

"How are your feet faring?" he asked, having no intentions of answering.

She was not surprised he did not answer and she knew enough not to pursue it. "My feet are well."

"You do not need to rest?"

"Not yet," she said, thinking it thoughtful of him to ask. Something one would not expect from the executioner, but then he was not out to do her harm.

"A storm brews in the distant sky," he said, stopping as they entered another area of open land.

Anin looked across the wide expanse of land and in the distance, just above the hills, the sky was darkening and gray clouds hurried across it. "We should seek shelter before the sky drowns us."

"There is a dwelling in the next forest we come upon, but we will have to set a faster pace if we are to make it there before the rain."

"Then we best hurry," she said.

Paine nodded and without hesitation set a strong pace. He was aware that her feet would suffer for it, but she would suffer worse if caught in a powerful storm. Once at the dwelling, she would be able to rest and from the look of the sky it might be more than a day's rest she gets.

Anin kept her focus on staying close behind Paine and also trying to avoid rocks that would worsen the injury she had already suffered to her feet. With a faster pace, it was not long before her feet began to pain her, but that could not be helped. They needed to make it to the dwelling before the rain fell.

The sky was almost as dark as night when they reached the small dwelling. The only thing inside was the round fire pit that sat in the middle of the one room.

"I need to get a fire going and hunt for food to sustain us through this storm," Paine said.

"I will gather wood while you hunt and there should be wild berries about that I can collect."

He issued a warning before leaving her. "Bog will remain with you, but stay close to the dwelling."

Anin wasted no time in doing her part to secure them against the approaching storm. She hurried and gathered broken branches and twigs and set them in the dwelling. She then gathered brush, enough for two, to serve as sleeping pallets and prevent the chill of the ground from creeping into them. It was not until she finished those two chores did she begin her hunt for wild berries.

Bog followed her every move, keeping close. She was quick at picking berries since she did it often and with great enjoyment, though today she did so out of necessity. A sky darkening as quickly as this one could bring heavy rain that could trap them here for more than a day. The land would not be easy to travel afterwards, mud would slow them down. It would take even longer to reach Pictland, not that she would mind the delay in meeting her fate. She would rather spend the time with Paine.

Her hand hovered over the berries she was just about to pick, the thought surprising her. She could well understand why Paine was feared, just looking at the massive size of him and his unique body drawings, not to mention the double-sided battle-axe he carried and the wolf that was his constant companion. He was not a man one approached without caution or at all. Yet in the two days they had spent together, she had discovered that he was not all he appeared to be. And she quite enjoyed discovering the man behind the executioner.

Anin looked down at Bog after picking a handful of berries. "I will get to know you both better and I hope we can be friends." She dropped the berries to the ground for him and he did not hesitate to enjoy them.

Once finished, she and Bog returned to the dwelling, arriving at the same time as Paine.

"Hunt fast!" he snapped at Bog and the wolf took off.

"He will return before the storm?" she asked worried for the animal.

"His instincts are better than ours." Paine pointed to the door.

Anin opened it and entered, leaving it open a bit after Paine entered so that Bog could enter when he returned.

Paine was surprised to see how much Anin had done. He had not expected her to prepare sleeping pallets for them or gather as much wood as she did. He turned to her. "Sit, you have done enough."

"Your cloak," she said, stretching her hand out to him. "You would not want the fire to catch hold of it."

Paine slipped it off and handed it to her. Anger stirred in him when she snatched the cloak from him, her hand purposely avoiding his. He turned away from her and got busy snapping the larger branches against his bent leg and tossing them into the fire pit. He should be angrier at himself for wanting to feel the touch of her hand upon him. She was right in avoiding his touch. It was not right for her to do so. She belonged to the King, not to him. Only out of necessity in keeping her safe was it right for him to touch her, and he best remember it.

Anin spread his cloak over the brush that would be his sleeping pallet. She was glad her back was turned to him, her brow having wrinkled with concern. His face had turned angry when she had taken his cloak from him and she wondered why. She was sorry that she had not rested her hand on his when she had taken the cloak, for then she would have felt what troubled him. But she had purposely avoided touching him for that reason.

"Get off your feet," he snapped.

Anin turned and sat on the pallet, not far from his, that she had made for herself. He did not look at her. He was too busy setting the meat to cook over the flames that had already begun to fill the small room with warmth.

Bog suddenly hurried into the dwelling and rushed behind the fire pit as if hiding from something.

"He hears the thunder that will be upon us soon," Paine said and went and closed the door and shoved a sturdy twig through the broken latch to keep it shut.

It was barely a few moments later when a clap of thunder shattered the silence and Anin could have sworn it trembled the dwelling. She drew her cloak more tightly around her.

"Are you afraid of storms?"

"Some more than others," she said and shuddered when another clap of thunder sounded as if it was right outside the door.

"You have nothing to fear from the storm. The sky is just reminding us of its power. Sometimes it boasts more loudly than other times."

She smiled. "You are much kinder when it comes to my fear than my brothers. They would tease me and even once they locked me away in a dark room when the thunder began. I was so very frightened. I cried the whole time."

"How many years were you?"

"I just passed my fifth year. My mum found me curled up tight and shivering in a corner. I remember wrapping my arms around her neck and refusing to let go."

"Were your brothers punished for what they did?"

"My da yelled at them and warned them never to do it again. Then he yelled at me for being afraid of something that could not hurt me. My mum agreed with him and I was left to sleep alone that night with the thunder still strong." Anin paused as if lost in the painful memory. "I did not sleep that night even when the thunder stopped, I was much too frightened. I felt so alone, as if I had been deserted by the ones who cared for me." She shook her head. "It was such a strange sensation. After that, I hid when a thunderstorm approached so that my mum or da would not be angry with me and my brothers could not find me."

He wished her brothers were standing in front of him right now, for he would thrash each one of them for failing to protect their little sister.

"I also did not want to listen to my mother repeatedly tell me that Lammok women were warriors and they feared nothing." Anin shook her head again. "I tried so hard to be as strong as my mum, but I fear I never will be."

A tremendous clap of thunder shook the small dwelling and fear had Anin jumping up and instinctively running to Paine.

He was already hurrying to her, his arms going around her, hugging her tightly against him, keeping her safe from her fear.

Anin tightened her arms around his waist and pressed her face against his chest and was ever so grateful for his strong arms wrapped so snugly around her. She never felt as safe as she did at this moment and she wanted to stay in his arms as long as possible. She did not give thought that her hands were pressed against his back until she began to feel his overwhelming need to protect her. She let the feelings soak into her, wrap around her, comfort her, and then she felt something else. It was tucked away almost as if it was kept hidden where no one could find it or perhaps was afraid to look.

He cared for her.

She wanted to reach deeper and feel it more clearly, but another clap of thunder startled her and she shivered in his arms.

Paine felt a chill of fear race through her and he lifted her just enough so that her feet did not touch the ground and brought her to rest in front of the fire pit. He turned her around in his arms, bracing her back against his chest and ran his hands down along her arms to take her chilled hands in his and hold them out to the flames to warm them.

The warmth of the flames coupled with the strength of him wrapped around her brought such comfort that she sighed aloud, and said, "I am most grateful. I have never felt this safe."

Paine fought the feeling that was consuming him, taking over every part of him, inside and out. It had been many years since he last felt it and he had sworn never to let himself feel again, for with such sensations always came pain. And there would be much suffering and pain if he allowed himself to care for Anin.

How many times must he remind himself that she was the King's intended? How many times must he warn himself not to touch her? How many times would he grow aroused when near her? How many times need he remind himself she was to be Queen and nothing could ever—never—be between them?

Not even one kiss.

The thought disturbed him enough that he eased back away from her and what made it worse was that he felt her reluctance to let him go. But then, it was fear of the thunderstorm that had her wanting to keep hold of him. The sobering thought had him stepping completely away from her. She had come to him out of fear, nothing more.

The loss of his warmth and strength left her feeling vulnerable, and she shivered.

"Take my cloak and wrap it around you. It will help chase the chill," he offered.

Anin nodded and did as he said, though it would never replace the comfort and safety of his arms. She sat on the pallet once again, her attention on her shifting thoughts. What was it about his embrace that made her feel so vulnerable and empty when he had moved away from her? After a moment of jumbled thoughts that made no sense, she thought herself foolish. He had helped her through her fear. There was no more to it than that and she had to let it be.

They ate in silence while the rain slammed against the dwelling as if trying to rip it apart. Anin jumped in fright now as did Bog. Paine remained calm.

Soon after they ate, they went to their sleeping pallets.

"Sleep well, you are safe," Paine said and turned on his side away from her.

61

Anin hugged her cloak to her chest and closed her eyes, hoping sleep would claim her immediately. It did not. She lay restless and fearful, the wind having grown in strength, whipping violently against the dwelling. Then the thunder returned, rolling over the land like a never-ending wave.

She hugged her arms tight and told herself over and over that it was all right, she was safe just as she had done when she had hidden away from her family during a storm. She felt as alone now as she had felt then. No one was there to comfort her, help her, care for her.

Thunder so strong rolled over the dwelling that she thought for sure they would be crushed and she jumped up, screaming for the one person who could keep her safe from her fear, "Paine!"

Chapter Seven

Paine sat up, his head turning to Anin and when he saw the fear that gripped her pale face, he did not hesitate. He hurried to her side and took her in his arms, tucking her close against him as he lay beside her on her sleeping pallet.

She clung to him and once again buried her face against his chest and mumbled, "Do not let me go. I beg you, do not let me go."

Her shiver ran through him and he went to turn away from her for a moment.

"No," she pleaded and made certain to keep tight hold of him.

"I am just reaching for my cloak to keep us warm. I will not let you go."

She kept herself pressed against him as he stretched his arm out to his side and his hand took hold of his cloak. He had seen fear in people far too often, he usually being the cause of it. But he never allowed it to disturb him or keep him from carrying out his task. He did what was necessary without thought and without care. Here and now, seeing the fear on Anin's face, feeling it in her every tremble, disturbed him and he wanted desperately to protect her from it.

After draping the cloak over her, he began to rub her back, hoping it would soothe her and it did. Her body, taut as a bowstring, began to loosen and go limp against him, though when another clap of thunder sounded, her body grew taut once again. He did not stop stroking her back even when her body turned limp, his large hand continued stroking, reassuring, comforting.

It was not until the thunder rolled off into the distance that Anin finally fell into an exhausted sleep still nestled in Paine's protective arms. He thought to let her go and return to his sleeping pallet, but her words resonated in his head.

I beg you, do not let me go.

Never had anyone said that to him. They usually begged him to let them go, some to let them die, the suffering too great for them to bear. Their pleas never stopped him from doing what had to be done. Nothing ever stopped him from carrying out the King's command, but then nothing ever stopped death from stalking him.

You lay with the future Queen.

The thought gripped him like a mighty hand, squeezing tighter and tighter. He would be made to suffer if the King learned of it. He had no right to touch her, hold her, and lay with her, though they did nothing wrong. But it was wrong, for no one but the King touched the Queen.

She was not Queen yet.

He shook his head. Future Queen or not, he could not dishonor her or wrong the King even though he did nothing but protect the future Queen from her own fears. It was not easy disengaging himself from her. She kept trying to slip back into his arms and he had a difficult time pushing her away, until finally he managed to settle her on her own.

A quick roll had him back on his own sleeping pallet, though not to sleep. He could not stop his thoughts. He told himself repeatedly that he had been tasked to bring the future Queen safely to the King. That meant doing what was necessary to protect her even from herself.

Or from him.

He shut his eyes against the thought. He needed no woman, nor did he want one, for it would only bring pain to them both. Why then did he grow aroused around her so often? A question he had no answer to nor did he want to dig too deep to find one.

She would be Queen or would she?

Paine knew King Talon before he became King. It had been easy to see that he was a man born to power. He was a fierce warrior, confident in his decisions and possessed great strength and courage and demanded the same of his warriors. He had dissolved two marriages since both failed to produce an heir and his two wives also had not cared for his insatiable need to mate. That was why this time when he searched for a wife, he made it known he wanted a woman of great strength. A Lammok woman, if possible, he had said with a touch of humor and a hint of command. One had been found for him...Anin.

How was it that Anin was nothing like her mother's people? She did not have their height or their skill with weapons. And never would a Lammok woman fear thunder. How was it that she was so different? And what would the King do when he discovered his intended was not what he expected her to be?

It was not his worry. He would see this task done, then be on to the next task. There was always another one, always someone who broke the King's law or someone who did something so foul that even death was not a good enough punishment for him.

Anin's fate was in the King's hands and with that thought on his mind Paine fell into a restless sleep.

Bog, scratching at the door, woke them both. Paine sat up and, after a stretch of his arms and a twist of his neck to both sides, he got up and followed the wolf outside. He was more surprised than relieved to see that not only had the rain stopped, but that dawn had brought the sun with it and also a little warmth. Bog had taken off, which meant he sensed no present danger and Paine was quick to see to his own needs before returning to the dwelling.

Anin looked ready to leave when Paine entered. Her hair was freshly plaited and her garments were brushed clean, her cloak already over her shoulders and clasped at her neck. She looked at him anxiously.

"The weather is good," he said. "We can take our leave." Her whole body seemed to sigh with relief and he wondered if she regretted begging him to hold her in his arms last night.

"That is good news." She looked away from him for a moment and then back again. "Last night—"

"Is forgotten," he finished. "Time to be on our way." She looked as if she wanted to say more, but he did not give her a chance. "Go see to your needs while I see to the fire pit."

Anin hurried past him and she was not surprised to hear him call out. "Do not go far." She needed no reminding, he had told her often enough. Though, today instead of not going too far, she wanted to run as far from him as she could.

She entered the woods and stood staring in the distance. She did not know why thunderstorms frightened her as they did. Over the years she had tried to conquer her fear, but to no avail. Last night, in his arms, was the first time she ever felt safe from them. She did not know if it was the strength in his powerful arms that comforted her or...

She shook her head and hurried to see to her needs, but when she finished and went to return to the dwelling, she stopped. The comfort of his strong arms had certainly helped, but it was what she felt while pressed so tightly against him that settled her fears while raising others.

He cared for her in a way she had never known anyone to care for her and she found herself feeling the same toward him, and it frightened her. She was promised to the King, but something in her felt for the executioner and it continued to stir in her, for when he had entered the dwelling she had felt a catch to her insides. And it grew when his green eyes met hers.

This was not good. It could never be between them. She was to be Queen.

"Anin!"

She gasped, her hand quickly pressing against her middle as if she could stop the fluttering inside. "I am here," she called out hastily and rushed her steps. As soon as she entered the clearing around the dwelling, he turned and started walking off. "Bog?" she called out as she hurried to follow.

"Will join us soon enough."

After last night, Anin decided it was best to keep to herself and ask no questions. The faster they reached Pictland, the faster this ordeal would be over. Or would it just be beginning for her?

They walked for half the day without exchanging a word and came upon a croft soon after.

Anin was thrilled to see it and hoped those who dwelled there would offer drink and food, the berries she had eaten while walking had not been enough to quench her hunger.

Bog drifted off well before they reached the dwelling. And as she and Paine drew nearer, Anin noticed an older man with sparse gray hair and a slim, older woman, his arm snug around her, standing near the open door. When she saw how they glared with fright at Paine, she understood why.

They feared the executioner had come for them.

"We have done nothing wrong," the woman cried out as she and Paine got closer to them.

"Hush," her husband warned lovingly. "King Talon knows that and he is a fair man."

"That he is," Paine said, stopping in front of them, "and he has not sent me for either of you."

The woman could not hide her relief, her stiff shoulders drooping and her wide eyes softening as she stepped out of her husband's arms and said, "May we offer you drink and food?"

The husband nodded, smiling. "Aye, you are welcome to share in what we have."

"That is generous of you," Paine said.

The older man took a step forward toward Paine and lowered his voice. "Should we serve your prisoner as well?"

"The woman is not my prisoner." He did not want it known that she was the future Queen, though he offered no explanation to her identity and none was asked.

The man nodded. "Then you must be tired from walking. Please sit and enjoy the warmth of the sun while my wife and I get you food and drink." He turned quickly and followed his wife into the house.

Paine pointed to a small table with one bench beside it and Anin hurried over to it, tired of being on her feet. The table was meant for two people and certainly not for one the size of Paine. When he sat beside her, there was no way of keeping the sides of their arms from not touching. His warmth seeped into her and though she did not want to acknowledge it, it felt good.

"Your feet?" Paine asked without looking at her.

"They are much better." They were better, though still pained her some, but she would not dare tell him otherwise. She did not want anything delaying their journey.

Paine had the urge to tear her shoes off and see for himself, but he let it be. This unexpected reprieve would at least give her a chance to rest them.

The man and woman fed them well and shared more than generously of their food; sour milk, cheese, bread, and goose eggs. The couple stood to the side like two servants waiting to be beckoned.

Anin wondered why they did not join her and Paine or at least engage them in conversation. After watching them for a few moments, she realized that it was Paine. His mere presence frightened them and they did not want to be near him or engage him in anyway. They had not even shared their names with him. They wanted him done and gone.

Anin grew uncomfortable sitting there, seeing the fright in their eyes as the couple watched as they ate. Anin looked away from them, her glance settling on the food on the table. Had they been so fearful that the couple had given them all the food they had? She found her hunger waning at the thought. Paine had no problem from what she could see, but then he paid the couple no heed. He focused on filling himself.

He turned his head and kept his voice low. "Eat. We have a long journey ahead of us."

Anin kept her voice to a whisper. "What if this is all the food they have?"

"Then they are fools for giving it all to us." He stopped her before she could argue with him. "Not another word—eat."

"Take what is left with you," the woman called out. Her eyes widened, as if suddenly realizing she said something wrong and quickly added, "When you are finished."

Her remark robbed the last bit of hunger from Anin. They were not truly welcomed there and she did not want to stay. She pushed away the near empty bowl of milk and looked at the woman. "My gratitude for your generosity." She slipped off the bench and walked away from the couple, looking off into the distance, wanting to be anyplace but here.

"We will take the bread and cheese," Paine said.

"I will wrap them in a cloth for you," the woman said and hurried to do so.

Anin did not glance back when she heard the couple call out, "Good journey." She followed behind Paine after he handed her the bundle to carry. They walked in silence, Bog joining them after they were a good distance from the croft.

The silence grew too heavy for Anin as did her thoughts and she could not help but say, "They feared you."

"Everyone fears me."

She did not think on her response, it slipped from her lips. "I do not fear you."

Paine stopped abruptly and turned, taking quick steps toward her.

Anin stood firm against his intimidating approach. With his battle-axe gripped tightly in his hand, the muscles taut along his arms, and his face set in a scowl, she probably would have been wiser to back away from him. But something held her firm.

He stopped so close, their bodies almost touched. "You should fear me."

"Why?"

"I bring great suffering, though more often death and that couple was well aware of it and kept their distance, for they had no wont of either."

"They had done nothing wrong, so why fear you?"

"It is death they fear and to them I am the harbinger of death. They give to me, I go away, and death does not touch them."

Anin stared at him as a sudden thought struck her. "That is why King Talon sent you to get me. No one would dare tempt death." She shook her head. "The Drust—"

"Tempted death and lost, and it is also the reason we must get you to the King without delay."

She tilted her head in question.

"Stay with me long enough and death will claim you as well."

Chapter Eight

Paine's warning haunted her well into the night, her sleep restless. She woke repeatedly from dreams that confused and frightened. She could make little sense of them, though one thing was clear throughout them all...a warning that she was in danger.

What danger and from who? She had no answer and once again drifted off into a disturbed sleep.

Anin ran, through a mist so thick that she could not see where she was going. She had to run. She had to get away, but who was chasing her?

Run, Anin! Run fast!

The woman's frantic voice was not familiar to Anin, but she heard only concern and caring in it, and so she ran.

"Hurry, Anin, you must get away from him!"

Anin ran faster, the mist beginning to fade. She heard it then—footfalls—behind her, getting closer and closer.

"Hurry! Hurry! The voice urged.

Her chest heaved and her legs grew so heavy she thought she would not be able to take another step and the footfalls drew ever closer.

"Anin!"

The voice was sharp and angry.

"Anin!"

She had to keep running. She had to find Paine. Paine would protect her. Paine would keep her safe.

"Anin!"

Her eyes sprang open and she jumped up and ran, hitting something solid and went tumbling with it to the ground.

Paine had not meant to frighten her awake or for her to run into him with such force. He had only meant to wake her from an obviously frightening dream. Now she lay stretched out on top of him.

Anin shook her head to clear her eyes of the mist that lingered in them. She braced herself on the solid mass that had tumbled to the ground with her, so that she could get up. The feelings hit her hard, pain and despair so strong that she wanted to cry, then nothing.

Death.

No. Wait, a spark. She saw it, felt it, weak as it was, and fighting to grow stronger.

"Anin."

This time when she shook her head, her eyes cleared and turned wide, and she saw that she was staring down at Paine flat on his back. She was lying on top of him. Her glance went to his lips, slim and slightly parted, and she got the overwhelming urge to kiss him.

His hand was suddenly at the back of her neck, taking firm hold. "Do not dare think it!"

His harsh warning snapped her out of whatever had taken hold of her and she pushed against his hard chest to hurry off him.

She turned away from him as soon as she got to her feet. Whatever was the matter with her? She had wanted to kiss him so badly, the need still lingering now. This was not right. Why would she feel that way?

He suddenly stepped in front of her. "You are to be Queen. You belong to the King. Do not make him send you to me for punishment."

Anin could find no words, his remark stealing what little sense was left in her confused thoughts.

"Gather your things, we leave," he snapped sharply and stormed away from her.

Anin hurried to do as he said, growing more confused and frightened than ever. What was wrong with her? Why were her feelings for Paine growing with every touch? And what would happen when she first laid her hands on the King. What would she feel? The thought sent a shiver through her. As the old couple had said, and many agreed, the King was a fair man. Or was he?

She shivered again, thinking on what Paine said about the King sending her to him for punishment. Would the King do that? More importantly would Paine punish her? She felt safe and protected with him. Would he truly hurt her? Her insides gave a turn and she was glad she had not eaten at all today.

Her thoughts plagued her as she walked. Why could she feel what others felt? Her mum had warned her to push the feelings away, fight against it, and tell no one of it, and she had since she was young. But meeting Paine had changed all that. Never had she felt with the intensity as she did when she touched Paine. And the strange part was that she ached to touch him again, explore what was inside him and discover what was fighting so terribly hard to break free.

After a while, her thoughts vanished as she found it necessary to be more watchful of her steps. The woods they traveled had grown denser, the path unclear. She was ever so grateful when Paine finally stopped. It took a moment for Anin to realize it had been a sudden stop and she grew alarmed.

"What is wrong?" she whispered.

"We are not alone."

"I heard no warning from Bog."

"He trails us. They approach us."

"The Drust?"

"No, Bog would have picked up their pungent scent."

"They may be travelers."

"A hopeful thought."

She did not ask him if he knew otherwise, she knew he did, and her alarm grew.

Bog suddenly appeared, rushing over to Paine and growling as he took a protective stance in front of him.

Paine lifted his battle-axe.

Anin would reach for the dagger in her boot if necessary since she felt her limited skill with the weapon might be more hindrance than help. She much preferred to reach out to the forest and ask for their help and protection, and she did silently.

"Stay near me," Paine ordered in a whisper as several warriors suddenly made themselves known a distance in front of them.

"What brings you so far from your tribe?" Paine asked as they drew nearer.

Anin was surprised to hear Paine speak another language. She did not know it, but she was familiar with it. She had heard her mother speak it with her sisters a few times. When she had asked her about it her mum had explained that it was the language of the dal Gabran Tribe to the south of Pictland. They were neither Pict nor part of the Pict Kingdom. The Lammok traded with them from time to time, though less since the Pict tribes unified. Now the King controlled most of the trading with the south.

The warriors were not as large as Paine and all had long hair. Their garments were similar to those she and Paine wore, though they wore fur capes. They carried bows and caches of arrows slung over their shoulders and they approached Paine cautiously, though they all kept glancing toward Anin.

"We search for one of ours who has been gone too long. With your King's permission, he was sent to trade with the Lammok," the one in the lead said his glance drifting to Anin again and again.

Paine doubted the man spoke the truth. King Talon would have sent his own warriors to find out what happened. So what was the dal Gabran doing this far north?

"You are the King's executioner, are you not?" the warrior asked.

Paine's intent stare was his answer.

The warrior grew uncomfortable, shifting from one foot to the other. "I only ask, for one who appears so young and innocent surely is not your prisoner, therefore, I wonder if I missed the announcement that the executioner has taken a wife."

The warrior was searching for information and the way all the warriors kept glancing at Anin, Paine assumed the warrior's interest was mostly in her.

"That does not concern you," Paine cautioned sharply.

The warrior bobbed his head, acknowledging the warning and saying no more. "We will be on our way. The path is clear to Pictland."

He seemed to pause, waiting for a response. Paine remained silent.

After a moment, the warrior said, "Safe journey."

The warriors tried not to stare as they passed Paine and Anin, but one by one their eyes kept darting to Anin, and she did not care for their obvious scrutiny.

Bog did not care for it either. His snarl deepened and grew and he fell into step a distance behind them as the last warrior passed by, making sure they kept walking.

Anin looked to Paine who had turned and watched the warriors disappear into the forest almost expecting him to snarl like Bog, he appeared so angry.

"First the Drust attacks, then dal Gabran warriors are in Pictland, far north of where they should be with a story that sounds far from the truth. Something is brewing." Paine was not happy. Something was wrong. Something had brought the dal Gabran here and it was not to search for a missing tribesman. And why did the warrior seem interested in Anin or if their destination was Pictland? That was the warrior's intention when he said the path was clear to Pictland. He wanted to learn where they were going. Something was definitely wrong. "We keep a good pace and you will stay close," he ordered Anin and began walking.

Anin gave a silent acknowledgement to the forest for keeping them safe as she hurried to do as he said. She was vigilant not only of her steps this time, but of her surroundings. Bog also seemed more cautious and kept close to her and Paine.

They did not stop once as the day wore on and Anin struggled through her hunger and the exhaustion that seemed to burrow deep inside her. She glanced down at her aching feet, wishing dusk was near so they would have to stop for the night. She suddenly collided with Paine's back, he had stopped so abruptly. He was quick to turn and place his finger to her lips.

She nodded and waited while he stood and seemed to be listening for something. Bog did the same, though he had taken a stance behind her.

A distance away several birds flew out from the treetops at the same time Bog began to growl.

Paine grabbed Anin, hurried her to a low tree branch and hoisted her up. He followed up behind her after saying to Bog, "Go and wait for my call." The wolf took off and Paine turned to Anin. "Climb high."

Paine moved past her when she struggled to reach the lowest branch of the thick old, oak and hoisted himself up. Once above her, he reached down and grabbed her hand to pull her up. As he eased her up, his other arm reached down to catch at her waist, yanking her up the rest of the way. He helped her to climb from there, higher and higher. They disturbed the bounty of colorful leaves that had yet to be shed for the harvest season, but it was necessary and Anin offered her gratitude to the tree for helping them.

She kept hold of Paine's hand as they continued to climb, letting his strength and courage seep into her.

Her thoughts went to the many birds that had taken flight at once. It had been a warning that something large had disturbed them and when she heard the heavy pounding footfalls growing closer and closer, she knew a troop of warriors headed their way.

Instinctively, she turned to Paine just as he reached out to pull her against him and tuck them both firmly into the crook of two, thick tree branches. She was relieved that he had not stayed to fight them, but then he was no fool. He knew he could not win against a troop of warriors whatever tribe they may be.

The footfalls stopped not far from the tree and voices drifted up between the branches, though not all of what was being said could be heard.

"Find them."

"Not far."

"Kill them both."

There was a rush of footfalls and it grew quiet once again, though Paine cautioned with a shake of his head and a finger to his own lips that she was not to move or speak. She nodded, understanding that they should wait to make certain they were all gone.

After what seemed like an endless wait, Paine motioned to her to stay where she was and he would be back. He slipped down, disappearing through the branches, his battle-axe snug in its sheath at his back.

Paine went as silently as he could, though stopped when he thought he heard footfalls. He gently brushed leaves aside not worrying that the rustle would catch someone's attention since a light breeze filled the air.

He waited sure he had heard someone approaching. After hearing nothing, he was about to lower himself to another branch when he spotted movement. He pulled back so as not to be seen, then silently as possible peered past the leaves and saw that one of the dal Gabran warriors stood beneath the tree.

The warrior appeared worried and confused as his head snapped from side to side, taking in everything around him. Then as if startled by a noise, he jumped and ran off. Why was one dal Gabran warrior going in the opposite direction of the others?

He took a moment to give thought to their circumstances and it did not take him long to make a decision. He hurried back up the tree to retrieve Anin and be on their way.

Her wide eyes told him she was anxious to hear what he had learned.

He kept his voice to a whisper. "It appears all are gone as we should be."

Anin stepped forward eager to be on their way and end this journey that turned out to be far more dangerous than she had expected.

Once on the ground, Paine summoned Bog with a call one would think was a bird. The wolf appeared as if out of nowhere.

Anin brushed away the few colorful leaves that clung to her.

"We need to go," Paine said, pulling his battle-axe from the sheath.

She heartily agreed, though was surprised when he turned to walk in the direction they had already been. "You go the wrong way."

Paine walked over to her. "The Drust are aware of the path we travel and now the dal Gabran is as well. We cannot continue the way we were going and we need to go now."

Anin did not argue. She agreed with Paine and trusted him and so she followed along quickly. Gone was her exhaustion and hunger. Her only thought was getting as far away from the Drust as possible.

Bog ran ahead and remained a distance from them as they hurried along. It was awhile before Bog returned suddenly and took a guarded stance a few feet from them.

Paine turned to Anin. "Take cover somewhere until I come for you."

"No, I go with you," she said as if it was settled.

Paine went to argue, but seeing the determination in her eyes he would only waste time. "Stay close," he ordered.

His order was easy to follow since she felt much safer being close to him.

It was not long before they come upon the dal Gabran.

Anin stared at the dead bodies scattered around the forest and saw her own fate if it had not been for Paine. She looked to him. "Why?"

Paine glanced over the senseless carnage and shook his head. "I do not know, but the Drust will not stop until they see their mission done."

And they both knew what that mission was...to see Anin dead.

Chapter Nine

They stopped just before dark, Anin nearly collapsing next to the trickling stream that had her parched mouth begging for the cool water. She bent over to scoop up a handful when her body simply surrendered to exhaustion and tumbled forward.

Her fall was broken just as her face was about to sink into the water.

"Drink," she heard Paine order, his arm having caught her around the waist to hold her firm.

Too tired and parched to hold herself up, she drank. When she finished, he eased her up and rested her back against him. Despite her hunger, she could have fallen asleep right there. His body's warmth seeped through hers, chasing away the chill that had taken hold of her. His chest pillowed her head nicely and his arm remained firm around her waist.

Paine continued to hold her. She needed to be held after the day she had been through and right or wrong, he did not intend to let her go, at least for a while. He would rest along with her, then see what food he could find for them. They both needed to keep up their strength.

He would take a short rest, nothing more. He closed his eyes.

Paine woke to find himself so close to Anin that their lips almost touched. He stared at her, peaceful and content in his arms and realized at that moment he felt content himself, something that had long escaped him.

His lips drifted closely to hers as if of their own accord, as if he could do nothing to stop them. Her eyes opened, returning him to his senses and he pulled away reluctantly and hurried to his feet, realizing they had both slept through till morn. His insides rumbled, reminding him that neither of them had eaten last night.

"I will find us food. You start a fire," he said and walked away, Bog by his side.

Anin stared after him. His lips had been so close to hers when she woke that she wondered if he had meant to kiss her or was it that she wanted him to kiss her. A dangerous thought with her being the King's intended.

She stretched her arms to the overcast sky as she sat up, chilled air nipping around her. Confusion had her shaking her head. She had always felt as if she did not belong, though her parents and siblings never gave her reason to feel otherwise. It was as though she was missing something, whether a part of herself, a connection, she had no idea...until Paine.

With him she felt whole as though she had been reunited with a missing piece of herself. It was strange, frightening in a way to feel so attached to someone that you felt something missing when parted. Her mum would scold her if she told her how she felt about Paine. She had warned her to always rely on herself and she had.

So why feel this need to be close to Paine?

Her thoughts continued to churn while she got a fire going, and she smiled when Paine returned with two fish ready to cook.

He did not speak while the fish cooked or while they ate, though neither did Anin. She was much too busy eating every morsel of the delicious fish.

After dousing the fire, Paine squatted down beside her—though not too close—at the stream and scrubbed his hands and face.

"Do you think the Drust will discover they do not follow us?" she asked, drying her hands on her cloak.

82

"At some point they will and I intend for us to be a distance from them before they do." He stood and turned. "We leave now."

The day stretched on endlessly, Anin keeping pace with Paine and cautious of her surroundings, concerned the Drust would appear out of nowhere. They were relentless warriors and the last of the tribes to surrender to King Talon.

By mid-day they were halfway along a narrow ridge when Paine suddenly stopped, Bog along with him. Anin halted her steps, worry settling over her as she watched Paine stare along the ridge to its end in the distance. She followed his stare and stopped herself from gasping.

Traveling up along the ridge were Drust warriors.

Something had her turning to look behind her and down the ridge. Fear gripped her when she spotted Drust warriors hurrying up toward them.

"Paine!"

He turned and looked past her. The Drust would have had to travel all night to have caught up with them, unless... Were there more following them than the troop that had passed them?

Anin turned to Paine. She did not say the obvious—there was no place for them to run.

His arm shot around her. "Wrap your arms around my neck and bury your head against my chest and do not let go."

As she did, he shouted something to Bog, then his arms clamped tightly around her and he pitched them to the side, sending them tumbling down the ridge. She squeezed her eyes closed tight and kept her head buried against his chest. His legs captured hers in a tight grip once they went over the edge, stopping hers from flailing about.

Her body was battered by stones, twigs, and forest debris, though not as badly as it would be if Paine was not locked tightly around her. She held on with all her strength, fearful of being ripped away from him.

They finally rolled to a stop, Paine asking anxiously, "Anin?"

Not sure how she felt, though knowing they had no time to waste, she gathered her wits and breath about her and said, "I am good, and you?"

"I am fine," he said, getting quickly to his feet, then reaching down to help her up. He held her steady as he glanced up along the hill to the ridge. It had been a long fall, but a necessary one. The Drust warriors stood along the edge, staring down at them.

They were a foreboding sight, their whole bodies covered in drawings with cloths wrapped around their waists, being their only garments. Some held their long spears high while others rested the weapon by their sides, but all eyes glared down on Paine and Anin.

Anin's glance had followed Paine's and she stood shocked at the frightening sight. "Where did so many come from?"

"I do not know, but they are determined to see that we do not reach Pictland."

"Why do they stay where they are? Why do they not run down at us?"

"They will not follow where we go."

"Why?" Anin asked, knowing there were areas in the Highlands no one dared to tread, not even the bravest of warriors and the thought sent a shiver through her.

He nodded behind her.

Anin turned. A short distance away was the edge of a forest and carved in the trees were symbols, warning anyone who approached to stay away, not enter. None were welcome there. It was the home of the Giantess.

"They wait," Paine said, nodding up at the Drust warriors. "We either fight them or enter the forest." He stretched his hand out around them. "You can see there is no way out except through the forest or back up the hill to the ridge and the waiting Drust, though their spears will stop us long before we reach the top.

Anin looked around the small clearing where they stood. They were trapped. To one side rose thick rock that reached to the top of the hill, while the surrounding area was all forest.

Anin had heard tales of the Giantess, a not so benevolent divine being, and her home. Her father would sometimes tell tales to all in the feasting house. She recalled one such tale. It would always begin with her da saying that King Talon's strength was beyond that of any mortal man. All would nod their heads in agreement. Her da would go on to say how the King could tame the wild beasts, calm an angry sea and that the land would tremble in fear when he walked upon it. Some joined in, shouting out how the King could split a man in two with one single blow of his mighty sword and that he rode a beast of a stallion that no one could go near but him.

It was, however, the tale of King Talon surviving his time with the Giantess that impressed everyone the most.

"Is it tale or truth that King Talon entered the home of the Giantess and survived?" she asked Paine.

"Truth. That is why some believe him more a God than mortal man, for they feel the Giantess blessed him with remarkable powers and allowed him to walk among mortals. Others believe she spared him, but cursed him for intruding on her home."

"What curse did she place on him?"

"You can ask the Giantess yourself if you are unlucky to meet her." Paine took her arm, cast one last look at the Drust warriors staring down at them, and hurried her along into the forest, Bog following behind, his ears back, his tail down, and a low growl rumbling in his chest.

85

Chapter Ten

Paine did not have to tell Anin to remain close. She pressed herself so tightly against his side that he wondered if he would ever be able to remove her. He could not blame her. The forest was denser than any he had ever passed through. Even if there was not an overcast sky, the trees and foliage was so thick he doubted the sun could break through them. That made it difficult to determine direction and with none but King Talon, that Paine knew of, having traveled this way no clear path had been forged.

"How do you know where to go?" she asked as his confident steps took them deeper into the forest.

"There are signs."

In her fear, she had forgotten about the signs that could guide you on your path. Her mum had taught her about them and she had learned quickly. Her mum had been proud. What she had not told her mum was that the woods had more secrets to share. The trees whispered to her and the birds and animals helped to guide and warn. Even the spiders helped, spinning their webs on the south side of trees. She never feared getting lost in a forest, but then that truly was not her present fear.

She feared the Giantess and feeling no such fear in Paine, she asked, "Do you not fear the Giantess?"

"No. She either allows us to pass or I slay her."

She felt not a trace of fear or sorrow in him. He would kill without thought, without repentance. That was his task. To take the last breath from a person and it seemed not to disturb him at all.

Bog walked beside her, his steps cautious and his eyes watchful.

She remained silent as they continued on and was reluctant to let go of Paine when he stopped every now and then. When he squatted down to examine several rocks, she knew what he was looking for...how thick the moss was on one side. The side that got the least sun would always have the most moss growing on it and that would be the north side. Though, with little sun getting passed the dense trees it might be difficult to tell.

While Anin waited, she decided to silently call out to the trees and request their help. She would do the same of the animals and birds. Though, before she did, she decided it was only fitting to acknowledge the person whose home they had entered without permission.

Anin closed her eyes and spoke silently. *Giantess, please forgive us for intruding on your home. It was a necessity or we would not have been so rude as to enter without your permission. We wish you no harm nor do we wish to disturb your peaceful dwelling. We would be most grateful if you allow us to pass through without incident. Blessings to you.*

"What are you doing?"

Anin opened her eyes to see Paine standing directly in front of her. "Making a silent offering to keep us safe."

"You were not silent." He took a step closer, keeping his voice to a whisper. "You did not speak in your familiar tongue."

Her brow wrinkled. "That is not possible. I know no other tongue."

"It was unfamiliar to me."

"It was probably nothing more than mumbles."

Paine did not argue with her. She had spoken clearly and he had heard her clearly. He would think on

87

it when there was time since it was another piece to the secret that was Anin. Her mum had been too anxious to keep Anin from wedding the King. The Girthrig Tribe had always been loyal to the King and it should have been an honor for Anin's mum to see her daughter become Queen.

He would gather what pieces he could on Anin and present them to the King. It would be the King's decision after that. Why did that thought disturb him?

Paine shook his head. "We need to keep going and be out of these woods as soon as possible." He instinctively reached out for her hand.

Anin took it without hesitation and continued on, Bog keeping close to Anin's side.

Anin always felt the trees whispering to her whenever she walked in the woods, but these trees did not merely whisper. They were clear voices, guiding her.

Watch where you step.

Go to the right of the large oak.

A stream waits ahead, passed the hedge and around the pine.

Drink your fill, then rest.

Anin tugged at his hand to go right at the towering oak tree. "We must go this way."

"Why?" Paine asked, stopping.

Anin remained silent for several moments, wondering how to explain to him what she was hearing, when Bog began to sniff the air. "I thought I heard a running stream and I believe that is what Bog smells."

She tugged at his hand again and he followed. His curiosity grew as he watched as she turned at a hedge, as if she knew her way, and went around a large pine to bring them to a flowing stream.

"How beautiful," Anin said, admiring the graceful curves as the stream meandered along stone banks with lovely purple heather hugging the stone. Slim birch trees were plentiful and an overcast sky seemed like a brilliant sun after the darkness of the surrounding forest.

They heard Bog lapping up water and saw that he had followed a path that took him to a sandy section where it met the stream.

Paine and Anin hurried along to drink of the cool water.

He finished before Anin and waited until she was done before asking, "How did you know this was here?" When it appeared she was not sure how to answer, he reminded her of what she had once told him. "You favor the truth from me, so I ask the same of you."

If she trusted him, why did she hesitate to answer him? She could not say and that troubled her all the more. Since meeting Paine, things had begun to change. Her secret, as her mum called it, was growing stronger and she no longer could hide it away...and she did not want to. She was beginning to realize that *the secret* was a natural part of her. How or why, she could not answer, but perhaps one day that secret would be revealed to her.

"Your delay in responding makes me think you keep something from me or is it that you do not truly trust me?"

Bog's head turned at the same time Paine's did.

"Footfalls," Paine whispered and Bog growled.

Fright gripped Anin. "Could the Drust have followed us?"

"Anything is possible, though I doubt they follo—" He suddenly pushed her flat on the ground, going down with her. "Drust."

She saw his lips move more than heard his whisper.

He used his hands to tell her to stay there that he would be back for her. She thought it odd that she did not argue with him that she felt safe with him leaving her there. She nodded and kept her eyes on him as he disappeared into the dark forest.

She waited, not moving, and listened for any sounds.

"What are you doing there kissing the ground?"

Anin bolted to her feet at the sound of the raspy voice and was shocked to see a short, slim, old woman, leaning on a wooden staff a head taller than herself. Her gray hair was sparse and hung untamed around her face and shoulders and her garments were worn. Her round face was abundant with wrinkles, yet her blue eyes appeared young and vibrant.

"Hiding," Anin responded and quickly asked, "Who are you?"

"Who are you hiding from and I am a guest here, are you?" the old woman leaned heavily on her staff as she shuffled over to a flat rock on the stone bank and sat.

"The Drust," Anin said, wondering how the old woman could be a guest of the Giantess. It was not as though the Giantess welcomed with open arms.

"Bah," the old woman said with a wave of her hand. "The Drust are too afraid to come here."

Anin was relieved to hear that.

"Are you a guest?" the old woman asked again.

Anin shook her head. "I am sorry to say we entered without permission, which we never would have done if there was any other way."

"That was rude of you."

Her scolding tongue had Anin wincing. "It was rude, and I am sorry, but we were left with little choice, and I mean no harm to anyone here."

"What of the warrior with you?"

"He intends no harm as long as no harm is done to us."

"Why would harm be done to you? I told you the Drust fear this place. So who would harm you?"

"I am unfamiliar with this forest, so I cannot say what might await us here."

"Why did you not speak the truth to the warrior when he asked?"

"You heard us speaking?"

"I hear everything," the old woman said with a cackling laugh.

Anin wondered who the woman was, though she had a feeling that the woman did not intend to tell her.

"Why not tell him the forest speaks to you?"

Anin eyes turned wide. "How do you know?"

The old woman ignored her question and demanded, "Why not tell him? Do you fear what he will think? What he will say?"

Did she fear how he would respond? She sat on a rock beside the old woman. "My mum warned me against speaking about it."

"Bah, pay her no heed. She knows not what she speaks."

"She is my mum. She cares about my well-being"

"Then she should encourage you to discover yourself, not hide away."

"I do not hide."

The old woman laughed again. "You hide from yourself. You hide from how you feel for the warrior, you hide from how you have yet to understand and accept how you feel about him, and you hide how you rely on the warrior to protect you when you have the courage and skill to protect yourself. You hide from everything instead of embracing everything."

Anin stood and snapped, "You know nothing."

The old woman laughed. "The truth will find you whether you want it to or not." Her laughed suddenly died. "Though, the truth is not something we always want to hear."

A chill settled over Anin and she shivered, rubbing her arms.

"Careful with your foolish fears," the old woman snapped with annoyance, "or they will lead you to foolish decisions."

Annoyed, Anin demanded, "Who are you?"

"Who are you?" the old woman commanded like a stern Queen.

Anin obeyed like a dutiful servant. "I am Anin of the Girthrig Tribe and future wife to King Talon."

"Are you now? Well, Anin of the Girthrig Tribe and future wife of King Talon, remember what I told you...foolish fears lead to foolish decisions or you will hide and keep secrets for your remaining years."

Curious that the woman spoke as if she could see the future, she asked, "Are you a seer?"

"I am no such lowly creature," she said offended.

It struck Anin then, her eyes turning wide as she stared at the old woman. Was it possible? With nervous breath, she said, "You are the Giantess."

"Finally, you realize who I am, unlike that fool Talon."

"I would think the King expected—"

"A giant woman," she snapped. "And the fool thought he would subdue or slay me and forever be remembered in endless tales, proving his prowess. He learned well his mistake. I gave him more prowess with his sword than he needs." She grinned pleased with herself.

Another shiver took hold of Anin. Did the Giantess know Paine thought to slay her if she did not let them pass through?

"Do not worry over your man. I will not harm him. I have no interest him. Death walks too closely to him."

"Yet you have made yourself known to me. Why?"

"You will discover why when you allow yourself to be who you truly are."

"Your words make no sense to me."

"One day they will make perfect sense." The old woman stood. "When you find your true courage it will help the executioner find his courage."

"Paine has much courage."

The old woman laughed. "We shall see. Your time here will bring you no concerns as long as you harm nothing here. There are plenty of berries to sustain you. Now go drink your fill from the stream. It is a distance to the next one."

Anin turned to the stream, her mouth once again parched. She turned back around to extend her gratitude to the Giantess, but she was gone. She shook her head. It was all so strange.

She heard footfalls approach and she looked to hide, but Bog appeared and she smiled, knowing Paine would follow and he did.

"So strange," Paine said, shaking his head.

Anin almost smiled, hearing him voice her own thought.

He approached Anin. "I thought for sure I saw Drust warriors, but I could find no signs of them."

She was about to tell him of her encounter with the Giantess, but stopped. Why did she hesitate? She had thought she trusted him. Had that changed? She did not believe so, then why not tell him of her meeting with the Giantess?

She had no answers to her troubling questions and it disturbed her even more that she remained silent, not sharing what she had learned.

"You saw or heard nothing?" he asked as he passed by her to stoop down and take another drink from the stream.

Anin stumbled for an answer.

Paine was suddenly in front of her, taking firm hold of her chin. "You hesitate to answer me. What do you hide from me?"

Hide.

Again she was reminded of hiding. Had the Giantess been right? Did she hide more than live?

"It is not a difficult question," he said, keeping hold of her chin and forcing her to keep her eyes on him.

It was more his eyes that held her than the grip on her chin. There was patience in them, as if he would wait forever for an answer. She felt a catch in her chest when he spoke as if he read her thoughts.

"I am a patient man. I will wait as long as it takes for an answer." He might wait, but it would not be an easy wait. It was difficult to ignore how much he favored being close to her or how a simple touch of her chin stirred him. Then there were her lips, softly inviting with a touch of moisture that made him want to taste them. How would she taste? Sweet? Potent? Delicious?

His stirrings soon turned to an arousal, something that was happening much too often when she was near. He should keep his distance, yet he ignored his own warning and foolishly brought his face closer to hers and whispered, "Tell me your secret, Anin."

The thumping in her chest, the flutters in her middle grew when he stepped closer. Did she trust him with her secret?

Her mum's warning echoed in her head. *Never tell anyone.*

The Giantess had told her differently. Who did she trust?

Revealing her secret to him was one thing, telling him what happened while he was gone was another. She said softly, "The Giantess made herself known to me."

"You are well? She did not harm you in any way?" he asked even though she appeared untouched, he had to be sure. There was no telling what the Giantess might have done to her.

94

"I am and she was pleasant enough, though abrupt at times. She informed me that we were safe to travel through her home as long as we did not harm anything while here. I assured her we would not. She also advised that the berries are plentiful and will sustain us, and it is a distance to the next stream."

"What else had she to say to you?"

"She told me I was rude for entering her home uninvited."

Paine nodded. "She said something similar to King Talon."

"Did the King truly wish to slay the Giantess?"

"It was a time when he needed to prove his strength and courage to the tribes. He wanted to prove he was worthy of leading them. Slaying the Giantess would have done that."

"She did say he wanted to prove his prowess and that she gave him more prowess with his sword than he needed." She was shocked to see the wide smile that surfaced on Paine's face.

"That she did and with more than one sword."

Anin's brow wrinkled, then suddenly it struck her. "Oh, his prowess with women." Sorrow filled her. "How sad for him to never feel so deeply for one woman that he must mate with many. He will never know the feeling, the joy that that one special woman can bring him or how it would feel to give the same to her. He will never hear someone say—"

"The King has forbidden any woman to say it to him." It was not his place to tell her and yet he felt compelled to do so. She needed to know so that she would not go on dreaming that someday it would be possible to hear the King admit his deepest feelings for her with a single word...*tuahna*. Once she wed the King, it would never be possible.

Hide.

It was as if the Giantess spoke to Anin silently and she nodded, agreeing with her. Only this time, it was meant for the King. What did he hide?

Chapter Eleven

They stopped at dusk and sat around the fire, eating the berries Anin had collected. Paine had not rushed their pace since there was no fear of the Drust finding them, and an easy pace would benefit them both.

Anin seemed to think the same. "I am grateful that we go slower today. It was nice not to rush or fear being followed, though I cannot help but wonder what will happen when we leave the safety of this forest."

Paine would have liked to ease her concern, but he would not lie to her when he was unsure of what they would face. "I do not know what awaits us, but we will face it together."

Somehow that thought comforted Anin.

A heavy chill settled over the land along with darkness and though Anin sat close to the fire, she still shivered.

Let him warm you.

Anin looked around, expecting to see the Giantess.

"It is the wind, though it did sound like strange laughter," Paine said.

"It is a bitter wind for harvest time." Anin wrapped her arms across her chest, rubbing them with her hands and hoping he would come and keep her warm.

Paine reminded himself that she was the King's intended and his task was to deliver her to the King safe and unharmed. He had grumbled at the task when it had been presented to him and had suggested that King Talon's personal guard be sent to collect her. King Talon had reminded him that death walks with the executioner and no one would dare tempt death.

Death did walk beside Paine. It was as if a burdensome demon followed his every step, waiting, watching, and claiming everyone he ever cared for. It was another reason to keep his distance from Anin and see only that she was delivered to the King.

"Stay close to the fire," Paine grumbled and stretched out on the ground, doing as he advised her to do, and kept the crackling flames between them.

Anin was disappointed and stretched out on the ground on her side, facing the flames, and keeping her cloak tugged snugly around her. Her thoughts went to what the Giantess had said about how Anin hid and that she did not understand nor accept how much she had grown to care for Paine. How wise was it to feed such a thought when she was promised to the King?

Have the strength and courage to be who you are.

Her mother had said similar words to her since she was young, but only the Giantess had encouraged her to be who she was. The question was...who was she?

This journey with Paine had allowed secrets to surface. Did she embrace them as the Giantess urged or keep them buried?

She shivered, the cold ground seeping into her body. She wished she slept beside Paine. She favored his arms around her, the warmth of his strong body next to hers, and that spark of caring she felt deep inside him and that was growing ever stronger.

A gust of wind had her cringing against the cold.

Suddenly Paine was stretching out beside her, wrapping his arm around her and easing her against him.

"I will not have you die from the cold or the King will have my head."

Anin smiled and snuggled her back against him. "I would not want you to lose your head because of me."

"Go to sleep. We set a brisker pace tomorrow. King Talon eagerly awaits your arrival." And he was just as eager to deliver her and see this task complete, though he suffered a strong tug to his middle every time he thought of it.

"I am curious—"

"Curiosity will only get you in trouble," he warned.

"That would depend on what a person is curious about."

Now Paine was curious. "Tell me."

"There is gossip that the King's first wife, Estra, now wed to the chieftain of the Malloch Tribe, is heavy with her husband's babe. Is this so?"

Tunnan, the chieftain of the Malloch Tribe and loyal supporter of the King had sent word to King Talon as soon as his wife had told him of the babe. King Talon did not receive the news well, for it only served to give his opponents even more reason to see him dethroned since it now seemed obvious he would never father a son to ensure the Pict reign. His opponents also made it known that not one woman, out of many, he had mated with had he gotten with child.

"Aye, it is true," Paine said, wishing for the King's sake it was otherwise.

"If the King's third wife does not bare him a child whether son or daughter, surely his enemies will seek to depose him."

"It is those against the Unification of the Tribes that wish to see him deposed. But there was endless chaos and bloodshed before the unification. There are also those tribes to the south who watched and waited, still do, to push north when the time is right and end the Picts. We are stronger now thanks to King Talon and we thrive as a people."

"What if I fail the King? Will he be rid of me and wed me to another as he did with his other two wives?"

"Go to sleep," Paine snapped, having no answer for her and not caring for the thought of what might befall her.

Anin did not argue nor did she sleep. She did not want to be Queen.

Be who you are.

As if that would help her, though if the King found her lacking, perhaps he would change his mind, she could only hope.

She had thought to rest her hand on Paine's arm and feel what he was feeling, but stopped herself. It was not right for her to intrude like that, no matter how badly she wanted to. She would not want someone intruding on her feelings, so it was not right to do so to him.

Between the heat of his body and the warmth of the flames, she found herself being lolled into a peaceful slumber.

~~

It is time for you to come home, Anin. Listen and you will know where to go. You will be safe. Come home!

Anin thought about her brief dream while she walked the next day, the pace hardier than the day before. She had woken with a start, jolting up, expecting to see the woman who had been calling to her in her dream standing there and strangely enough wishing she had.

Somehow the voice was familiar to her, but she could not recall where she had heard it. One thing she was sure of was that it was not her mum's voice calling her home. Why then did the woman urge her to come home? What home?

They continued walking and both were surprised when they reached the edge of the forest. Beyond was barren, rocky land, spreading as far as one could see, leaving it easy for the Drust to spot them.

If it was close to dusk, Paine would have remained in the safety of the Giantess's forest, but there was much light left and he did not want to waste it.

He turned to Anin and her soft smile brought a forbidden thought. It was not that the thought had not come to him before, but this time it was stronger than it had ever been, making it more dangerous.

He ached to kiss her, taste her lips stained red from the berries she had eaten a short time ago. She would taste like the berries, more tart than sweet, the way he liked them.

"Is something wrong, Paine?" Anin asked, stepping closer to him and resting her hand on his arm before giving her action thought.

A jolt of desire struck her so hard that it frightened her and she jumped back away from him. His eyes took on a hardened glare that had her taking another step back.

"Keep aware...we do not know what awaits us," he ordered and stepped out of the forest, knowing it was much too dangerous for them to remain one more night there with how he was feeling toward her.

Anin followed, more worried about what she had felt from him than the Drust.

Chapter Twelve

A chill had Anin keeping her cloak snug around her as they walked over rocky, pitted land. It was difficult to stay aware of her surroundings and watch her footing at the same time, but if she did not, both could prove harmful.

They stopped shortly before dusk, having come upon a small river. While Bog went off to hunt for his meal, Paine saw to catching fish for theirs. It was a quiet evening they shared together, little being said. Sleep claimed them early, though Anin woke shivering from the cold and it was not long before she felt Paine wrap himself around her. She sighed gratefully and returned to a peaceful slumber.

They started the next morning just after dawn and kept a good pace, again little being said.

Paine preferred the silence. Too often Anin's questions left him thinking about her fate and the possibilities often disturbed him. She was a kind woman and many times more trusting than she should be, and the King would not be disappointed with her features. She was beautiful.

Too beautiful for the likes of himself and that thought disturbed him the most. Such a thought should not enter his head and yet he could not chase it away no matter how hard he tried.

He shook his head, trying to rid himself of his troubling thoughts.

"Something wrong?" Anin asked behind him.

"Keeping my head clear." Her soft laughter brought a quick smile to his face and he got annoyed. No one had made him smile as easily as Anin did in a long time.

"My mum once told me that I would have to shake my head senseless to clear all my countless thoughts."

"So you burdened your mum with endless questions?"

"No, she would not suffer my questions and said as you have that curiosity would get me in trouble. Though, I am grateful you were thoughtful and did not forbid me to ask questions as my mum did. Naturally, I could not stem my curiosity so I asked questions of others, though not too many questions of one person, so as not to annoy or have them remark to my mum."

"So you are also stubborn."

Anin laughed again. "At times. What kind of child were you?"

"A dutiful one. I helped my da work and protect the land and my mum and sister."

"You have a sister, how wonderful! Are you kind to her? My brothers still torment me."

Why had he mentioned his family? He had buried them and the memories long ago. Why had he allowed them to surface?

"My family is no more," he snapped and hurried their pace as if he could outrun the heartbreaking memories.

Anin felt a sting of pain for him and hurried to keep pace. "How horrible for you to lose your family, I am so sorry."

Paine stopped abruptly and turned almost colliding with Anin. "My family was not lost to me. They were brutally taken from me. Now enough talk. I need to get you safely to the King."

He turned and hurried his steps. Anin followed, saying nothing. What could she say? She did not want to ask him what happened, for she would not want him to relieve the horror of losing his family. She did, however, wonder if he was trying to right the wrong done to his family every time he swung the executioner's axe.

It was not long before dusk when they climbed a small hill and saw a village below.

"It is the Corsar Tribe. They are loyal to the King and fought with honor beside him. They will give us food and shelter for the night and protection from the Drust if need be."

Anin smiled grateful they would have food and a safe place to sleep.

The overcast sky grew darker as she, Paine, and Bog entered the village. The few people that were about began whispering and one scurried off as soon as his eyes fell on the executioner.

Anin wondered if they would be treated as the old couple had treated them, willing to give them food, yet avoiding them. She watched as more people emerged from their dwellings, eyes wide with concern, and began following them.

She kept her chin high as she walked beside Paine. She wanted everyone to know she walked beside him proudly and willingly. Though, she wondered if it mattered since all eyes were on Paine.

Anin stopped along with Paine when a tall, slim man approached them. His tunic fell just above his knees and a fur cape hung over his shoulders. Fur wrappings encased his lower legs and body drawings covered both arms. He had fine features, though the many wrinkles around his eyes and mouth marked him as an elder and his long gray hair signified him as a man of importance.

"It is with pleasure I welcome the King's executioner to our home," the man said with a nod. "I am Conmar, Chieftain of the Corsar Tribe."

"We need food and shelter for the night," Paine said.

"Of course, I will gladly provide whatever you need."

Anin watched the exchange between the men. Conmar seemed cautious and anxious. Anin felt the same of the tribesmen that had gathered around them. Something was not right and she instinctively took a step closer to Paine.

"Do you need a place to keep your prisoner?" Conmar asked.

Anin bit on her bottom lip to keep from speaking. She wanted to acknowledge Paine as her friend, but that was not possible with her slated to be Queen.

"She is not my prisoner," Paine said and offered no further explanation.

Anin rubbed her arms, a sudden chill coming upon her and her unease grew.

Fear.

That was what she was feeling, an overabundance of fear.

"What goes on here?" Paine demanded, feeling the unease himself and Bog agreed with a low rumbling growl.

Conmar raised his voice for all to hear. "It is a sign from the spirits that you were sent to us. We need your help. Please, come sit and eat and I will explain."

Anin was surprised when Paine ordered Bog to follow them into the feasting house and Conmar did not object.

Food and drink were provided even to Bog, and Conmar presented his wife Phillia, a thick woman who barely struck a smile. Conmar made no mention of the help they needed until the meal was done.

Phillia approached Anin and said, "I will show you to your dwelling where you may rest."

"Anin stays with me," Paine said to her relief.

Phillia bowed her head and left along with others, leaving only Conmar with Paine and Anin.

"Tell me," Paine ordered. He did not care for the unsettling feeling he had gotten upon entering the village. He knew well how he brought fear with him when he appeared, but fear had been here before he arrived. Something was terribly wrong and he had no intentions of letting Anin out of his sight.

Conmar leaned closer to Paine and kept his voice low, though there was no one about to hear him. "Several passed moon cycles some of our smaller animals had been found dead."

"That is not uncommon. Death strikes us all."

Conmar shook his head. "Not like this. The animal killings stopped after we found one of our own dead in the woods, gutted viciously just like the dead animals. At first, we thought nothing of it. A wolf probably had gotten him. We changed our minds when we found the next body and realized that an animal would have eaten at least part of his kill. We knew then it was no forest animal. We have lost five tribesmen in the same way since the last moon cycle. Fear has taken hold of our village and turned friend against friend, no one trusting one another. No matter how many sentries I post it does not stop the killings and since the killer eludes us many believe that a demon is responsible. They fear that the demon will not stop until the whole tribe is dead. Be it demon or man we search for, I beg of you to help us."

Anin shivered at his words. She had heard stories of demons that rode in on the shadows of the night claiming innocent people. And if hungry enough, would stay and feed on the fear and death.

"Find the demon and take his head so that we may finally be rid of him."

It was not an easy task Conmar asked of Paine, but he was the King's executioner and would be responsible to see it done.

"If you have not found this creature, what makes you think I can?" Paine asked.

"You are legend, whether warrior or executioner, nothing stops you from your task. You serve the King and his people with honor and do what must be done, what no one else wishes to do or dares to do."

Anin held her tongue. She wanted so badly to speak up and tell Conmar that Paine was all of that and more, and yet no one called him friend.

"Do you know what you ask of me? What I will do to find this demon?" Paine said as if in warning.

Conmar thought a moment, his hands beginning to tremble. "I know you will bring suffering, but my people already suffer and you arriving here when I was about to reach out to King Talon for help is a sign. The spirits sent you to help us."

"When I am finished, you may think it more the devil that sent me."

Conmar drew back away from Paine and clasped his hands tightly to stop them from trembling.

"Who found the slaughtered bodies?"

"Various tribesmen."

"Where were they found?" Paine asked.

"Mostly on the outskirts of the village."

"And no one saw or heard anything?"

"Nothing. That is why most believe it is the work of a demon. He makes no sound as he stalks his prey, then steals their voices before slaughtering them so they cannot scream for help."

"Where do you think this demon came from?"

"I do not know, though there has been talk that the young man who joined our tribe just before our troubles began brought the demon with him," Conmar explained.

"And he was found over the one body, blood soaking his hands and garments and weeping. He says he came upon Hendrid and was trying to help him."

"Take me to him," Paine ordered, standing.

"I will have Phillia see to Anin."

"I will not say it again. Anin stays with me." Paine held his hand out to Anin.

She took it, gripping it tightly. They thought they would seek food, shelter, and safety here for the night and what had they found...death many times over.

"Stay close," Paine whispered as they followed Conmar outside.

He did not have to tell her. She had no intentions of leaving his side, and she was also relieved that Bog kept close to her as well.

People were gathered in small groups, their eyes following Paine.

"See to your daily tasks," Conmar ordered.

"Will the executioner slay the demon for us?" someone shouted.

Silence followed as Conmar looked to Paine and waited along with his tribesmen, wanting to hear the executioner say it for all to hear.

"I will see it done," Paine called out.

Cheers filled the air and smiles surfaced as people dispersed, fear not feeling as heavy as it once did, though by no means was it gone.

Conmar took them a short distance passed the feasting house and around a gentle curve in the village and came upon a young man busy pounding the black stone that was broken and shaped into arrowheads for spears.

He stood as soon as he saw Conmar approach. He was short with thick arms and a barrel chest and short red hair and beard both neatly kept. His eyes turned cautious and curious, and he gave Conmar a respectful nod when he stopped in front of him.

"Dunnard, the King's executioner wishes to speak with you," Conmar said and stepped aside.

"I did nothing wrong," Dunnard said, taking a step back.

"I did not accuse you of anything," Paine snapped so sharply that it caused Dunnard, Conmar, and Anin to jump and Bog to step forward with a growl.

Dunnard took another step back.

"Take another step and I will think that you wish to run from something," Paine said.

Anin did not blame the young man for backing away from Paine. If his sharp tone did not intimidate, his size surely did. He towered over Dunnard.

Dunnard wisely took a step forward. "Forgive me. How may I serve the executioner?"

Anin admired the young man's bravery, though his fear was obvious in his trembling hands.

"Tell me where and how you found one of the men who were killed."

Dunnard cringed and shook his head slowly. "Hendrid. He was a kind man. He did not deserve to be gutted like an animal. I found him just inside the woods not far from the village."

"Do you know what he was doing there?" Paine asked.

"I do not know. I was looking for hardy branches to make spear poles when I came upon his—" He stopped abruptly. "He was barely alive when I found him."

"What did you do?"

"I tried to stuff him back together, but there was so much blood. He begged for help," —he choked on his words— "I failed to help him." Tears ran down his face.

"Did you go for help?"

Conmar answered. "I and two other men came upon him."

Paine turned to Conmar. "I did not ask you.

"It is as Conmar said," Dunnard was quick to say.

"You heard nothing or saw nothing?" Paine asked.

"Nothing." Dunnard shook his head as if disappointed in his own answer.

"He was alive when you found him?"

Dunnard nodded.

"With his last breath he did not speak the name of the man who robbed him of his life?"

"He could barely say anything."

"Yet you heard his pleas for help clearly?"

"He was afraid to die," Dunnard said.

"Are you afraid of death Dunnard?" Paine did not wait for a response. "We will talk again."

Dunnard's eye turned wide. "I told you everything."

"Perhaps or perhaps not, we shall see." Paine turned to Conmar. "Take me to the others who found the bodies?"

He turned away, stopped, and glanced back at Dunnard. "You make your arrowheads sharp." He did not wait for a response. He turned and walked away, leaving Dunnard's whole body trembling.

Conmar shook his head as he walked alongside Paine. "He is a skilled arrow maker and helpful to the tribe since his arrival. Will your torture reveal if a demon has taken hold of him?"

"Torture reveals the truth more often than not. Were the others alive like Hendrid when found?"

Conmar shook his head. "No, not a breath to them."

"I will speak with Dunnard again."

"You will torture him to get the truth, will you not?" Conmar asked.

"If necessary."

"Do whatever you must to end this evil."

Paine always did what had to be done whether he liked it or not. One thing he never strayed from, though, was talking with his prisoners before beginning torture. Sometimes he got the answer he wanted after a short conversation. He did not like to torture. Most people confessed to anything to end their suffering and that did not always get the truth, and the King demanded the truth. He would see what each man told him, then decide if he should proceed with torture.

Anin lagged behind Paine, turning her head several times as they walked away to get another look at the young man. He stared after them, his eyes so wide she thought they would burst from his head. Could he do such a horrible thing to one of his tribesmen? Or was it as he said, he tried to help the dying man? She could find out with one touch. She had to contain the overwhelming urge to rush over to him and lay her hand on him. She would know then if he killed the man or not.

She chastised herself for the foolish thought. Her mum had warned her repeatedly not to pay heed to such nonsense that it would not serve her well. It had been difficult to do as she had cautioned and since meeting Paine, her urge to touch, to feel had grown too strong to fight against.

"Anin!"

She jumped and turned to Paine.

"Three times I have called you."

His words were stern and she thought him angry, but his eyes held concern. "Endless thoughts," she said, offering an explanation and went to his side, Bog keeping close to her.

Anin followed Paine from place to place and listened intently as he spoke with the men who had found the bodies. He asked several of the same questions more than once and Anin began to see how the men would sometimes answer differently.

By the time Paine finished questioning the last man, he turned to Conmar and said, "See that Dunnard is tied securely for the night."

"You believe Dunnard brought this evil down on us?" Conmar asked.

"Tomorrow I will know for sure and do what must be done."

Conmar nodded. "I am relieved to hear this." He showed them into a small dwelling, pleasantly warm from the roaring flames in the fire pit.

"I will see Dunnard secured, though I would ask you to see for yourself that we secured him well enough."

"Let me know when it is done."

Conmar hurried and took his leave, anxious to see to the task.

"Do you believe Dunnard guilty?" Anin asked, drawing closer to the fire pit and holding her chilled hands out to warm them.

"I believe that it is odd that he came upon Hendrid still alive and saw or heard nothing. All the other men had been found well after they had died. Also the evil did not start until after he arrived. He will tell me more when I speak with him."

She saw concern in his eyes and gentle warmth spread through her or was it the fire's heat that warmed her? "Dunnard's words seemed heartfelt."

"I have heard such heartfelt talk before only to discover it lies."

Shouts from outside drew their attention and a knock sounded at the door. Paine opened it to find Conmar's wife, Phillia standing there.

"Conmar says you must hurry. The tribesmen are calling for Dunnard's head."

Anin hurried after Paine as well as Bog.

"Cut him open like he did to others," one man shouted.

"Nay, let him rot on the stake for a few days before we slit him open," another cried out.

"I did nothing. Nothing," Dunnard shouted.

Anin stood shocked after breaking through the crowd with Paine. Dunnard was naked and pressed against a tall stake in the ground as rope was coiled around him from his ankles to just below his shoulders. Blood marred his head and face where swaths of his beard and hair had been cut away.

"I did nothing," Dunnard pleaded again and a stone struck him, bouncing off the rope. Several more followed, some catching his flesh, leaving him bleeding.

"Enough!" Paine shouted and went and stood in front of Dunnard. "You will leave this man to me or suffer for it, and I will see that your suffering will be far greater than his. Now leave and do not return here."

People scurried off afraid of what the executioner could do to them.

Paine walked up to Dunnard. "Think on what you will tell me tomorrow."

"I told you everything. I beg you to believe me."

"Think on it, for I will get the truth from you," Paine said and turned away to stand in front of the young man until everyone had gone. When the first drop of rain struck the ground, Paine took Anin by the arm and hurried her to their dwelling.

Anin stood again by the fire pit warming herself, though she did not know if her chill came from the cold the rain had brought with it or from seeing Dunnard suffer so badly.

"I do not believe he killed those men," she said.

"Because his words are so heartfelt? Great suffering and fear can force the tongue to say anything."

She shuddered, thinking of the poor young man, rain pouring down on him and darkness falling.

Paine went to her and took her hands in his, rubbing them. "Many claim themselves innocent when they are far from it."

"Have you found none to be innocent out of all those you have tortured and beheaded?"

He stopped rubbing her hands, released them, and took a step away from her. He had no right touching her with hands that had brought so much pain and death.

"Not one innocent person?" she asked when he failed to answer.

"There was a woman" His brow scrunched in thought as a memory surfaced. "I was sent to a village where a healer was accused of stealing the breaths of some recently born bairns. The tribe wanted her to suffer before I took her life. She had been beaten badly, burned on parts of her body, and her long gray hair chopped short.

"When the torture began, she did not beg for her life or scream out her innocence. She begged for help for two bairns that were due to be born. She feared for their lives. She pleaded with me to send for a healer from another tribe to tend the births." He shook his head. "The torture continued and still she begged for those bairns to be protected. That night one of the women started birthing. She and the bairn were soon in trouble. It was the chieftain's sister who was giving birth and she begged for the skilled healer to help her. He granted her permission, but only if I attended the birth and made certain she did not steal the bairn's breathes.

"I watched the healer soothe the mum, though she herself suffered from what had been done to her, and coax the baby out with little difficulty. The caring smile on her beaten face was something I will never forget. If I had not turned my head away for moment, I would not have caught or stopped the healer's helper from smothering the bairn with her hand over his little mouth and nose.

"It did not take long for her to confess to what she had done. Angry at not having bairns of her own, she wanted no other women to have them."

Anin felt relief for the healer and sadness for the woman. "What happened to the healer?"

"There were some who believed the healer helped the woman even though the woman insisted otherwise. I advised her to leave the tribe and she agreed. She is now King Talon's healer."

Anin smiled, happy for the healer. "If one proved innocent, could not others?"

"We have no time for this."

She walked over to him and laid her hand on his arm. "There is always time for the truth." A tingle of desire rushed through her and tender warmth hugged her. She had touched him without thought or consequence, but was glad she did. She let her hand stay as it was, enjoying the comforting feeling that drifted from him into her.

Paine stepped away reluctantly, her simple touch causing far too much feeling to stir in him. "Remember do not leave my side while we are here."

"As you wish," she said. He did not have to tell her to stay close, she wanted to do so. Oddly enough, she felt that she belonged beside him and she did not know what she would do when he finally left her.

"Sleep, for we are lucky to have sleeping pallets and shelter from the rain tonight," Paine said.

Anin did as he said and not soon after fell into a peaceful slumber.

She did not know what woke her, the crackle of the fire or the stillness around it. Paine slept a distance from her and Bog slept in front of the door, though his head shot up when she sat up. Something disturbed her. She did not need to think on what it was, she knew.

One touch and she would know if Dunnard was innocent. One touch could save him.

Quietly Anin got to her feet and so did Bog. Keeping her steps light, she approached Bog and leaned down close to whisper, "Not a sound."

He seemed to understand and since he had been given no order to stop her, followed her out the door.

The rain had stopped, taking the chill with it and leaving a heavy haze behind to greet the morn. Confident she could find her way to Dunnard, she took a step into the thick mist.

Chapter Thirteen

It was strangely quiet. Anin listened for any little sound, the hoot of an owl, the drip of water the rainstorm left behind, the scurry of nocturnal animals, but there was nothing. It was as though the mist snuffed out all sound.

She took cautious steps, Bog so close to her side she felt him rub against her leg. Her ear finally caught a sound and she stopped and listened.

"Help me! Help me!"

Anin followed the faint pleading until she was able to make out a shadow not far from her. When a low growl erupted in Bog's throat, she stopped. Had the shadow moved? Was there someone there with her? She looked around, the mist so thick she could see nothing, not even the shadow that had been there. Had she been foolish in her thinking? Could a demon be following her ready to rip her apart as he had done to the others?

The pleading voice called out again, more anxiously this time. She decided there was nothing left for her to do but follow it and learn the truth. If she did not have Bog with her, she may have thought differently. She took several steps when the pleading stopped, though she did not. She followed where she believed the sound had come from and soon came upon Dunnard.

He gasped when she stopped in front of him.

"I mean you no harm," she said softly.

"Please, you must help me. I swear I killed no one."

It was frightening enough walking in the thick mist, not able to see anything around you, but to be tied to a stake helpless had to be terrifying beyond measure.

Anin raised her hand to place it on his bare shoulder, to comfort and to discover the truth. She brought her hand down gently to rest on his wet, chilled skin. Cold seeped into her at first, then suddenly terrifying helplessness gripped and twisted her insides. It changed so quickly almost as if she had never felt it. Instead, a strange sensation took hold of her, pleasure from inflicting horrible pain on others. She had to fight her way through the horrible sensation, feeling smothered by the evil that was rising up and surrounding her.

A hand suddenly clamped around her wrist, yanking her hand off the young man and spinning her around.

"Did you not hear me when I ordered you not to leave my side?" Paine asked with sharp anger.

Anin glared at Paine, unable to say anything, wanting desperately to let him know that he was right. Evil resided in Dunnard.

"Are you feeling unwell, Anin?" Paine asked concerned that she appeared as if she wanted to speak but could not.

Dunnard spoke up. "She is a seer, is she not? Is that not why she touched me, to see the truth for herself? And the truth has left her speechless, for she knows I killed no one."

"She is no seer," Paine said, though looked at Anin questioningly. Could it be possible? Could she be a seer? Could that be the secret her mum had been hiding?

"She is a seer," Dunnard insisted. "A seer sees the past and the future. What is my fate? Please tell me."

Paine's hand fell off Anin's wrist to quickly reach out and grab Dunnard's hair, giving it a hard yank. "I am your fate!"

"I did nothing. I beg you to believe me. I did nothing!" Dunnard pleaded.

"I will see you soon and you will confess the truth," Paine said and turned, taking firm hold of Anin's arm and hurrying her away. Once they reached the dwelling, he opened the door roughly and shoved her inside. "Do you wish me to suffer unspeakable torture before I lose my head?"

The thought turned her sick and she shook her head and was glad her voice had returned to her. "Never would I want you to suffer and I most certainly do not wish death upon you."

Paine took such quick steps toward her that she scurried away from him, her back hitting the wall. He planted both hands on either side of her head and brought his face close to hers. "Never, ever, disobey me again. If I fail to deliver you safely to the King, he will see me suffer far beyond any suffering I have brought on others."

Anin reached up and laid a hand to his warm cheek, flushed hot from anger. "Forgive my thoughtlessness. I will not diso—" Her words died instantly when Paine's true feelings rushed over her. *Fear.* Not for himself, for her. Fear that something had happened to her. Fear that he failed to save her. Fear that he would never see her again.

Paine had never seen such tenderness and caring in anyone's eyes as he did in Anin's. One look could soothe and—his eyes flared when suddenly her eyes looked at him as if she had just discovered something—about him.

Her fingers drifted off his cheek to his lips and he warned himself to stop her, but he did nothing. He stood still, not moving, his breath caught somewhere inside him. And when her fingers drifted faintly across his lips, he whispered her name in warning, "Anin."

His warm breath kissed her fingers, sending a rush of tingles through her. She instinctively, without thought or consequences, went up on her toes and brought her lips to meet his.

Paine grabbed her by the arms, intending to push her away. Instead, he yanked her against him, settling his lips over hers in a hungry kiss.

Anin felt something in her spark and fire to life, as if she had never truly been alive until this very moment. When he slipped his tongue into her mouth to mate with hers, she felt herself slip deep within him, where spirit stirs, and somehow lock there. They were one now and would always be and nothing would ever change that. It was a strange sensation, a rhythm of sorts, almost as if their hearts beat together as one.

Anin's breath was suddenly ripped out of her when Paine shoved her away. She stood there a moment, her hand to her chest, fighting to regain her breath and her wits.

Paine turned away, fighting for breath, feeling as if it had been torn out of him. He turned back in haste. "I know of seers who can rob a man of his breath and thoughts. Are you one of them? Is that why your mum did not want you to wed the King?"

His words pierced her chest, hurting so badly that she dropped down on the bench to the side of the door. "I am no seer."

He could still feel the taste of her on his lips, hot and hungry. He rarely kissed women. It was a good poke he would have with those willing, but not a kiss did he share. A poke was a poke, but a kiss meant much more. He had not intended to kiss her, so why had he?

"You wanted to kiss me as much as I wanted to kiss you."

"You know my thoughts," he accused.

She wanted to tell him that she felt everything he felt for her, but her mum's warning rang clear in her head.

Tell no one.

And this time she listened. "I know what I see on your face and," —she placed her hand on her chest—" I know what I feel."

Paine turned away from her again and walked around the fire pit, so that it separated them. He was trying to find an excuse to explain it all when he knew full well what he had felt, still felt, and feared he would always feel. And the kiss had proven it to him. It had reached down so deep in him he had thought their spirits touched and united, joining them together forever.

It had shocked him and that was why he had shoved her away and for no other reason, not even that she was to be Queen.

He turned slowly to face her. "This cannot be. You are meant to be Queen." He raised him hand, stopping her when she went to respond. "It is done. We speak of this no more."

Anin held her tongue. It would do no good to tell me that she was meant to be his and he was meant to be hers. How she knew that she could not say, but as sure as light graced the land each morn, she knew it to be true.

"Dunnard will tell anyone who will listen—and many will—that you are a seer. I will have to tell the King of this incident or he will hear of it from someone else and demand to know why I did not tell him."

"If I was a seer, I would have been able to warn you about the Drust attacks before they happened. I am no seer."

"Why did you go see Dunnard?"

How could she explain to him what she could not explain to herself? She chose to tell him a partial truth. "I believed Dunnard innocent and wished to talk with him."

Paine walked around the fire pit to stand a safe distance from her with his arms folded across his chest. "I do not believe you. Now tell me the truth."

He was good at getting the truth from people in any way he could. She had seen that when he questioned the tribesmen who had found the bodies. She worried that a few choice questions might reveal what she wished to keep hidden. She had to be careful of her responses.

"I think you are right about Dunnard. He lies easily."

"And what brought you to this conclusion?"

"That he claims me a seer, thinking it will save him. As you said yourself, he will tell everyone that I am a seer and convince them I know of his innocence."

"He will not have time for such claims." He tilted his head, seeing a slight scrunch of her brow. "Is there something else you have not told me?"

His ability to see more than most frightened Anin. It could prove difficult when harboring a secret. "I do not know if it matters or not, but I recall seeing a shadow pass by near Dunnard as he begged for help."

He wanted to reach out and snatch her up against him and never let her go, for fear of something dreadful happening to her, but he did not move. He simply shook his head and ordered, "Never again will you place yourself in danger."

"Bog was with me," she said as if there had been nothing to fear.

"He did not go after the shadow?"

"He growled, but never left my side."

Paine looked to Bog and nodded. "Good work, Bog."

The wolf jumped to his feet from where he lay by the door and started growling just before terrifying screams pierced their dwelling.

Paine grabbed his battle-axe and Bog waited anxiously at the door. Anin followed both of them as they rushed out of the dwelling and into chaos.

"The demon struck again," a woman screamed, joining the others who were running frantically through the village.

Paine grabbed Anin's hand and she held on tight, fearful of being torn away from him in the rushing crowd. Mist still lingered, though not as heavily, leaving it easier for them to follow the others. It was on the outskirts of the village, near a stream where everyone gathered.

Paine pushed his way through the crowd, though they parted as soon as they saw it was the executioner and his wolf.

"He has struck again," Conmar said as he turned and spotted Paine. "How is this possible with Dunnard tied to the stake?"

"Dunnard is possessed of a demon who takes to flight whenever he wishes," someone yelled out.

Others agreed with similar shouts.

Paine turned a powerful voice on them all. "Go to your dwellings and stay there until otherwise told and do not go near the prisoner."

All eyes turned to Conmar.

"Innocent or guilty, Dunnard needs to die now to stop the fear and madness that grips my tribe."

"Dunnard will die when I command it," Paine ordered. "Have them obey me or suffer for it."

Fear gripped Conmar as strongly as it did the tribe and he threatened, "I have a village of warriors."

"And who do you think they will obey when I take your head in one swift blow and hold it up for all to see?" Paine raised his battle-axe to his waist.

Conmar was quick to shout, "Do as the executioner says. Return home."

Grumbles filled the air as the crowd began to disperse reluctantly.

Paine looked to Anin and ordered, "Turn away."

Anin did so without protest. She had no desire to look upon the horrific scene. And she was pleased when Bog sat beside her after Paine ordered him to guard.

A few steps took Paine and Conmar to the body and he crouched down to get a better look. "His name?"

"Rolson...a good warrior who many of the lasses favored."

"Is he one of the added sentries you posted last night?"

"How did you know I added sentries?"

"You would have to be a fool not to."

"He was one of several, though the heavy mist made their task more difficult," Conmar confirmed.

"Who found Rolson?" Paine asked.

Conmar nodded toward a woman sitting beneath a tree, her head slumped. "Young Areanis came upon the awful scene."

"Bring her here," Paine ordered.

"Areanis, come here," Conmar called out and she stumbled to her feet to hurry and do as he ordered.

Anin felt sorry for the young woman as she watched her approach. Her eyes were red and swollen from crying and she wore no shoes. Her hands and feet were covered with blood and blood was splattered all over her tunic.

"She tripped over Rolson and by the time she was able to get to her feet, she was drenched in blood. She is frightened that death has touched her and will claim her next," Conmar explained before the young woman reached them.

"You found Rolson?" Paine asked and Areanis started trembling.

She bowed her head. "The mist was so thick I did not see him. I thought I had tripped over a fallen tree. When I saw Rolson and all the blood on me, I started screaming and tried to get the blood off me. She demonstrated, rubbing her hand on her tunic frantically.

"What were you doing here?"

Areanis seemed reluctant to answer.

"Answer the executioner!" Conmar ordered sharply.

"I was meeting Rolson."

"You saw nothing, heard nothing before finding him?" Paine asked.

Areanis shook her head. "I could not take my eyes off Rolson. His insides were spilled out around him." Her trembling increased and tears pooled in her eyes. "The demon got him and he is going to get the rest of us. You must save us, please," she begged tears running down her face.

"This madness cannot be allowed to continue," Conmar said.

"Death touched me. He will come after me next. I will die like all the others," Areanis cried, her shoulders slouching in defeat and her tears clearing a path through the blood on her cheeks.

Shouts rang out. "Dunnard broke free. He broke loose. The demon is free."

Chapter Fourteen

"The demon is coming for me," Areanis cried out and ran into the woods before anyone could stop her.

Paine looked to Conmar, "Gather your warriors and meet me at the stake." He hurried over to Anin, taking her arm. "I do not want to leave you, but I must go after Dunnard. I will see you safely to our dwelling and you will wait there until I come for you."

The village was in chaos, people running and hurrying inside their dwellings, shutting their doors tightly. Warriors rushed to gather at the stake, spears and swords in hand.

Anin hurried inside as soon as Paine opened the door. "I will have your word that you will stay here until I come for you

"You have my word I will remain here."

The door shut and a shiver ran through her.

"It is a shame you will not be able to keep your word."

Anin froze in fright for a moment before forcing herself to turn and see Dunnard standing there naked. Dark spots marred his body where the stones had hit him and areas of his skin were peeled raw from where the rope had been drawn tightly around him.

"Your cloak," he said, holding out his hand and taking a step closer to her.

Anin quickly slipped it off and tossed it to him.

"Did Areanis run?" he asked as he fashioned the cloak around his waist, providing cover to his lower parts.

Anin nodded

"Good, she waits for us," he said with a chilling grin.

"You kill together?" Anin asked.

He laughed. "You knew that as soon as you touched me. Is that why the executioner is so good at his chore? He keeps a seer by his side."

"I am not a seer."

"Why do you deny it? I could see it in your eyes when you touched me that you knew what I did, though I was not sure if you saw Areanis slip through the mist to help me or heard the plans we made." He stretched his arm out to Anin. "Touch me and see your fate."

"I am not a seer."

"Deny it if you wish, but I will have you tell me of my fate."

He rushed at her, grabbing her, and she instinctively tried to push him away. He twisted her arm and she yelped in pain and his pleasure shot through her like a stab to her chest. He twisted it again and before she could cry out once more, she felt the brutal sting of his hand to her face twice. Blood pooled in her mouth and ran down her chin. She swept her tongue faintly across her lower lip to find it split near the middle, blood continuing to run from it He enjoyed making someone suffer and the more pain, the more enjoyment for him.

"Tell me!" he demanded.

She saw eagerness in his eyes to hit her again and felt it seep into her until she thought it would choke her. She responded quickly even though there was no truth to her words. "You and Areanis survive."

"And the executioner, what is his fate?"

Anin hesitated and it was the excuse he needed to make her suffer once again. This time he delivered a blow to the side of her face, catching her eye and cheek. The pain shot through her like a piercing arrow, causing her to cry out and for that he slapped her again, and she tasted more of her own blood. She had to answer quickly and tell him what he wanted to hear if she was to survive.

"You slaughter him as you did the others," she said her insides twisting at the thought.

"I cannot wait to see how the executioner responds when I slit him open and he watches as his entails spill out."

A rap shook the door and Dunnard grabbed her chin, squeezing it and whispered, "Watch your tongue or I will make sure you lose it here and now."

"Who is there?" she demanded.

"Willum, I was sent to make certain all remain inside their dwellings until the demon is caught."

"I will remain where I am," Anin assured him. Dunnard sent her an evil look and she was quick to call out. "Where do the warriors search?"

"The woods where the last body was found. Be safe."

"You as well," Anin called out and Dunnard grinned.

He pressed his finger roughly against her lips and she cringed from the pain it brought her and he pressed even harder, causing more blood to flow from her wound.

After a few moments, he whispered, "You will open the door and peek out just enough to see that no one lurks about."

She did as he said, hoping that once free of the dwelling she could somehow escape him. She peeked out, pushing the door open a bit further. "I see no one."

With a tight grip on her arm, he shoved her out further past the door until he could see for himself and once sure no one was about, he squeezed her arm even harder as he hurried her around the dwelling and into the woods.

Anin tried not to cringe from the pain in her arm, but when his fingers dug deep, she could not keep from wincing.

"That is nothing to what I am going to make you feel," he said with such pleasure that her insides sickened and she was glad she had yet to eat or she would have lost the food there and then.

He enjoyed every step he forced upon her and every squeeze to her arm, or jab to her back if she did not move fast enough.

"Hurry, Areanis waits for us."

Anin kept going, not knowing what to do. Paine thought her safe in the dwelling and would not return to her until Dunnard was caught. But he was closer to the village not where they were searching, so how would Paine ever find him?

Call to him. He will hear you now that your spirits have touched and become one. He will know how to find you.

The voice was soft yet strong in her head. Could it be? Would he hear her?

She called out silently. *Help me, Paine. Hurry, there is not much time. Dunnard has me.*

Dunnard yanked on her arm, causing her to stumble and giving him an excuse to squeeze her arm until she thought she would scream with the pain. She closed her lips tightly to keep from crying out and cringed, forgetting her wound. The taste of blood was strong in her mouth and she forced herself to ignore it, and the agony she suffered, as she continued to silently reach out to Paine.

I am waiting for you. I know you will come for me. You will always protect me and keep me safe from harm. You too, Bog. Come now, I need you both.

~~~

129

Paine stopped abruptly and listened. He had thought he heard Anin call out to him for help, but that was not possible. She had given him her word. She was waiting for him where he had left her.

He looked around. They had found no signs, no track of Dunnard, and Paine wondered if they had missed something.

Bog began to whine, startling Paine. The wolf never whined.

He heard something again. He shook his head and whispered, "Anin?"

Help me!

Her voice was as clear as if she stood next him and he knew Bog heard it as well since his whine increased. "Find Anin, Bog!" he ordered and the wolf took off.

Paine ignored Conmar's shouts to him and rushed to keep up with Bog, silently calling out her name again and again.

~~~

A strong wind suddenly swept through the forest, shaking tree branches, dropping some of the leaves to swirl around Anin and Dunnard as they walked.

Each leaf that swirled past Anin whispered her name and she had to stop herself from smiling upon hearing Paine's voice. He was coming for her.

Dunnard stopped suddenly and looked around, then called out softly, "Areanis, are you here?"

"What delayed you?"

Dunnard turned, tugging Anin along with him, to see Areanis walk from behind a tree, a dagger dripping with blood held tightly in her hand.

"You killed without me," Dunnard said annoyed.

"I had no choice. The warrior came upon me gathering the sack I hid for our escape. I had to get back here fast to meet you, so I took his life quickly," Areanis said with disappointment, though a smile surfaced slowly. "What of her? We can enjoy her and leave her where the executioner can easily find her."

Dunnard smiled as well. "True enough, and then it will be the executioner's turn."

Areanis's smile widened. "Suffering has been his friend. I wonder what he will do when his friend turns on him."

Areanis approached Dunnard, her smile fading when she saw Anin's bloody lip and the swelling at the corner of her eye and cheek. "You have enjoyed yourself some with her already."

"A little, but now we can enjoy her together," Dunnard said and he Areanis both turned and grinned at Anin.

~~~

Paine ran, ducking to avoid branches, jumping over fallen trees and large rocks to keep up with Bog, though the animal kept far ahead of him. It was a matter of keeping him in sight and usually Paine had no trouble keeping pace with the wolf, but Bog was traveling faster than ever before and that could only mean one thing. Anin was in grave danger.

He had been a fool to leave her. Never again. Never again would he leave her side. He had known an unbearable loss when he lost his family. It was a horrible lingering ache he had never wanted to experience again. A hint of such a loss had struck after leaving Anin alone at the dwelling. It had overwhelmed him so much that he had almost turned back. Now he wished he had.

Paine, hurry!

131

Her frightened voice tore at his insides and he ran faster.

~~~

"This will be fun," Areanis said, rubbing the bloody blade of her dagger on her tunic.

With Dunnard's grip so strong on Anin, it would be impossible to break free, so how did she stop them from torturing and killed her before Paine got here to save her? She spoke hastily when a thought came to her. "You would be fools to harm me."

Dunnard gave her arm a hard yank. "Why is that?"

Anin raised her chin, trying desperately to ignore the vicious pain in her arm. "I am to be Queen." She was pleased to hear their loud laughter and pleased to listen as the trees carried the sound far beyond where they stood. Hopefully, Paine would hear it.

"I am Paine's mission. He is to see me safely to King Talon."

Dunnard sunk his fingers into her cheeks squeezing tightly. "It appears that the executioner is going to fail the King." He released her face with a hard shove.

"That may be so," Anin said, "but what do you think the King will do when he discovers the future Queen and his executioner were killed? He will send his warriors to hunt you down. There will be no place for you to go. No place for you to hide. Once you are found, you will know more pain than you ever thought possible and you will beg to die. Of course, the King will not let you die easily. He will see that you suffer a brutal death."

"She is lying," Areanis said.

"All knows the King searches for a new Queen, one who will give him many sons. My mother gave my father four strong sons before she birthed me. My father

132

is Cathbad of the Girthrig Tribe, Lord of the Western Region, loyal servant of King Talon. My father will join in the hunt for you both and will not stop until you are found."

"There has been talk that the King has found a woman to be Queen," Areanis said, no smile on her face now.

Dunnard did not seem convinced. "Why not send his personal guard to bring her safely to Pictland? Why send only the executioner?"

"Who could protect her better?" Areanis argued. "And who would think that the future Queen would walk alongside the executioner, the man whose constant companion is death?"

"She could be lying."

"Then do what you will to her, but I will take no part in it," Areanis said. "It will be you the King hunts, not me."

Dunnard gave Anin another hard shove and she fell to the ground. "We leave now together."

Areanis shook her head and backed away from Dunnard. "I will not travel with you. When you laid your hand to her, you sealed your fate. The King will see you suffer."

Dunnard paced in front of Anin, his hand frantically rubbing his head. "This is wrong. She told me she is a seer and that we—"

Anin spoke up. "I told you I am no seer, but you would not listen, so I told you what you wanted to hear."

"The King would wed no seer," Areanis said, taking another step away from him.

Dunnard reached her in two steps, grabbing her arm. "You will not leave me. We go together."

Areanis shook her head. "I will not be hunted by the King. It is certain death."

It happened so fast that Anin could not believe her eyes. Dunnard grabbed Areanis's hand that held her dagger and drove it into her middle and yanked it up, splitting her open.

"No one leaves me," Dunnard said then pulled the dagger out and ran it across her throat and let her drop to the ground.

Anin stared at Areanis as she laid there gurgling, her eyes wide as her life slipped away.

Dunnard turned to Anin. "The pleasure of a good kill leaves me hard and ready for a good poke. Since Areanis is not here to satisfy me, you will have to suffice." He yanked her cloak off him and tossed it aside. He stroked his aroused member and smiled. "This might be more pleasurable than I thought. I can do more painful things to you than Areanis had allowed me to do to her."

Anin scrambled to her feet, reaching for anything that she could use to defend herself. She grabbed a good-sized rock.

He laughed. "That will not stop me."

She glared at him as she released a scream that echoed through the forest, the leaves and trees carrying it far and wide.

Dunnard charged at her and she threw the rock, hitting him in the chest and sending him tumbling back, but remaining on his feet.

A sneer tore across his face and he scooped up the dagger off the ground. "You are going to beg me to die." He charged at her again.

Anin went to run when suddenly Bog jumped in front of her, snarling and snapping at Dunnard, forcing him to back away.

"It is you who is going to beg me to die," Paine said from behind him.

Chapter Fifteen

Dunnard turned, dagger raised, and Paine knocked it from his hand with his battle-axe then delivered a vicious blow to his face, sending him sprawling to land flat on his back.

"Keep your sword at his throat until the others get here to tie him up," Paine ordered one of Conmar's warriors who had managed to keep pace with him.

Anin did not wait for Paine to come to her, she ran to him. He caught her in his arms and tears threatened her eyes. His arms welcomed her with such caring and concern that it was as if she had come home. She refused to let go of him, hugging him tightly, and resting her head on his solid chest. She did not want to be separated from him. She belonged there with him and he belonged to her just as she belonged to him and nothing would change that.

"Anin," he said softly. "I must look at you and know you are unharmed."

Her muffled voice was not easy to hear. "I am well now that I am with you."

"Anin," he said more forcefully and eased her away from him.

She shook her head. "I will not be separated from you."

"I will not let that happen." His own words surprised him.

"I will have your word on that."

He gave it without hesitation. "You have my word."

Anin reluctantly raised her head to look at him, though she did not let go of him.

Paine winced when he saw her face. Her lip was split and swollen, though it no longer bled. Her eye was swollen as was her cheek and both were turning dark.

"It is nothing," Anin said. "I am well."

"You are not. He dared to lay his hands on you."

"I am alive, you saved me and that is all that matters."

"He harmed you and that is what matters."

Anin was surprised to feel such strong anger within him.

"He will suffer for this," Paine said, running his hand down her arm.

Anin gasped when his hand touched where Dunnard had squeezed repeatedly. She gasped again when she felt rage take hold of him. "He squeezed my arm too often," she explained, hoping it would calm him. It did not.

Paine remained silent for a few moments, then he asked, "Did he harm you in any other way?"

Anin shook her head. "I am still fit for the King."

He leaned his brow down to rest on hers. "I do not care if you are fit for the King. I care that he did not harm you."

She raised her hand to rest on his cheek. "I am not harmed. I am safe here in your arms."

He asked the question that plagued him. "Was he waiting for you in the dwelling?"

Anin nodded.

Fury filled Paine's eyes. He was angry with himself for having left her alone, and he would see Dunnard suffer for all he did.

Conmar burst upon the scene, tearing Paine and Anin apart.

"You found him," Conmar said, looking upon Dunnard who had yet to revive. He turned wide eyes on Areanis's body, shaking his head. "Not before he killed again."

"They killed together," Anin announced, keeping close to Paine as they approached Conmar.

Anin told Conmar all about the couple and what they had done to his tribesmen.

"I am forever grateful that you and the executioner happened upon us. I will send a message to King Talon, letting him know how his executioner saved the Corsar Tribe."

"Time to finish it," Paine said. "We will drag Dunnard back to the village and there in front of all I will free you of the demon."

His warriors shouted their approval.

Dunnard began begging for his life after a short time of being dragging over rocks, fallen branches and through leaf and twigged filled ruts. No one paid him heed.

When they reached the village, Dunnard was hauled away and a horn blew, letting the people know they could safely come out of their homes.

Paine walked Anin to their dwelling and entered with her. Once he looked about, he turned to her. "Do you want to see what I do to Dunnard?"

She shook her head and could not stop a shudder that rant through her.

Paine went to her, looking over her wounds. Under her eye was turning dark and around her mouth was caked with blood. He wanted to stay and tend to her wounds himself. He had the skill, many times having to heal prisoners only so that he could continue torturing them. But he had Dunnard to see to. "I will leave Bog with you, having him with you is like having me with you. He will let no harm come to you."

The wolf stood away from the door he sat braced against and walked over to sit pressed against her leg.

She reached down slowly and when he made no move to stop her from touching him, she patted his head. "I feel safe with Bog and eagerly await your return."

"I will not be quick."

Anin shuddered again, knowing he intended to see Dunnard suffer and knowing the tribesmen would want it that way. "It will give me time to see to my wounds."

Paine reached out, not able to help himself from running a tender hand over her darkening cheek. "I will have the healer sent to you."

Anin cherished the gentleness of his touch and could not comprehend how soon his touch would bring such pain.

"Dunnard deserves what he will suffer."

She nodded, though wondered how he knew her thoughts. She took hold of his arm as he went to turn away. "We will stay another night here?"

He moved his arm so that her hand softly drifted down along it until their hands met. Once they did, he threaded his fingers with hers. Her hand was warm and soft and he never wanted to let it go. But he would have to and the thought pierced his chest like a mighty sword. "It would be wiser and safer to renew our journey in the morning."

She nodded again, wanting to leave this tribe and the memories behind, but he was right. They would be safer here for another night.

"Besides having the healer brought to you, I will also have food brought."

"I will wait for you to eat."

He looked about to argue, then simply acquiesced with a nod. He went to the door, turned and looked at Bog. "Guard!"

Anin felt safe when the door closed behind him. She told herself to be grateful for another night of shelter and food. Her only thought though was of her being

138

alone with Paine. No thoughts of tomorrow or what it would bring, only her and Paine alone together. She was caring for this man more than she ever thought possible and she could not understand why.

He was not someone she would have ever thought she would feel so strongly for and yet the thought of never seeing him again left her feeling—frightened.

What was happening to her? Why was she feeling this way?

Be who you are. The answers will come.

Surely, there was something wrong with her, hearing her mum and the Giantess so clearly in her head.

She jumped, terrified when the first agonizing scream penetrated the walls. Bog followed her as she paced around the room, hugging herself more tightly as the subsequent screams grew more horrifying. Finally, she could take it no more and dropped down beside Bog and hugged him, planting her face in his fur.

He did not growl or show his teeth, he simply rested his head against her.

The healer did not arrive until after a loud cheer rang out. Anin knew then that Paine had taken Dunnard's head. Bog growled when a tap sounded at the door and, try as she might, Anin could not get Bog to stop nor would he allow her to open the door.

She finally gave up and called out to the woman to get the executioner.

Paine's command had Bog moving away from the door. When he entered he looked to Bog. "The healer is here to help Anin. Guard them both!" He then looked to Anin. "I will return shortly."

When the door closed behind him, the healer, a spry elder, said, "It is good the executioner found someone who cares so deeply for him. Not many women can care for a man whose hands bring so much suffering and death."

Anin thought to correct her, tell her what a good man Paine was, but she did not. She remained silent. It was better to say nothing then say something that could possibly be harmful to them both.

The healer left as Paine entered, Conmar following in behind him and servants behind him.

"Are you sure you do not wish to join in the celebration?" Conmar asked. "Everyone would be pleased to have you there."

"I am sure. Anin needs rest after the ordeal she has suffered and before we take our leave in the morn."

"You are welcome to stay as long as you like. We would be pleased to have you both," Conmar offered.

"We must be on our way," Paine said curtly, ending the exchange.

"I will have food ready on the morrow for you to take on your journey."

"The King is grateful for your support."

"We owe you much, executioner, and I will let all know how you brought peace to our tribe." With a respectable bob of his head to Paine, Conmar left.

A small table and two benches had been brought into the room and in the middle of the table laid a large fish split open resting upon flat bread. Two fine bone horns rested in antler holders and a full drinking pouch sat there as well.

As soon as the last servant left, Paine went to Anin. He ran his hand softly along her chin. "You are well?"

"Some small discomfort, though not enough to complain about." She went to rest her head on his chest and he stepped away from her.

"Sit and eat, he said, turning and walking to the table.

"We cannot ignore what is between us," Anin said as she went to join him.

He swerved around and brought his fist down on the table hard. "There is nothing between us."

"You cannot deny the truth."

"The truth is that you are promised to the King. I serve the King and my task is to bring you to Pictland and that is what I will do."

"You gave me your word we would not be separated," Anin reminded.

"I will always be there to serve you."

Anin took a step toward him with her hand pressed to her chest.

"Stop!" Paine ordered sharply. "We will speak of this no more. I do and say what I must to get you safely to the King. I feel for nothing or no one." His arm shot out from his side, his finger pointing at the door. "I am no different than Dunnard. I gutted him like he did to the others, though I did it slowly, knowing exactly what to rip out of him so he would not die quickly, so that he would beg me to end the pain, would beg to die." He held his hands out to her. "These hands are evil."

Anin shook her head. "No, they are not and you are nothing like Dunnard."

"I am worse than Dunnard."

"You are not," she insisted.

"I am far worse." He held up his hands. "Look at them. These hands bring no caring only suffering and death. I will never take a wife, for I would never submit a good woman to my evil touch."

"That is nonsense. You care," —she tapped her chest— I can feel that you care."

"Enough!" he yelled and pounded the table once again. "We will speak of this no more. Sit and eat." He sat and pointed to the other bench. "Now!"

Anin did as he ordered, knowing there was no choice left to her...for now. She sat, though had no appetite to eat.

"You will eat," Paine ordered angry with himself for upsetting her, though it had been necessary. He had touched her, though innocently, too many times and the more he did the more he wanted to. And when she kissed him—the memory stirred his manhood. She was right. He was caring, caring far too much and what happened today proved it was growing far too troublesome.

He never let anything interfere in his task as an executioner. He did what needed to be done without guilt or repentance, and never did he find joy in killing as Dunnard did. Today, however, had been different. Today it brought him great joy to see Dunnard suffer for what he had done, not to those he killed, but for what he had done to Anin.

He was sent to protect her, but never had he thought he would need to protect her from himself.

The meal was eaten—what little was eaten—in silence. They retired afterwards, saying nothing and the silence continued between them the next morn after Paine ordered her to remain watchful once they took their leave of the Corsar Tribe.

Anin paid heed to her surroundings and her steps and when her thoughts became too burdensome, she reached out to the trees, the foliage, and the animals for comfort as she had done since she was young. The trees began to whisper and she spotted two squirrels busy at play. Several leaves drifted off branches, whispering a soft melody as they fell past her face. Feeling embraced by caring spirits, her burdensome thoughts grew lighter as did her steps.

With her thoughts clearing, a question came to mind. "Is it true the King would not wed a seer?"

Paine responded without looking back at her. "As you said yourself, if you were a seer you would have known of the Drust attacks."

"I am not saying I am a seer, I but wonder why the King would not wed one. Would she not be of great help to him?"

He gave a hardy laugh. "What do you think?"

It took only a moment to realize how foolish her question had been. "She would know everything he did. He could keep nothing from her."

"That could prove difficult, in many ways, for the King."

"And for his wife. She would know everything he did, every woman he took to his bed... unless, of course, it mattered not to her."

He stopped himself from asking if it would matter to her. It did not concern him. She was to be Queen. Annoyance poked at him. He needed no more reminders of that, since it did little good anyway. He still found himself coveting the King's intended. With his annoyance growing, mostly at himself, he threw a question at her that suddenly came to mind.

"Do you know the secret your mum hides?"

"My mum hides a secret? What makes you say that?" she asked and wondered if the secret concerned her.

"She was willing to suffer whatever was necessary to keep you from being found, so there was no chance of her confessing, but then there was never any chance that she would. She saw to that by to sending you away without knowing where you went. She was determined to protect you at great cost to her. Most mums would find it an honor that their daughter was chosen to be Queen. So her adamant refusal tells me that there is a secret she keeps that she fears once the King learns will place you in danger."

"I know nothing of any secret," Anin said, though wondered again if he could be right. Her mum had gotten so upset when she had learned the King wanted

Anin as his Queen. She had known her mum to be stubborn, but the news had made her more obstinate than ever before. Her mum and da had argued, he trying to make her see the benefits of such a union, not only for their daughter, but for the tribe as well. She had refused to listen.

"It must be a powerful secret for her to be willing to die for it," Paine said.

Tears sprang to Anin's eyes. "I would never want my mum to do that."

He stopped and turned to face Anin, wanting to see her when he asked, "And you are sure you know nothing about a secret that pertains to you?"

She shook her head. "My mum said I was born in the midst of a thunderstorm and was a good *bairn*, giving more than demanding. There is nothing special about me."

"In that you are wrong. There is something very special about you." He took a step toward her.

Anin did not know what made her do it, his words, the look in his eyes, or was it what she felt rushing from him into her? He was only a few steps from her, but she could not stop herself. She hurried forward to meet him.

"Stop!"

He had not raised his voice, but his warning rang so strongly that she stumbled slightly, coming to a fast halt.

"I can see in your eyes what you intend and I can tell you now if you dare kiss me again, it will not stop there this time, and then we are both doomed."

Disappointed, but heeding his words, she asked, "Why then did you approach me?"

He remained silent, staring at her.

Anin smiled softly, sensing again what she felt before. "You wanted to kiss me as much as I wanted to kiss you, but I frightened you off."

"I do not frighten. You but brought me to my senses, but since you knew my intention and are not a seer, then I would say that there is something special about you. I only hope it is nothing that will force me to take your head."

Chapter Sixteen

They walked until almost dusk and then ate sparingly of the food Conmar had given them, wanting to make it last. Night had brought a sharp chill with it and Anin was grateful that Phillia had given her a cloak. It was not as warm as her own had been, though it provided some warmth against the cold night air.

She turned on her side from time to time, letting the fire between her and Paine warm her front and back. She had thought Paine would join her after a while as he had been doing of late, wrapping himself around her and keeping her warm, keeping them both warm. But he remained where he was with his back turned to her.

Anin thought on what he had said about her mum and a secret. Was the secret about her? Was her mum trying to protect her from others learning about her strange ability to feel what others felt when she touched someone? How, though, could that prove dangerous to her?

She would know how the King felt every time she touched him. She would know if he cared for her or felt nothing for her, which could prove difficult for her. But if she laid her hand on others, she would know how they felt toward the King? Would that not be beneficial to him?

Or would it prove too much for the King for his wife to know more about him and those around him than he did himself? How could any man? Was that why her mum had warned her against letting anyone know?

Through the ensuing years her odd ability had manifested several times and while she had tried to conquer it, she was never successful. She simply learned to keep from touching others. That had all changed upon meeting Paine. Once she touched him, she wanted to touch him again and again. She had never felt things as potently as she had since meeting Paine, and what she felt when she touched someone now seemed to be growing even more powerful.

What would the King think of it all when he found out?

Anin shivered. Perhaps her mum had been right, though perhaps if she informed the King of her strange ability, he would choose not to marry her. What then? Would he allow her to return home or would he make use of her odd skill? And did she dare take the chance of telling him or having him find out?

Troubling thoughts delayed her sleep until she thought for certain dawn would wake before she slept. Exhaustion finally claimed her and not even the cold earth that seeped into her body could disturb her as she fell into a deep slumber.

Paine watched her eyes finally close and he fought the persistent urge to go wrap his body around hers and keep her warm. If he was honest with himself, he would admit that it was more than warmth he was looking for from her.

His disturbing thoughts kept him from a sound sleep. He dozed and woke, and dozed and woke again, each time keeping a keen eye on Anin. He would not let her out of his sight again.

~~~

Paine woke with a groaning stretch, his eyes opening to gray skies. He turned to see if Anin was awake, wanting to get a quick start on the day. He bolted to his feet when he saw that she was not there. He glanced about, his head turning faster than his body, but still no Anin and no Bog as well. Was Bog with her or had he gone off on his own?

The crunch of footfalls on fallen leaves had him reaching for his battle-axe until Anin stepped from behind some large foliage.

She smiled upon seeing him, though it vanished when she saw his green eyes ablaze with anger and she retreated several hasty steps back as he advanced on her rapidly.

He grabbed her by the shoulders before she tumbled back into a prickly bush. "What did I tell you about remaining by my side?" He gave her a hard shake. "Never do that again."

Anin's hand went to rest on his chest and she was startled to find not anger but fear rushing through him like a mighty river about to overwhelm the land. That he should feel that way for her meant only one thing...he cared for her more than he wanted to admit.

"I am sorry," she said softly. "I was not far."

"If I cannot see you, it is too far."

"I will remember that."

"Make certain you do."

"I did not mean to upset you."

"Yet you did."

She ached to step closer to him, to slip her arms around him, to rest her head on his chest, to feel his caring, his strength, his passion that she felt mounting, and to kiss him, if only her lip was not sore and painful...if only he would allow her to.

Paine eased her away from him and the prickly bush. Reluctantly he let his hands fall off her, then turned and walked a few steps away. He told himself it did not matter that her eyes filled quickly with desire or that the heat of her touch branded his chest so deeply he was sure she had left her mark on him. He had to ignore it. He had to keep his distance from her. He had to stop feeling the way he did about her or he would do something foolish.

Try as he might, he could not stop his chest from pounding, his arousal from growing, or his need to kiss her from flaring. He balled his hands into fists, fighting the urge to turn and go to her and—what? What would he do? Make the situation worse? Condemn them both with his foolish actions?

"We go!" he commanded and stumped on the last of the embers in the cold fire, trying to stump out his desire for the future Queen.

"Paine," Anin said softly.

He turned and once again advanced on her, though he did not lay a hand on her this time. "Do not look at me with such wanting or speak my name with such caring, not only for your own sake but for mine as well." He turned and walked off.

Anin hurried after him, Bog joining them after a few moments from wherever he had gone off to. Tears welled in her eyes. Why did she care for this man so much? Why did it feel that they were joined as one? She knew he felt the same. She had felt it herself when she had touched him and it was stronger than the last time. They were growing to care more deeply for each other as each day went by. But if she truly cared for him, she would have to curtail her feelings or chance placing them both in danger.

A single tear fell from her one eye and ran down her cheek and before she could wipe it away, Paine stopped, turned and was in front of her, wiping her tear gently away with his thumb.

"It cannot be. It can never be," he said and pressed his cheek to her damp one, lingering for a moment, as if branding her as she had done to him, before turning and walking away.

Anin followed along behind him, her hand faintly touching her cheek where his had touched. She had never felt anything so wonderful and she had never felt such unbearable pain as she did when he stepped away from her. He was lost to her and part of her had gone with him.

~~~

It was hours yet before dusk would touch the land when Paine stopped, his brow narrowing as he looked around him, then he sniffed the air. "Do you smell that?"

Anin took a deep whiff and smiled. "A delicious scent. Is there another tribe nearby?"

"Not that I recall."

"You know this area?"

"I came to know it."

"So no tribes occupy this area?"

Paine shook his head. He had traveled this particular path, knowing that after the Corsar Tribe, they would not come upon any other tribes. "I can recall none, though perhaps it is a group of travelers." He turned a stern look on Anin. "Must I remind you—"

"Stay close, do not leave your sight," she finished with a soft smile.

"See that you do," he snapped and turned away.

They crested a small rise not long after and they both stared at what they saw in the glen below, remnants of a dwelling that weather and significant time had claimed. Only part of the front had survived, supported by the trees and foliage that grew around it. The door stood open as if still welcoming people to enter.

Anin followed Bog who was already headed down the rise and Paine trailed, keeping watch around them.

"Do not go through the door," Paine ordered when she approached it.

"Why?" she asked, turning to him.

"It is not wise to step through a door whose dwelling no longer exists."

"Why?" she asked again.

"You may not find your way back again."

Anin smiled. "That is nonsense. Beyond the door are the woods, you can see that yourself." She pointed at the thick forest visible beyond the open door.

"It is not nonsense. I have heard warriors tell tales of such things. We will walk around it and follow the scent."

"It is easier to go straight through the door," she argued.

"I will say no more, we go around."

Anin thought it foolish and was about to step away from the door when a tug so strong pulled at her that she hurried through the opening, Bog following her.

Paine rushed after her and his wolf, having to duck his head to get through the open door. He intended to give her a good tongue lashing when he got hold of her. The thought died when he almost barreled into Anin.

"It is a village and a thriving one," Anin said her eyes wide with surprise.

Paine turned quickly and saw that the open doorway was gone. What had they fallen into?

He turned again and looked to see Anin was right. It was a thriving village. Several dwellings circled a large feasting house and people walked about engaged in their daily chores. To one side of the village lay planting fields. Many had already been prepared for the coming cold, while others were busy being harvested. Anin waited to see if Paine would say what she thought.

"This is not only a thriving village, but an established one," Paine said his eyes showing caution rather than surprise. It was obvious from the many dwellings, worn from time though well-cared for, and the large planting fields that the village had not recently sprung up.

Anin got the urge to explore the village yet there was also reluctance to do so. It was as if she was being tugged toward it and yet something else pulled her away from it.

"How is this possible?" Anin voiced what Paine thought. "This village has been here for many," —she gasped and grabbed Paine's arm— "It is a Wyse village, but why do they show themselves to us?"

He had thought the Wyse Tribe a myth. It was believed the Wyse kept their villages cloaked from sight, letting no one see them unless they chose to be visible. He knew of no one that had ever come upon them. It was a tribe believed to be steeped in secret knowledge and potent powers. A tribe feared yet their secret knowledge and potent powers coveted by many, including the King.

"We shall find out," Paine said and took hold of her hand, gripping it possessively as he proceeded into the village, Bog at his side. The gesture was meant to protect Anin, to make all that saw them believe she belonged to him.

Relief settled over Anin as soon as Paine had taken hold of her hand. There was strength and confidence in his grip and a fierce desire to protect her. She felt not a bit of fear in him, causing her own fear to dissipate some.

She had heard many different tales about the Wyse. Some believed them good and some believed them evil. Which one were they? The trees started whispering, but too softly for Anin to hear what they were saying. Were they warning her away or urging her forward?

"Welcome," a woman, the first one to spot them entering the village, called out with a smile.

"Pleasant day," another woman said, bobbing her head at them.

A man carrying a large basket braced on his shoulder smiled when he crossed their path, "Greetings."

"They welcome us most pleasantly," Anin whispered to Paine.

Paine knew that could change in a moment and remained cautious, keeping firm hold of Anin.

An elderly woman approached them. She was tall and slim with long, pure white hair that lay in a braid on her chest. She had soft, gentle blue eyes and lovely features. She wore a plain white tunic that fell to her ankles and a green shawl lay over her shoulders. She wore no shoes.

"Welcome to our village, I am Esplin."

Paine responded, "I am—"

"Paine, the King's executioner," Esplin finished and looked to Anin. "We heard you had a condemned person with you, but seeing how you hold her hand, I would say that busy tongues were wrong. We are pleased to welcome you and your woman to our village."

"Anin," Paine said, presenting her, though did not bother to correct the woman. It was safer for Anin that others believed she belonged to him. That way, busy tongues would spread what they had heard and none would know for sure whether it was truth or tale.

Paine was about to ask what tribe it was that greeted them when Esplin said, "You are welcome to stay with us as long as needed."

"Till morn will do."

Esplin looked up at the gray sky and wrapped her shawl more tightly around her. "Rain and cold will claim the land tonight. You may want to stay a day or two longer."

"If it proves necessary," Paine said and was about to once again ask what tribe welcomed them and how was it that the village could not be seen from the rise, but he waited. There would be time for questions later.

"You look to have been on the road for some time. There is a small pool of water just beyond the feasting house that has yet to completely chill. A quick dunk and wash might be just what you need. Afterwards, I will have a fine meal waiting for you."

Anin was quick to accept. "That would be wonderful." Her mum had scolded her for spending too much time in the streams or lakes when given the chance. She had warned Anin that her flesh would melt off her body with all the time she spent in the water. Anin had laughed, always feelings wonderful after a short dunk or a lingering one.

Paine's narrowed brow and tight lips told her that he did not feel the same.

Anin smiled. "If you prefer not to, you need not join me."

He turned a smile on her that stole her breath, tightened her chest, and just as a ripple of pleasure passed through her...he yanked her up against him.

"You know I cannot be long without you."

Though she was aware he spoke such endearing words to her for appearance sake, she took advantage of the moment and pressed her cheek to his, and whispered, "Nor I with you."

Her warm breath tickled his ear and her words were spoken with heartfelt truth that tore at his insides. He released her slowly and with much reluctance, though he kept hold of her hand.

"It is so nice to see two hearts joined so strongly together," Esplin said. "Now give me a moment to gather some cloth and a crock of salve that helps scrub the body and hair clean, then I will take you to the small pool to enjoy."

Paine leaned down to whisper, "You will behave, Anin."

"See that you do the same," she said, looking up at him with a smile.

"Think of our fate if we both do not behave," he warned.

It was a sobering thought and the lightness she felt in her heart quickly vanished. What did not vanish were Esplin's words.

Two hearts joined so strongly together.

Whether Paine liked it or not, their hearts had joined and could never be separated, even if they were.

Chapter Seventeen

"Take off your garments."

"As you wish." Anin reached to pull her tunic over her head and not surprisingly Paine turned his back to her.

"Let me know when you are done and while you dress I will take a quick dunk." He sat on the ground to remove his boots and leg coverings.

Anin did as he said, draping her garments over a bush. She snatched up a cloth and the small crock of salve Esplin had left them with once they had arrived at the small pool of water. It was a lovely spot with trees, bushes, and rock formations that lent the area privacy. Bog had joined them, sniffing around and wandering about.

After laying the two items on the ground near the pool, she scooped up some of the salve and rubbed it into her hair, leaving extra to use on her body. Then she hurried and stuck her foot in the water. It held a chill, but was not icy cold.

"Are you in the water yet?" Paine called out.

"Testing to see how cold it is."

"How cold is it?"

"Not as bad as I expected, though it is chilled."

"Then hurry and get in and be done with it," Paine ordered annoyed. He could not get his mind off her standing there naked and the thought of the things he would do to her to bring her to pleasure. Naturally, his wicked thoughts aroused him and he cursed himself. He listened to her splashing around and he almost slipped his hand beneath his tunic to pleasure himself and relieve the temptation to bury himself inside her.

Her sudden shout stopped him and spun him around. "What is wrong?"

"Nothing. I am delighted that the water is so much warmer out here in the middle of the pool."

"Be done with it," he grumbled loud enough for her to hear.

Anin did not want to hurry. She enjoyed the soothing water, she always had. She taught herself to swim when she was young and had fallen into the body of water not far from her home. She had thrashed about fearfully, swallowing mouthfuls of water until she thought for sure death would claim her when suddenly she felt as if hands lifted her, held her, and told her what to do. She had been swimming from that day on, growing stronger and stronger at it. She was proud of herself, though two of her brothers were annoyed that she learned to swim before them.

"Hurry," Paine shouted again.

Anin sighed and ducked her head under the water to rinse the last of the salve from it. The water was so warm beneath that she decided to take one last dive. She had learned to breathe under water for a good length of time often frightening her da and mum, so she was not worried about going too deep too long.

Paine watched her go beneath the surface for a second time and as soon as she resurfaced, he intended to order her out of the pond. She was too far from shore, too far from him. He grew worried when too much time passed and she could not be seen. He had seen too many men not resurface once they had gone under and by the time someone had gotten to them it had been too late.

He yanked off his tunic and ran into the pond, his strokes powerful and fast. He reached the spot he had last seen her and looked frantically around, hoping she had surfaced. When he did not see her, he dove beneath. When he could hold his breathe no longer, he resurfaced and not seeing her, he dove beneath again to search.

He popped up out of the water, his chest screaming for a breath when he thought he heard Anin call out to him.

"Paine. Paine are you all right?"

He coughed and spit water out as he twirled around in the water to see her swimming toward him. Relief so strong almost stole his breath, but anger saved it. As soon as she got close enough, he grabbed hold of her arm.

"Never again! Never again do that to me!" he yelled at her, words he seemed to repeat much too often to her.

She grabbed onto his shoulder, his tight grip making it hard to remain afloat. "What did I do?"

"You disappeared beneath the water for far too long."

His fear rushed through her, twisting her insides. She felt the pain of him thinking he had lost her and the overwhelming relief that he had not and she felt terrible for having put him through such suffering.

"I am so sorry," she said, moving closer to him. "I should have told you that I am adept at swimming."

"Adept or not," he argued, "I will not have you out of my sight for that long or so far away from me."

She felt it, his fear of not reaching her in time, in not saving her. "I will not do it again."

"So you say, but you never do." He gently dropped his brow against hers. "I cannot lose you. It would mean..."

"Losing your head," she finished when he did not, though it was not what he had intended to say. She felt what he had stopped himself from saying—*losing the woman who has stolen my heart.* She felt such a joy so strong sweep through her that she could not help but press her lips to his.

"Do not," he ordered, raising his head, ready to push her away.

"Just this once...I beg of you."

Her plea was so soft, so heartfelt that he could not deny her. He did not want to deny her, but he had no right. She was to be Queen. She did not belong to him, she belonged to the King.

He turned away.

"Paine."

His name whispered with such sorrow, yet such hope, broke his resolve. He turned and captured her lips with his.

They tasted softly of each other, taking their time, exploring until their hunger grew and they could not control it. Their arms encircled each other, their legs moving in unison, keeping them afloat and their bodies drifting close until they finally touched.

Anin groaned against his mouth when her body rested against his and his hard, thick manhood nestled between her legs. She wanted to join with him so badly, feel him deep inside her and feel his seed spill into her.

Paine could not get enough of her, not her taste, or the feel of her breasts pressed tightly against his chest. He let his hand drift down to her backside and he pushed her hard against him, his manhood slipping between her legs. All he had to do was lift her just a bit and slip easily into her, join with her and—the taste of blood in his mouth brought him to his senses.

He pulled away from her and seeing the blood drip down her chin, swore beneath his breath. The kiss had split her lip wound open.

"You are bleeding," he said with concern and wiped gently at her chin with his thumb.

Anin stared at him, tears threatening her eyes, overwhelmed by his desire that had flooded her like a mighty wave. Though, it was how much he cared for her that had left her unable to utter a word.

"I made you bleed," he said annoyed wiping more blood away as it ran from her lip.

She wanted to tell him that she did not care. All she cared about, all she wanted was him. Her heart ached at the thought of never joining with him. She wanted no other man. She wanted only Paine.

She knew she would never have another moment like this, another chance to tell him how she felt, so she did what her heart told her to do. She drifted closer to him, pressed her cheek to his, and whispered, "*Tuahna*."

Paine had thought he had suffered unbearable pain when he had lost his family, but hearing her tell him that she cared for him more deeply than anything else in life brought him tremendous joy and an equal amount of sorrow.

They could not be. They could never be and for him to acknowledge he felt the same would only make their parting that much more difficult. He pushed her away. "Never say that to me. That is meant for the man—"

"I willingly give my heart to, the man who will always keep my heart safe, never harm it, and never bring it pain."

"I would do none of that. I would only bring you pain."

She shook her head, moving toward him.

"Stop!" he ordered. "You and I will never be. This foolishness must stop. My ache for you is because I have been too long without a woman. I will find a willing one tonight and bring this madness to an end." His words were hurtful, not only to her but to him as well, for they were far from the truth.

160

Anin felt as if he had struck her with his battle-axe. He could not mean it. She was not wrong how he felt about her.

"Go and let me know when you have finished dressing." When she remained as she was, he shouted, "Go now!"

Anin turned to swim away, stopped and turned with tears in her eyes. She so badly wanted to tell him the truth that when she touched him she felt what he felt. That she had been able to feel what people felt with one touch since she had been young. She wanted to tell him it was why she went to Dunnard, to touch him and know of his innocence or guilt. To tell him he could lie to her all he wanted to, but one touch would tell her the truth. It already had.

She could say none of that without placing her mum in danger for keeping the secret, but she did cry out, "You lie. You lie how you feel about me. I want you and only you. I will not wed the King."

Paine stared at her stunned as she swam to shore. How could she know how he felt? She could not. She did not know. She wanted to believe it was so and she was right, but he could never let her know that. And that she would refuse to wed the King? She did not know what she was saying, what she could suffer if she refused the King. He grew angry.

"Anin!" he shouted, needing to make her understand she could not refuse the King.

She ignored his shouts and hurried to finish dressing. She needed to be away from him if only for a while. She ran into the woods.

"Anin! Do not dare leave! Anin!" he shouted and kept shouting as she disappeared into the woods.

The trees began to whisper, drowning out Paine's angry shouts and offering her comfort. She listened to them as she kept running, running from Paine, running from the hurt, running from fate...if only she could.

~~~

Paine was on the shore and dressed in little time. He looked around for Bog, but he was nowhere to be seen. He shouted out for him, needing him to track Anin, but the wolf did not appear. He did not dare wait a moment longer. He went in search of Anin.

~~~

Anin felt her breathing growing much too heavy and she slowed her pace until she finally came to a stop. She dropped down, the leaves crunching beneath her. Why? Why was she cursed? Why did she have to wed the King? Why did she have to care so deeply for Paine? Why had she confessed with one powerful word how she felt about him...*tuahna*? And what had been his response? That he had been too long without a woman and he would find a willing one to ease his ache, when it was her that he truly ached for.

She shook her head. She had felt how deeply he cared for her, felt their spirits join, and nothing—nothing—could ever change that.

She had once asked her mum why she had the ability to feel, with one touch, what others felt. Her mum had told her it was no ability but a curse and that she should fight against it, chase it away and never ever give it power. She had asked her mum who had cursed her and why, but her mum had no answer for her and told her to let it be, nothing good would come of anyone knowing she was cursed and so it became their secret.

Suddenly a wind blew through the trees and Anin realized it was a frantic whisper. She hurried to her feet as she listened.

Danger. Danger.

Anin was not sure what to do. She would not be in danger from Paine. Could it be the Drust? She realized too late that running off on her own had not been a wise thing to do. She did not even know if her wild run had taken her out of the Wyse settlement. She listened for footfalls, but heard none. She thought to run, but in what direction? She listened some more and her skin prickled when she heard it, a low growl.

Run back to Paine.

She turned and took off as fast as she could. She could tell from the sound behind her that it was more than one wolf and they were gaining on her. Her legs were tired from her first run, but she forced them to run even faster than before. If she did not, the animals would catch her and tear her to pieces.

This time she screamed out for Paine. "Paine! Paine!"

She kept running, ducking under branches while some struck her in the face, jumping over fallen trees or large rocks and hoping she did not fall. The wolves remained close behind her, waiting for one or all of them to lunge at her.

"Drop!"

She immediately obeyed Paine's forceful shout and fell to the ground. She heard him throw his battle-axe as he kept running toward her and the horrible screech when it caught the one wolf. Bog appeared out of nowhere, jumping over her and attacking another wolf. Then another agonizing cry split the air and Anin knew that Paine had killed the third one.

"Get up!"

Anin scrambled to her feet and turned to see fury raging in his eyes.

He grabbed her arm and all but dragged her along with him. "I will not waste words of warning on you again."

She knew what he meant. He would not warn her again about leaving his side. She wanted to tell him it was his fault for speaking falsely to her, but her words would be as wasted as he felt his had been on her.

Esplin spotted them when they entered the village and went to them. "I have food waiting for you."

"We require time alone," Paine said his strong tone leaving no room to argue.

Esplin nodded and led them to a dwelling, stepping aside after opening the door. "All you need is within."

Paine nodded and shoved Anin inside, following her and shut the door behind him.

The inside was a good size with a raised sleeping pallet against one wall, a soft blanket covering the stuffing beneath. A fire pit sat in the middle, its flames sending warmth to all corners of the room. A table, food aplenty on it, and two benches sat against another wall.

Unfortunately, Anin had lost any desire to eat, to talk, to argue. She was tired, her limbs sore from all the walking and unexpected running she had done since dawn, and from the fear of almost being torn apart by wolves. She did what she wanted to do most. She sat on the raised sleeping pallet and almost sighed with pleasure from how soft it was.

Paine paced in front of her. He was still seething from her not only running away from him, but her near deadly encounter with the wolves. When he heard her scream his name in terror, he thought he was too late to save her. His fear had him running faster and it was good that he did, for the wolves had been about to lunge at her.

164

He stopped pacing, though his heart kept pounding, and he glared at her. "This madness must stop. You cannot refuse the King. No one refuses the King."

"He will care not that I care nothing for him or that my heart belongs to his executioner?"

"You do not know what you say."

"I know I care for you."

"Why do you care for me?" He stuck his hands out at her. "These hands bring only anguish, they know no caring."

Anin went to take hold of them and he yanked them away, stepping back, keeping his distance, and it hurt her that he did so.

"You are a good man and you care for me, I know you do," she said, wanting to go and touch him, feel the truth of her words, but he would only push her away, so she stayed as she was.

"Understand this well, Anin...we will never be. I have warned you about this far too many times. Accept your fate and let this be. I foolishly kissed you because I was in need of a woman. That is all. I care nothing for you. You will be Queen and I am and always will be the executioner. Now eat and sleep and do not leave here." He looked at Bog as he walked to the door. "Guard and stay!"

Anin dropped back on the sleeping pallet as soon as the door closed behind him. Why did she feel as strongly as she did for Paine? And how had it happened so quickly? It was as if she knew he was meant for her, but how? How could that be?

She knew little of him, only that he was the King's executioner and that he was feared throughout the land. How could she care so deeply for a man feared by so many, and whose companions were misery and death? She had no answers.

She only knew that she was not meant for the King. She was meant for the executioner.

Chapter Eighteen

Paine walked through the village, not knowing where he was going and not caring. He should have never kissed her. Why had he? She was to be Queen. He had no right to kiss her. If the King learned of it, he would take their heads. He knew this and yet he had kissed her anyway. He had been a fool and he was growing more foolish. He had to stop this madness between them before it was too late.

He rubbed the back of his neck, an ache having settled there and let his glance wander over the village. The people were well-groomed and welcoming, not a suspicious glare from one of them and not a sign of worry. They all seemed confident that they had nothing to fear from the King's executioner.

With dusk near at hand, the last of the chores were being finished and some were already headed, while laughing and talking, to the feasting house. Never had he been in a village as pleasant as this one.

Could this truly be a Wyse Tribe? There was not much known about the Wyse, mostly myths from what Paine had heard. There were some who believed that they were the first people to settle this land, discover its secrets, and learn how to use them. It was also believed that some Wyse tribesmen lived among the other tribes, but never let it be known. They were sent to keep watch.

King Talon had sent warriors out across the land to try and find one of the mystical Wyse settlements, but without success. If this was a Wyse Tribe, Paine needed to find out what he could about them before taking his leave, though more importantly he had to convince the chieftain to meet with the King.

"What is it you search for, Paine?"

He turned to Esplin. "Why do you think I search?"

"Your eyes, they question."

He let his question be known. "What tribe is this?"

She smiled. "Why ask what you already know?"

"I prefer to hear it from a Wyse tribesman."

Her smile remained as she nodded. "You are among the Wyse."

"I am honored," Paine said. "I know all are not welcome in your tribe."

Esplin laughed softly. "All are welcome, though all are not worthy."

Her words surprised him. How was he—the executioner—worthy?

Esplin took his arm. "You need nourishment. Come eat and we will talk."

He thought of Anin alone and cast a glance over his shoulder.

Esplin patted his arm. "Anin sleeps. It is what she needs after such trying events."

"How do you know she sleeps?"

"I keep watch over her."

Bog would never allow anyone into the dwelling, so how did Esplin know Anin slept?

"I will answer what questions I can."

"I have many."

"Everyone does," she said as they entered the feasting house.

Paine found it odd that there was no table of honor for the chieftain. There were only tables and benches, fitting six people, circling and spreading out from the large fire pit. The tables held an abundance of food, the delicious scents causing his stomach to grumble.

He wondered about the chieftain. It was believed that there were several Wyse settlements. If that was true, in which settlement did the High chieftain reside and did he travel from settlement to settlement?

Esplin took him to a table where a family sat, a mum, da, and two children, a lad and a lass. She presented Paine and he was surprised when they welcomed him with smiles and kind words and were not at all upset that they shared the table with the King's executioner. The lad held out his crudely carved animal, that had yet to take recognizable shape and proudly announced that he was going to be a master carver like his da.

Paine felt a twinge of a memory, recalling how he thought when he was young he would one day do the work his da did, but he never got the chance.

He smiled at the lad and told him he was doing a fine job.

The family seemed to know after that that Esplin and he wanted to talk for they kept to themselves. Paine had many questions, though he asked none once he took a taste of the food. He was too busy eating the delicious fare.

When nearly finished, a vessel of fine wine in his hand and the table to themselves, he said, "Tell me about the Wyse Tribe."

"That would take some time, since our history goes further back than most and our tribe is rich with beliefs."

"Why hide your settlements from others?"

"We are there for those who see us and for our own kind when they wish to return home."

"So the Wyse do walk among the other tribes."

"They do and other tribesmen live here among us as well."

"By choice?" Paine asked startled to hear that.

169

Esplin laughed. "We do not take prisoners and our own tribesmen are free to explore outside our boundaries."

"Many believe the Wyse learned the secrets of this land and have unnatural powers. Is that true?"

"This land has much to offer if one is willing to listen. The Wyse women and men listened and became sensitive to the land, sensitive to touch. The land and all on it speaks to them and one touch allows them to feel what others feel. There are some that are born more sensitive than others. They usually become our leaders."

"King Talon would be most grateful if he could speak with your chieftain."

"When he is worthy."

Paine came to his King's defense. "He is a good man."

"But is he a worthy man?"

Paine had no chance to answer, a young lass approached the table.

"Forgive me, Esplin, for intruding, but Dorsa is close to birthing."

Esplin stood. "Hurry back to her, I will be right there." She turned to Paine as the lass hurried off. "I must see to welcoming a tiny *bairn* into our tribe, the first for Dorsa. If there is time before you leave, we can talk again."

Paine nodded, though wished they had not been interrupted. He had not learned nearly enough about the Wyse and he still wished to meet their chieftain. He swallowed the last of his wine and left. A chill had arrived with the darkness and he realized he had not worn his cloak. Not that it mattered, he had suffered through far worst cold. What disturbed him more was that he carried no weapons. He was never without a weapon and yet he had not given a weapon thought when he left the dwelling.

Tall torches on poles buried in the ground lit a path through the village and made it easy to see his way back to the dwelling. He opened the door slowly and was pleased when he met resistance from Bog's body. He was sleeping in front of the door and he stretched as he moved away to drop down next to the fire pit.

"Well done, Bog," he commended, but the wolf's eyes had already closed.

He glanced over at the sleeping pallet and saw that Anin was curled up tight, a slight shiver to her body. She had fallen asleep without a blanket over her and the fire in the pit had dwindled. He saw to both, adding more wood to the fire and taking the blanket from the end of the bed and draping it over Anin.

He wanted to climb in beside her and wrap her in his arms and keep her warm as he had done for the last few nights when the cold ground began to send shivers through her. He could do that no more, not after today, not after their kiss, not after feeling her naked body fitting so perfectly with his.

With a shake of his head, he reluctantly left her and went to the door, lowered himself in front of it, and dropped his head back against it. He had thought this would be an easy mission for the King. Collect the future Queen and deliver her safely to the King. Nothing had gone easy since he had found Anin hiding in a tree. Together they had faced far more danger than he ever would have anticipated, and in doing so he discovered a woman who was more fearless than she realized.

Anin was a woman who had the courage to dare fate and lose her heart to a man who did not deserve it. And though he protested, he could not deny how he felt. He had lost his heart to Anin...to a woman he could never claim as his own.

~~~

Anin woke with a stretch and a smile, lingering on her sleeping pallet, though she did not remember it being this soft. Had her mum had a new blanket made for her? If so, she favored it greatly. Reluctantly, she opened her eyes, knowing she should be up and about and seeing to her daily chores. She sprang up when she saw that she was not in her room and looked around, and it all came rushing back to her.

Paine, the pool, the kiss, and how his words had hurt though they were false, at least how he felt about her was false. She knew full well the truth. He could not hide that from her, though he was not aware of that. However, she did not know if he had truly meant that he would find a willing woman to ease his ache. She hoped it proved false as well.

She gave the room another glance, surprised to find herself alone, neither Paine nor Bog were there. She hurried off the raised pallet and ran her fingers through her hair. It felt smooth and free of the grime it had collected during her journey. She quickly plaited it and placed the braid over her shoulder to rest on her chest. She brushed at her garments to chase the many wrinkles away as best as she could and grabbed her cloak to hurry outside.

With the sun not high in the sky, it was not long since dawn. Anin breathed deep of the chilled air. She looked around as she walked, wondering where Paine had gone and wondering why he had left her alone. Unless he thought it was safe to do so.

She walked around the village, enjoying the scents and sounds and the people, so warm and welcoming. Her stomach grumbled while speaking with one woman who was busy fashioning a basket. She was quick to give Anin some food, which she did not refuse. She continued on, though stopped from time to time to chat with people, only to be given more food.

The village reminded her of home and she felt a catch in her chest. It surprised her that while she missed her home and family, she missed Paine upon waking this morning the most. She wondered again where he had gone off to. Had he not returned at all last night? Had he spent it with whatever willing woman he had found? Bog had been there when she had fallen asleep, but not when she woke, so who had let him out? Paine could have earlier, after he left the woman.

There was only one way to find out. She had to touch him, but where was he? And why had they not left yet? It was passed dawn and they usually started their journey shortly after dawn. Had he decided to remain another day? It would not bother her if he had. She was not in a hurry to meet the King.

"Good, you are awake. We need to be on our way."

Anin turned around and could not stop herself from smiling when she saw Paine approaching her. She truly had missed him, though it was not right for her to feel that way—she could not stop herself. She could not change how she felt.

She hurried to him, reaching out to take hold of his arm. "Did you get enough sleep?"

He backed away from her. "Not nearly enough."

She moved closer and got upset when he once again backed away from her. "I did not hear you return."

"You slept soundly. You did not even stir when I placed the blanket over you or stirred the embers."

She slowly stepped to the side of him, hoping to reach him before he could step away again. "I am grateful you looked after me."

He was quick to put further distance between them. "It is my mission."

A spark of annoyance had her snapping, "I thought you wanted to leave at dawn."

"With all you have been through, I thought to let you rest a while longer. Once we leave here, our pace will be rapid with few stops and little rest."

Anin asked what she truly did not want to know. "How long before we reach Pictland?"

"Keeping a good pace, we will reach the border of Pictland in three sunrises."

They both turned quiet and Anin did not need to touch him to see that his words had brought him as much displeasure as they did her.

She tried once again to get close enough to touch him, and once again he put distance between them.

"Meet the most recent member of our tribe, Serene."

Anin and Paine turned to see Esplin with a small bundle cradled gently in her arms.

Anin hurried to take a peek. Paine remained where he was.

"She is so beautiful and so tiny," Anin said eager to hold her.

"Here take her. You will have a daughter of your own soon enough."

Anin went to hold out her arms, but Esplin walked over to Paine and shoved the tiny lass at him, leaving him no choice but to take hold of her.

Anin almost laughed. Never had she seen him look fearful, but he did at that moment. He held the tiny lass as if he was afraid he would somehow hurt her. Then she recalled what he had said about his hands. *They bring nothing but misery*. He should see now that that was not true.

Paine felt terror rip through him. His hands were soiled with evil. He should not be holding an innocent bairn. The tiny lass squirmed in his large hands and

Paine gently moved her to the crook of his arm, keeping her close to his chest, fearful not to crush or drop her.

She settled herself against him with what sounded like the purr of a kitten, her tiny, fisted-hand going to rest under her chin.

"Now you will not fear holding your own daughter when she is born," Esplin said.

Paine was stern when he spoke. "I will have no children."

Esplin laughed softly. "You will have three daughters and a fine son."

Her words stirred sorrow in Anin. She wished she could be the one to give Paine three daughters and a fine son.

Paine caught himself before he snapped at Esplin, not wanting to disturb the sleeping bairn. "How do you know this?"

"Our future is written upon us. All you need to do is look."

"You are a seer," he said that making more sense to him.

"I am no seer. I simply see what others refuse to." Esplin reached to take the sleeping lass.

Paine, to his surprise, found himself reluctant to let the tiny bairn go.

Esplin turned to Anin. "I must return her to her mum, but you can hold her for a moment."

Anin reached out eagerly and took the little lass in her arms. A lovely, soothing peace settled over her and she wondered if all bairns felt that way after birth. She returned her to Esplin who held out her arms. "She brings such peace."

"That she does," Esplin agreed. "I must get her to her mum and see to another who is about to give birth to a little lass."

"You are so sure it will be a lass?" Paine asked.

"The firstborn of all Wyse women is always a daughter. It is just the way of it." She looked from Paine to Anin. "You will be leaving us soon?"

"We will gather our things and be on our way," Paine said. "We are most grateful for all you have shared with us."

"I wish I had more time to speak with you both," Esplin said. "The next time will be different. We will have more time to talk."

"I would like that," Anin said and feeling the need reached out and gave Esplin a hug, careful not to disturb the sleeping bairn.

Stay strong.

Anin rested her hand to her chest after stepping away from Esplin and stood there while Paine spoke with her about the Wyse Chieftain meeting with the King. She barely heard what he said, she was too stunned at what she had heard and felt.

She was certain Esplin spoke to her, but she had heard it only in her head. As her words had faded, a strange sensation had taken hold of her when she laid her hand on Esplin's back. It felt as if Esplin was part of her and she part of Esplin long before they had ever met each other.

"Safe journey to you both," Esplin said. "We will see each other again."

Anin hoped so, for there was much she had to ask the woman.

Chapter Nineteen

Anin wondered why Pain had a length of rope looped over his shoulder. She found out when they reached the top of the rise where they had looked down and first seen the Wyse settlement. It was visible no more.

"The King will be pleased that his future Queen met with the Wyse Tribe," Paine said and slipped the rope off his shoulder.

Anin had the urge to take a step away from him. "What is the rope for?"

With deft hands, he worked on the rope. "To tether you to me."

"That is not necessary."

"After the wolves almost tore you apart, I told you I would not waste words of warning on you again." He held up the rope. "Now you will have no choice but to do as I say."

Anin stumbled back away from him. "That is a hangman's loop."

"It will fit perfectly around your waist. Now come here to me."

Any other time he would have ordered her to come to him she would have done so without hesitation, but the hangman's loop made her think twice.

Paine did not like the worried look in her eyes. Did she truly believe he would harm her? Was it not better for them both if she finally doubted him, finally saw him for who he truly was?

He held the deadly loop up, shaking it at her. "You are lucky I am not slipping it around your neck and tether you as I do prisoners."

"You would never—"

Paine rushed at her, grabbing arm so that she could not move away from him. "Never be foolish enough to think I would not do what was necessary or commanded to do."

Anin cringed when he slipped the rope over her head and it brushed her neck as he spread the loop wider to push past her shoulders.

"Lift your arms," he ordered.

She did as told and he settled the rope around her waist. His actions and words frightened her and she quickly laid a hand on his arm as he pushed the knot tight against her waist. She shivered at the dark emptiness she felt within him. It was what she had felt when she first met him. She gripped his arm tighter, fighting to get through the emptiness, fighting to find what she had felt several times before that he cared for her more deeply than she thought any man ever could.

"Paine," she whispered and the emptiness began to fade and beneath it she could feel tender warmth and— he yanked his arm away.

"Never touch me again," he said, though it sounded more like Bog's snarl. "I have been too lenient with you, but no more."

"Which is it you truly fear, keeping me close or keeping me at a distance? Or is it both?"

Either way he would suffer. Keeping her close would bring the King's wrath down upon him and keeping her at a distance meant he would never have her. That she understood meant she was aware of his lies, but then she had been aware of his lies at the pond as well. It was almost as if she could reach inside him and know what he felt.

He did not respond. He did not need to. She understood all too clearly. He wrapped the other end of the rope around his waist, knotting it. He left enough length between them so that they would not be so close that she could touch him, but close enough that she could not go far from him. Satisfied, he turned and walked along the top of the ridge.

Anin followed, seeing Bog run ahead of Paine.

"I should punish you for this by remaining silent," she said after a few steps.

"You call that punishment?" he said with a rough laugh.

Her words brought the laugh she had hoped for from him. She wanted no anger between them their last few days together. She wanted good memories of him.

"You do not enjoy my endless chatting and questions?" she asked sweetly.

"Not in the least. I relish the quiet." He felt his lie twist at his insides. "You should be watching for the Drust, not talking."

"You think they will not give up? They will continue to follow our trail?" she asked, foolishly having given them no thought. They were no longer in the safety of the Wyse or in the protection of the Corsar Tribe. They were completely on their own.

"The Drust grow in warriors since their first attack. It shows they are intent on seeing their mission finished as planned."

"With my death." She shivered, recalling her struggle with the Drust warrior and the hatred she had felt spewing from him and how much he wanted her dead.

"That will not happen, and do not disturb me with more questions."

Anin remained quiet for only a short time. "Why do you not want bairns of your own?"

179

He shook his head.

"Do you not want to live on through your children and their children, ever remembered?"

"No! What bairn would want to be the son or daughter of the King's executioner? I would not stain an innocent child with my blood."

"You do not have to remain the King's executioner forever."

"I serve the King. It is the chore he has chosen for me."

"Is it truly or is it the punishment you have chosen for yourself?" Anin asked.

"You speak foolishly."

"I speak what I see and feel. It matters not since you will have three daughters and a son." Again Anin felt a twinge of envy for the woman who would birth his children.

"Esplin is wrong. I will have no children. Enough talk. It distracts and we must remain watchful." Paine waited a moment, knowing she would speak again and said, "Not another word, Anin." He waited again. "I mean it."

Anin shut her mouth with a pout, though it turned quickly to a smile. He knew her well, knew she would continue talking without looking back at her. They truly were meant for each other. Why had fate not seen that? Why was she made to join with a man she cared nothing for?

She pushed the troubling thoughts away to remain watchful as Paine had said. They traveled over a barren stretch of land where you could see anyone approaching from a distance away. While the land appeared unwelcoming in its stark emptiness, there was also a beauty to it. With the cold not many full moon cycles away the land was preparing for sleep, the leaves falling from the trees to blanket the land and nourish it during its slumber and the harvest taking the last of what the land had to give.

While this journey had not been easy or wanted, she was grateful for it. She had gotten to see more of the land and its people, and she had gotten to meet Paine and feel what it was like to lose her heart.

Sunrise to sunset saw no incidents.

Paine had her sleep close to the fire and he slept the length of the rope between them. He did not move close and keep her warm like he had done before. He kept his distance and it hurt Anin that he did. It was not his warmth that she missed most, it was him. She slept and felt more peaceful when he slept wrapped around her.

They woke to a gray sky and Anin argued with Paine when he refused to remove the rope so that she could see to her morning needs.

"I will turn my head," he said.

After endless arguing and her need growing ever stronger, he finally gave in and removed the rope from around her waist, though he warned he would remain close by.

The rope went back on her as soon as she was done. She did not protest. It would do no good. He would have his way.

The gray skies lingered throughout the day. A storm was brewing and Anin hoped it did not bring thunder with it. They entered small patches of woods that once again opened on to barren land and it went that way for a while until they were about to emerge on open land once again.

Bog stopped suddenly, the hair on his back rising. Paine approached the edge of the woods cautiously, having warned Anin with a finger to his lips to remain quiet. He peered from behind a tree, beyond saplings and foliage to a stretch of open land where a group of Drust warriors were gathered. Some squatted, their eyes searching, while others stood glancing around slowly.

They appeared to be waiting, but for who? Not for him and Anin. The Drust would wait in hiding, follow, and strike when the time was right, not remain in the open where they could be seen. Also, he had changed the path Anin and he had taken, making it more difficult for the Drust to find them.

He turned to Anin and motioned to her once again to remain silent. He did not have to instruct Bog, the wolf would follow his lead. If they lingered, their chance of discovery would grow, but he needed to see if this truly was a meeting, then who did the Drust expect?

It was not long before he got his answer. A horse and rider approached from the distance, opposite of Paine. The Drust turned as soon as one of them alerted the others to the rider's approach. Paine was surprised and disappointed to see that the rider wore the cloak of the King's warriors, though not his personal guard. Paine was unable to see his face, his hood drawn down too far. He remained on his horse as he spoke to the Drust warriors as if he was in command of them. He pointed toward where he had come from and then back at the Drust.

Paine wished he could hear what he said, but they were too far away. After a short time, he turned and rode off, and it was not long after that that the Drust followed in the same direction. They would be there waiting for him and Anin, but how did they know he and Anin would come that way? Or was there one of many Drust troops waiting for them?

It was not until they were a distance away that Paine spoke, though he did not tell her of the man wearing the cloak of the King's warriors. That did not concern her. It was meant for the King alone.

"This shows that it is not a rogue group of Drust warriors," Anin said. "Something is afoot."

"And the King needs to know about it."

"With the Drust ahead of us waiting, where do we go from here? Or does it matter? Do the Drust lie in wait for us wherever we go?"

"We go a back the way we came and take a different path that may delay our arrival at Pictland another day unless we keep a good pace."

Anin would not have minded the delay if it were not for the Drust. "I will match your pace," she assured him.

"Be sure that you do, since you are tethered to me. If you go down so will I."

"Release me."

"Never!" he snapped.

Anin felt a jolt to her chest from the impact of his one word. He was not speaking of the rope attached to her. He was speaking of how he felt about releasing her from his heart. He would never let her go, separated or not she would always be part of him. She reached out to lay a tender hand on him and he backed away.

"You will be Queen," he said reminding them both and hurried past her, setting a quick pace.

Anin rushed along with him, tired of being reminded of her fate and angry she could do nothing about it. It was her duty and she had been willing to fulfill her duty, but not anymore. Not since she met Paine.

Her thoughts faded quickly, having to pay attention to where she walked, avoiding pits and rocks, worried she would fall and drag him down with her.

They did not stop until after dusk. Paine refused to light a fire, concerned that if there were any Drust in the area they would see or smell it. They shared a quick meal from the food Esplin had given them.

As much as Paine had warned himself against getting too close to Anin, tonight could not be helped. It was cold and with no fire to warm them the only heat they would get was from each other. He bedded them down behind a large boulder with trees close behind it. No one could reach them without him hearing their approach. He also had Bog to keep watch.

Anin settled against him when he wrapped himself around her like a warm, comforting blanket. She rested her hand on his arm, having ached to touch him all day, whether to reassure herself what he felt for her or simply to enjoy the comfort his closeness brought her, brought them both.

She fell into a quick, deep slumber, Paine having to shake her awake when the sun rose. He had not wanted to disturb her or the pleasure he got from having her in his arms. But he could not delay their departure. If they kept the same pace, they would reach the border of Pictland by dusk. As soon as sentinels spotted them, word would be sent to the King and he would send his personal guard to collect them both. It would be over, his mission complete, and Anin gone from him.

"We will keep a good pace and reach the border of Pictland as dark falls," Paine said before hurrying her along.

It was not what Anin wanted to hear, but there was nothing she could do and so she kept pace with Paine all the time wishing fate had chosen differently for her.

The gray clouds that had been following them since yesterday began to grow darker and Anin thought she heard thunder in the distance. A storm was brewing and not a small one.

They stopped once for a brief rest.

"There is a dwelling we can seek shelter in once across the Pictland border and the next day the King's personal guard will meet up with us and escort us the remainder of the way."

Anin nodded, unable to speak, knowing her time with Paine would soon end. She did not allow herself to think when they were once again keeping a strong pace. She emptied her mind, though it would have been better for her to empty her heart, but that was not possible. It would never be possible.

Watch where you step!

The voice in her head warned too late. She suddenly found herself falling down a dark hole.

Chapter Twenty

Paine was yanked back off his feet. He immediately flipped himself over and grabbed at the rope, digging his heels into the dirt to stop from being dragged. Once he had balance and firm hold, he got to his feet, keeping a taut hold on the rope. His heart pounded against his chest, then slammed against it when he saw Anin was gone. The end of the rope she was attached to disappearing down a hole.

He shouted for her. "Anin!"

His worry grew when he got no answer. He wanted to hurry and pull her up and out of the hole, but without knowing if she was hurt or that anything stood in the way of harming her if he did, he remained where he was and called out to her again.

"Anin!"

"Paine!" Her shout was strong.

"Are you hurt?" he called out as he turned slowly letting the rope coil around his waist from where he held.

"I do not think so."

He shut his eyes a moment, hoping that was true and, keeping the rope taut, started walking toward her. "Is there anything around you that could cause you harm if I pulled you up?"

Her answer was a terrifying scream.

Paine pulled the rope hand over hand while yelling out her name as he rapidly approached the hole. Once he got to the edge, he quickly peered over it.

Anin thrust her arms out frantically to him.

He reached down, grabbed her arm just under her shoulder and yanked her up and out of the hole. She threw herself at him, burying her face against his chest as her arms went around his waist, hugging him as if she would never let go.

His arms circled her and feeling her tremble, he held her tighter. Her scream had pierced him as painfully as a spear piercing his heart. He had feared the worst and he was never so relieved to hold her in his arms. "You are safe now. There is nothing to fear. I have you and I am not letting you go." He was not sure if his words were meant to calm her or him.

His words cut away at her fear to settle deep inside her and ease her trembling. Paine was there with her. He had saved her. He would keep her safe. He would always keep her safe. She was so upset that she was not sure if it was her feelings she felt or Paine's.

When her trembling had subsided, he eased her face away from his chest and lifted her chin to look at her. "What frightened you?"

She shuddered. "Dead Drust warriors surrounded me, sitting there with their spears in their hands."

Paine did not want to think of what could have happened if she had fallen on one of the spears. It also troubled him that a Drust death trap had been uncovered so close to Pictland. All battle with the Drust had been fought on their land during the conflict, so what was one doing here?

Paine explained what she had seen. "After a battle, the Drust bury some of their dead on enemy land. The Drust feel that as long as a Drust warrior has a weapon in his hand that he will continue to fight even in death."

She gripped his arm. "A battle with the Drust has recently been fought here?"

"No," he said, shaking his head.

187

"I screamed because at first glance I thought the Drust down there," —she pointed to the hole— "were alive, for they have yet to rot."

Paine did not allow his surprise to show. "I need to go down and have a look."

"Why would you want to do that?" she asked, gripping his arm tighter as if somehow she could stop him.

"To see if any of them are the ones who attacked us."

"That would mean—"

"That the Drust still battle the King." He loosened the loop around her waist and did not want to think what would have happened if he had not placed it there.

Her hand quickly grabbed his. "I want to stay tethered to you."

If only she could, he pushed the impossible thought from his mind. "And you will, after I use the rope to go down in the hole and have a look." He kept an arm around her waist as he stepped away. "Are you all right to stand on your own?"

She suddenly felt ashamed. She was the daughter of a Lammok warrior. She should fear little. "I am fine."

He stepped closer. "There is no shame in fear."

He understood, which made her feel all the more inadequate. "My mum would be appalled by my actions."

"You are not your mum, Anin. You are who you are and should not be ashamed of it. Now we have wasted enough time. We need to see this done and be on our way. The clouds grow heavy overhead. Soon the rain will come and we need to reach shelter before then."

She cast a quick glance to the sky and saw that the clouds had darkened considerably. Rain was not far off, though she hoped thunder did not come with it.

"What can I do?" she asked.

188

"Stay by the rope in case I should need help and keep a watchful eye. If you see anything that causes you alarm let me know." He hurried to tie one end of the rope around a nearby tree and the other remained around his waist, then he lowered himself carefully down into the hole.

Paine did not take long. It took little time to see what he needed to see.

Anin waited anxiously and was relieved when he emerged from the hole.

"They are the ones who attacked us."

"They send a message to the King that they still war with him?"

"The King must be made aware of this immediately," Paine said untying the rope around his waist to fasten it around her waist once again, wondering as he did who of the King's warriors had betrayed him and sided with the Drust. "We must be on our way," Paine said, securing the loop firm around Anin's waist. "We need to reach shelter before the storm breaks."

Anin nodded, the wind having picked up and the clouds having grown even darker.

They took off and as the sky continued to darken, Anin begged the sky spirits to keep the thunder away and it did, though not the rain. It started with only a few sprinkles, grew heavier, and then it seemed as if the sky opened and dropped buckets full of rain on them.

It was dusk before they came upon the dwelling Paine had mentioned. She was drenched and shivering when they entered and Paine saw to setting a fire in the pit. She immediately held her wet, chilled hands out to the flames to warm them.

With the glow of the flames, Anin was surprised to see that the dwelling had a raised sleeping pallet with blankets piled at one end. A small table and bench sat on the opposite side of the fire pit, and Anin wondered whose home they had intruded upon.

"Get out of those wet garments and set them to dry by the fire pit while I go make certain no one lurks about," Paine ordered and he and Bog were out the door before she could respond.

Anin was too cold to even think to argue, the storm having brought a sharper chill with it. She shivered as she peeled her wet garments off and draped them on the stone surrounding the fire pit to dry. She quickly wrapped a blanket around her and shivered again from the warmth that settled over her chilled skin. She remained close to the heat of the fire pit and worried what the night would bring. Sending out blessings to whoever would listen, she begged for the thunder giant to stay away.

~~~

Paine looked about, not so much for Drust since they had crossed over the Pictland border and he doubted the Drust would follow, at least not yet. He wanted to make certain the sentinels saw him and knew he had returned. They would report his presence to the King and an escort would be sent for them. But it was impossible to see anything in the slashing rain.

He wanted to give Anin time to get out of her soaked garments. He had learned that remaining in wet garments could bring illness and his task was to protect the future Queen from all things and once again reminded himself that that included him as well.

He shut his eyes a moment not only at the thought of her naked, but at the thought of how he and she had enjoyed the kisses they had shared. How much she had wanted to kiss him. How much he wanted her kiss. Her

190

blue eyes had been heated with such strong desire, her lips so moist and inviting that he could not deny her.

He shook his head. He had betrayed the King by kissing the woman who was to be his Queen, but if he confessed he would not only be condemning himself, but Anin as well. That he could not do. This would all be over soon. He would deliver her to the King and it would be done. He would see her rarely. The thought troubled him more than relieved him. He would miss her. Miss her curiosity, her smile, her touch.

The thunder struck so hard and unexpected that Paine jumped, startled, and Bog cringed as if in fear, a rare response for him. Then Paine realized why, more thunder was about to follow.

Anin.

Paine took off running, Bog trailing.

Another clap of thunder sounded as if it split the earth in two and his insides twisted.

Anin.

His only thought was of her alone and full of fear. He ran faster.

~~~

Anin stood frozen in place. The small dwelling shook from the thunder or was it her shaking with fear.

Paine.

Where was he? Why had he not returned yet?

Stop, Anin, you must stop this! Thunder cannot hurt you!

Her mum's scolding voice rang in her head. How many times had she heard it? How many times had she tried to fight against it? How many times had she tried to tell her mum how the sound of the thunder made her feel? It was as though the thunder itself rippled through her and she could feel its urgent need to strike the earth again and again. She envisioned an angry giant pounding the earth over and over until his temper abated. But no one would listen and her mum would scold her repeatedly until finally she would run and hide from the angry giant.

Another clap of thunder had her cringing and her body trembling badly.

"Paine," she whispered, "Paine, please, I need you."

She covered her ears at the next loud clap of thunder, the blanket falling away from her as she did, leaving her naked. "Paine!" she screamed not only for him but to stop the endless pounding that echoed through her.

The door burst open and Paine rushed in along with Bog.

Anin did not stop to think, she stretched her arms out to him.

Paine gave no thought as well. He rushed over to her and threw his arms around her and her slim arms went around him, pulling him tightly against her. Her trembling worsened and Paine realized his wet garments were doing her no good. He pushed her away, but she fought against him, refusing to let go.

"My wet garments. I need to get out of them."

Reluctantly, she released him, but remained so close that the rainwater from his garments splashed over her as he hurriedly pulled them off. She was back in his arms as soon as he was naked, pressing her body against his before he could grab for the blanket. She was far too frightened for him to push her away again. She needed comforting. She needed to feel safe.

His arms tightened around her and held her firm.

"Do not let me go," she begged.

"Never."

His voice was strong and confident, his body solid against hers, and his arms snug around her. Never. Never would he let her go. Nothing could harm her when he held her, not even the mighty thunder giant.

Thunder broke again, sounding louder than before and Paine ran his hand soothingly down along her back and up again. He continued stroking her back and it was not long before he felt heat returning to her chilled skin. It was then he realized how smooth and soft her skin felt and how delicate the slight curve in her back. If he allowed himself to follow it all the way down he would...

He warned himself to stop, not go any further, but the need to touch her intimately warred with reason. It took all his strength to ease his hand off her.

Shortly after, she began to shiver once again and his hand returned to stroke her back without hesitation. Another warning echoed in his head and if he did not pay it heed, they both could very well lose their heads for betraying the King.

He pushed her away so quickly that she had no time to protest. He reached down and grabbed the blanket and hastily wrapped it around her. He left her for a moment and grabbed the other blanket on the sleeping pallet and tucked it around his waist.

She was back in his arms as soon as he did and just in time, for another clap of thunder sounded. She buried her face against his naked chest and he was relieved that she hugged her arms tight against herself. Her hands and arms would dig into him rather than her breasts that tempted.

He stroked her back again, though through the blanket this time, all the while thinking King Talon must never learn of this. The King would find nothing unfitting in Anin seeing Paine naked, he and his warriors, women warriors included, having gone into battle naked at times or practiced on the practice field naked. There was nothing like *painted people*, as the

Picts were called by others, rushing at their enemies naked, screaming, and weapons raised high, to instill absolute fear and complete confusion in them. But Paine, holding the future Queen naked in his arms, was not something the King would abide.

He waited until the thunder rolled off in the distance and felt her body ease before stepping away from her. She did not want to let him go and he had to be more forceful than he cared to be as he pushed her away from him.

"The thunder is far off now. There is no more to fear," he encouraged firmly, though felt a twinge to his chest when he saw the fright that continued to linger in her eyes and how pale she had grown.

She nodded and stepped reluctantly away from him, though not as far as Paine would have liked.

"We should eat."

"I am not hungry," Anin said her insides upset as always when a thunderstorm rolled around.

"You should sleep. We leave at first light," Paine said. "We are on Pictland land now and the King's warriors will spot us soon enough and an escort will be sent to take you the rest of the way."

"You will leave me?" she asked the thought sending a fright so strong through her that her legs weakened.

"Once I present you to the King, you will see me rarely."

She stepped away from him and though it was not far, he felt as if there was a chasm between them and this time he felt as if his insides were being torn apart. He turned away from her and saw to feeding the fire, keeping the flames plentiful and the small dwelling warm against the chilling rain.

Anin did not know what to make of how she felt. The thought of being separated from Paine hurt so deeply that she wanted to cry. What was it about this man that stirred these feelings in her? Why had she found more comfort in his arms than she had ever felt before? Why did she have this overwhelming need to remain with him, never leave him? How was it that she had whispered, *tuahna*, expressing how deeply she felt for him? And how was she ever going to wed the King when she felt as she did for Paine?

She fought the tears that threatened at her eyes. She had to stay strong. She would not cry. She could not cry. She swiped roughly at the first tear that spilled from her eye.

"Anin," Paine said softly and she turned. His chest tightened when he saw a tear slip down her pale cheek. He took a step toward her.

Anin raised her hand, stopping him. "I must fight my tears. Lammok woman do not cry. My mum would be terribly angry with me if she knew I showed any weakness. She tried so hard to make me strong, scolding me every time I shed a tear, every time thunder rumbled. And here I am failing her twice."

"You cried often?" he asked, taking a step toward her.

She nodded. "Over foolish things as my mum would remind me, but for some reason I could not stop my tears. They were always the victor."

"There is no shame in shedding tears."

"Do you shed tears?" she asked, wiping another one away.

"Not for many years."

"At least you have cried. I believe the last time my mum cried was when she was born." She could not stop the next words that came to her lips. They rushed out of her as if worried she would stop them. "I will miss you."

Her words struck him hard in the chest, though he responded harshly. "No one misses the executioner."

195

"You are not the executioner to me. You are a man who made me feel safer than I ever felt before, and I will miss you terribly." The tears came then. She could not stop them.

Paine could not stop himself from taking her in his arms. He wanted to wipe her tears away and let her know that she could cry in front of him anytime she wished and he would not think any less of her. Most of all, he wanted desperately to kiss her and claim her for himself. He restrained himself from doing any of that and simply held her close and let her shed her tears.

How would she ever walk away from him, never to feel his arms around her again? She purposely pressed her hand against his chest, wanting to feel what he felt, know what was deep inside him, and know if it hurt him to part from her as much as it did her?

She stopped herself from gasping, feeling something unexpected. She felt an ache similar to hers. He would miss her as much as she would miss him.

The words rushed out as before. "You will miss me."

Paine pushed her away. "Do not speak such nonsense or you will suffer for it."

"I am to be Queen," she said with heavy sadness.

"And you forget that too often," he said harshly. "Now go and sleep." He pointed to the sleeping pallet.

Anin did not bother to argue. He was right. It did not matter how either of them felt. Fate had decided for them. She lay down, turning her back to him and let silent tears fall. At least the thunder had rumbled off and hopefully it would not return.

Paine sat with his back braced against the wall, keeping his eyes on the fire pit. Her words had disturbed him. How did she know that he would miss her? He never let anyone see how he felt, but then he had not allowed himself to feel anything for a very long time, not until he met Anin.

He closed his eyes and rested his head back against the wall, trying to chase all thought away when his remark to Anin's mother suddenly struck him. *I will learn your secret and may mercy be with you if I must return here.*

He opened his eyes and looked over at Anin, her back to him. There had been more to her mum's refusal to have her daughter wed the King, but his task had nothing to do with that and so at the time he had paid it no heed. But now after spending time with Anin he began to wonder.

She was nothing like a Lammok woman warrior, not in features, height, skills, or strength, and a Lammok woman would never fear thunder. Her long dark hair was the only likeness to the Lammok Tribe. Then there was the way she was so aware of how the older couple felt toward him that she could not finish eating. And how often had she seemed to know what he felt? Esplin's words suddenly returned to him.

The Wyse women and men listened and became sensitive to the land, sensitive to touch. The land and all on it speaks to them and one touch allows them to feel what others feel. There are some that are born more sensitive than others. They usually become our leaders.

Could Anin be one of the Wyse? But how? Her mum was Lammok.

His thoughts scrambled around in his head until he reached a conclusion.

Anin was her mother's secret.

Thunder suddenly split through the silence. Paine was on his feet as Anin called out to him and was at her side and had her in his arms before she finished his name. He stretched out beside her, keeping her close and stroking her back. The thunder continued, though not as loud and by the time it rolled away Paine and Anin were asleep—in one another's arms.

Bog's growl woke Paine and Anin the next morning, but not quickly enough.

The door burst open, the latch breaking, and in walked a warrior. He stared at them naked together on the sleeping pallet, and angrily demanded, "What goes on here?"

Chapter Twenty-one

"Are you a fool?" the warrior yelled at Paine.

Bog stood, his teeth bared at the man and a deep growl rumbling in his chest.

The warrior ignored him, continuing to yell. "Poking the future Queen? The King will have your head for this." The warrior turned dark eyes on Anin, "But first he will have you take her head."

Anin spoke before giving her words thought. "Paine would never hurt me."

The man's dark eyes bore into her for a moment, and then he looked to Paine. "Outside and shut that wolf up or I will." He turned and walked out the door, closing it forcefully.

Bog stopped as soon as the warrior was out the door.

Paine stood and Anin stared at him, but it was not his naked body that had her thoughts churning, but what could possibly happen to him because of her foolish fear.

As he hastily donned his garments, she hurried to say, "We did nothing wrong."

Paine grabbed his battle-axe and looked at her. "We may not have joined, but it was wrong of us to sleep together—naked." He went to the door. "Have no fear, Anin, I will keep you safe."

He would keep her safe, that she knew, but at what cost to him?

She hurried to slip into her garments, some still damp, though she paid no heed to the discomfort, her thoughts on the man who had angry words for Paine and had completely ignored her.

He was one of King Talon's personal guards, one of the finest, fiercest, and most skillful of warriors. They were as equally admired and feared and many preferred to keep their distance from them.

The one who had burst into the dwelling had fine features and dark eyes that matched his long, dark hair plaited at the sides then drawn back to knot at the back of his head. He was tall, though not as tall as Paine and his body lean, though muscled. He wore the dark garments of the King's personal guard, which meant his body markings were specific to his back, chest, arms, and neck. And there was a forceful presence about him which led Anin to believe he was in command, meaning?

He was Wrath, the powerful leader of the King's Personal Guard, the warrior who rode at the King's side and was like a brother to the King. He was named such, for once he let loose his anger few remained standing.

~~~

Once outside Bog ran off, though he knew the animal would remain close in case he was needed. Not that any of the King's guard would dare touch Bog. They knew Paine would kill them if they did.

Wrath stood beneath a pine tree, his arms folded across his chest and anger still simmering in his dark eyes. Wrath and Paine were more friends than foes, having fought in endless battles together with the King before he was King.

"Tell me that that beautiful woman bewitched you so that we may save you from losing your head," Wrath said when Paine came to stand in front of him.

"Nothing happened between us."

Wrath threw his hands in the air. "Oh, so all is well because you did not poke the future Queen, you only slept beside her naked." He glared at Paine. "King Talon will not be happy to learn what went on here and he will learn of it."

"I will tell him myself, though I believe he will be more interested to learn that we were attacked by Drust warriors and that I saw someone garbed in the hooded-cloak of the King's warriors speaking with the Drust and if that isn't enough, a small troop of dal Gabran has been slaughtered on our land by the Drust."

Wrath took a quick step toward him and lowered his voice. "Tell me all."

Paine explained all to him and Wrath was pacing in front of him by the time he finished.

"There have been rumblings about dissent among a few who believe that King Talon will never produce a son to continue Pict rule and so he should be removed from the seat of power and replaced with a man capable of continuing the Pict reign."

"Then I would suggest there may be some who wish to hasten his departure by showing that he cannot control the Drust."

"The King needs to know of this." Wrath placed his hand on Paine's shoulder. "And hear why you found it necessary to sleep with his future wife."

Paine kept his voice low. "There is more to Anin than the King knows."

"Do not tell me she is not fit to wed the King," Wrath said annoyed. "The search will have to begin again and will only give those who oppose the King more reason to incite others."

"That will be for the King to decide."

"Which means you do not intend to share with me what you know?"

"I do not know enough yet."

Wrath gave a nod toward the door. "She is beautiful, though I thought she would favor the woman of her mother's tribe. I see no Lammok in her except for the dark hair. And she appeared fearful when I entered the cottage. A Lammok woman warrior would have attacked me as soon as I entered. Do her mother and father need to be called before the King?"

"Possibly, but not at the moment."

"Tell me why you slept with this woman who will, or was, to be Queen," Wrath demanded more than asked.

"That is for the King to know," Paine said firmly.

Wrath's brow pinched and his eyes narrowed. "What are you not telling me?"

"What I choose not to tell you," Paine said and turned away.

"I will find out."

Paine gave an abrupt laugh. "I have no worries about that."

"And what does that mean," Wrath asked, walking up beside him.

"Your quick anger blinds you to what is easily seen."

"My anger saved your arse more than once," Wrath reminded.

"And my calm attention saved your arse far more."

Wrath grabbed his arm and brought them to a halt.

Bog was suddenly at Paine's side, snarling and snapping at Wrath.

"Why does he not like me?" Wrath asked, letting his hand fall slowly off Paine.

"Go guard," Paine ordered and Bog ran to the dwelling door and sat in front of it, snarling in warning. "You can be so blind to the obvious."

Wrath's tone took on an edge of anger. "I am not blind to the fact that I fear this may be one time I cannot save your arse."

As he walked off, Paine wondered the same thing.

~~~

As soon as Paine entered the dwelling, Anin asked softly, "Will you take your leave of me now?"

"No, as I told you, I will deliver you to the King and then take my leave. Are you ready? It is time to go."

Anin could not explain the deep ache in her chest and how it spread and seemed to consume her at the thought that once Paine presented her to the King, he would be gone out of her life.

"Anin."

She looked to see that he held the door open. She did not want to leave this small dwelling. She would have preferred to remain here with Paine and what? He had repeatedly reminded her that his task was to present her to the King and he would see it done. He had also told her that he would keep her safe and he had done that. Now it was time for her to do what she must—become the King's queen.

Anin pressed her hand to her middle that fluttered with worry. This was not what she wanted, though fate had thought differently. It was difficult for her to believe fate would be so cruel. She had felt how Paine felt when she had laid her hand on him. He cared as much for her as she did for him.

"There is no time to waste, Anin. The King waits."

Anin reluctantly stepped outside and stopped abruptly when she saw the enclosed cart that waited for her. The two narrow slits on either side of the cart would provide only a modicum of light and air. It would be like being locked in a cell and that she could not bear.

"I will not ride in that," Anin said and took a step back, bumping against Paine.

"You will, the King has ordered it," Wrath commanded and nodded to one of the warriors to open the door.

Anin shook her head. "I will not be closed away in there."

"You fear riding in the cart?" Wrath asked as if the thought was ridiculous.

"I am not comfortable in closed, tight places," Anin said, keeping her back pinned against Paine.

Wrath's brow knitted as he asked, "You are part Lammok, are you not?"

"I am," Anin said.

"Then how can you fear anything?" Wrath snapped and not waiting for an answer ordered, "You will ride in the cart as the King ordered."

"I will not!" Anin shouted her body beginning to tremble.

Wrath and his warriors stared at her, shocked by her adamant refusal.

"Let her ride a horse," Paine said from behind her.

Wrath glared at him. "Few have the skill to ride a horse. Besides, the King's orders will be obeyed." He walked straight at Anin, his hand reaching out to grab her as he got near.

Paine's hand snapped out and clamped like a metal shackle around Wrath's wrist. "Do not touch her."

Anin was squeezed between the two men and she braced herself back against Paine to keep Wrath's body from touching hers. The short distance between her and the fierce warrior did not however stop her from sensing his anger. It raged around him like a thunderstorm ready to unleash fury. No wonder he was called Wrath.

"I was ordered by the King to keep the future Queen from harm and deliver her safely to him. If riding in the enclosed cart causes Anin harm, then she will not

204

ride in it. I—like you—keep my word to the King."
Paine released Wrath's wrist.

"You tread on dangerous ground, my friend, watch
your step," Wrath warned and turned away.

Anin had to stop herself from turning around and
throwing her arms around Paine in gratitude. But he
would not wrap his arms around her in front of Wrath
and his warriors. It would not be proper.

He stepped around her and, without saying a word
to her, went to look over two horses a warrior brought
forth.

Once again, she felt empty when he left her side.
She and Paine were part of each other. And how did one
live missing a part of oneself?

She looked down at Bog, standing beside her and
whispered, "I will miss you, Bog."

The wolf moved closer so that his body pressed
against her leg. She smiled, pleased he seemed to feel
the same way.

Paine lifted her onto a horse. "Just follow the
animal's lead."

Anin did not bother to tell him she was familiar
with riding a horse. She rode her da's horse often,
though he had scolded her whenever he discovered her
doing so.

He mounted his horse and rode in front of her
beside Wrath. The cart traveled behind her and warriors
behind it. Bog kept pace with Paine, though kept his
distance from the horse and he glanced back now and
again at Anin as if keeping close watch on her.

As the day wore on so did Anin's loneliness. No
one spoke to her. It was as if she traveled
unaccompanied. She had felt less lonely when she had
left her home and traveled by herself to her mum's
people. She had felt the companionship of the forest and
the creatures that inhabited it. At least they had

welcomed her. Wrath and his warriors were there out of
duty to the King and had bid her no welcome.

It was not until well after the sun was high in the
sky that they stopped for a brief rest. Anin hoped Paine
would come and sit with her, but she sat in solitude
under a tree with no one paying her heed. She watched
as the warriors talked among themselves and Paine and
Wrath huddled not far from the narrow stream in
conversation. Bog had gone off to do as he pleased and it
gave Anin the notion to do the same.

Since Paine had found her, she had not done as she
pleased and her freedom would certainly be curtailed
once she was Queen. This would be her only chance to
do as she wished and she wished to take a brief walk in
the woods and relish the comfort it always brought her.
Seeing that no one looked her way, Anin stood ready to
slip quietly behind the tree and into the woods and
welcome the peacefulness of the forest that was sure to
surround her.

She froze mid-step as Bog's lone howl echoed
through the forest, sending gooseflesh rushing over her.
She waited, fearful another would follow. And it did.

Anin was about to turn and run to Paine when a
Drust warrior burst out of the woods, his spear raised
and aimed straight at her. She was suddenly shoved
aside. Falling to the ground, she watched as Paine's
battle-axe deflected the spear, then quickly brought it
down on the screaming warrior, silencing him with one
blow.

Paine reached down, yanked Anin up by her arm,
and shoved her against a tree where she was quickly
surrounded by some of the King's guard. Knowing they
would give their lives to keep her safe, he rushed off to
fight along with Wrath and the other guards.

The attack ended quickly and deadly for the few Drust warriors. Paine and Wrath easily dispensed of them, Bog arriving to help with the last one.

Wrath turned to Paine when all was done. "The Drust was not in favor of the tribes uniting, but to openly attack the King's guard and on Pict land makes no sense. They know the King will have no choice but to retaliate and they cannot hope to defeat him and the united tribes."

"They attacked with one purpose...to kill Anin," Paine said with a glance at her, the King's guard still surrounding her.

"Why?" Wrath asked the question puzzling. "No attempts were ever made on the King's two previous wives. What is different about Anin?"

"That is the question I have been asking myself."

"And one that needs a quick answer before war settles upon the land again. If we keep a strong pace, we can make it to the King's stronghold before the sun sets on this day." Wrath did not wait for Paine to agree. He turned and ordered his warriors to mount, then turned to Paine. "She rides in the cart where she will be safe."

"She will not get in the cart."

"Then put her in it," Wrath ordered.

"No," Paine said.

"She must be kept safe."

"Her safety is for me to see to. Your task is to aid me in that," Paine reminded.

"And how do you intend to do that?"

Paine walked away from Wrath without responding, though his actions answered for him. Paine hoisted Anin onto his horse and mounted behind her.

Wrath rode up beside him. "I wonder what the King will think when he sees you mounted on the horse behind his future Queen."

Paine wrapped his arm firmly around Anin's waist. "He will know I do what is necessary to keep her safe."

Chapter Twenty-two

They arrived at King Talon's stronghold at dusk and Anin's breath caught at the sight of the place. She had heard talk of the structures the King had had built at Pictland, but she thought them nothing more than mere tales, thinking it impossible. Seeing it herself proved how wrong she was.

They came upon a wood fence taller than three men standing atop each other. The tops of the fence had been carved into points as sharp as spears and torch lights flickered from various spots along it, making it appear as if the fence went on forever.

Two large wooden gates opened as they approached and once inside Anin's eyes fell on the large structure that dominated the middle of the area. It was like none she had ever seen. It stood two stories high, large posts running in intervals up the front of the dwelling. Two large doors stood in the middle of the lower level. Smoke drifted out of several holes in the turf-thatched roof and tall torch posts stood like sentinels along the front of the structure. Several other dwellings sat nearby, some appearing to be work structures.

People stopped what they were doing to stare at Anin. No smiles crossed their faces and she wondered if it was because she rode with the King's executioner.

When they stopped in front of the large dwelling, Paine quickly dismounted and hastily reached up to take her by the waist and slip her off the horse. She purposely placed her hands on his arms, wanting to feel what he was feeling.

The sensation was so strong it startled her and sent her insides churning. He did not want to be separated from her. He did not want to let her go, though he did, and with haste when her feet touched the ground.

The loss of his touch was almost too much to bear. Once again, she felt as if he took part of her with him.

"What is wrong?" Paine asked, stepping closer to her.

She raised her head, not realizing it had drooped with her heavy thoughts. What could she say to him?

The two large doors opened, sparing her from responding.

Wrath walked up to them, glancing from one to the other. "Are you ready to face the King?"

A shiver ran through Anin, though Paine ignored the question and stepped to her one side. Wrath stepped to her other side. She felt imprisoned by the stature and width of the two strong men and dutifully followed along as they walked toward the open doors after Paine ordered Bog to wait outside.

She entered to find it a feasting hall, though a much larger one than she had ever seen. Long tables and benches sat in rows. Huge logs crisscrossed the ceiling and others ran along the walls, waddle and daub snug between them. A sizeable stone fire pit occupied a far corner of the room, the smoke going up through a hole between the posts. Not far from it sat a long table with no bench in the front of it. Behind it stood two men, the tall one's back turned to them. The other man only reached his shoulder, though his face was not aged with lines and ruts, his short hair was pure white. He stared at them, no sign of welcome on his face.

Anin's insides churned again. The tall one had to be King Talon. It was said he stood two heads above most men and his long, dark hair signaled he was of the ruling class. He wore a sleeveless, long, dark leather tunic and though his arms were leaner than Paine's they were defined with thick muscle. It was said his strength was beyond that of any mortal man. Many believed he could tame the wild beasts, calm an angry sea and that the land would tremble in fear when he walked upon it. There was talk that he could split a man in two with one single blow of his sword and he rode a beast of a stallion that no one could go near but him.

To Anin it was more tale than truth...until seeing him for herself.

The white-haired man gave the King a nod and stepped aside and that was when King Talon slowly turned around.

Anin stared unable to take her eyes off the King. She did not know if it was his fine features that captivated or it was the markings that ran down along the right side of his face. She had heard that no one had ever seen such strange markings and it was believed that he was born with them...born to be King.

His bold green eyes were just as strange and alluring. Once drawn in by them, they were difficult to escape. Though, as tempting as this man might be to most women, Anin did not find him so. To her, he frightened more than attracted and she found herself moving closer to Paine.

"Do not keep me waiting," King Talon ordered sharply and walked around to stand in front of the table.

Anin reluctantly kept pace with Paine and Wrath, her worry mounting with each step she took. They stopped a short distance from the King and Anin continued to stare at him. It was difficult not to. He was an impressive man. His leather tunic sat open from below his neck to the middle of his chest, lean with muscle. A leather belt was drawn tight at his slim waist, keeping the remainder of his tunic that fell to his ankles closed.

Paine spoke. "King Talon may I present—"

The King interrupted abruptly, "I will hear about the Drust attacks first, and then you will clarify why you were found naked on a sleeping pallet with the woman who *was to be* my future Queen."

Relief and fear stirred in Anin. If she no longer was to be his queen, then what was to happen to her? And how had he known about Paine and her?

Paine did not bother to look accusingly at Wrath. He would not have betrayed him when he said he had told him he would explain to the King. It was one of Gelhard's men and that was where his eyes went...to the white-haired man, the High Counselor to the King. Gelhard had men everywhere and they kept him abreast of all that went on, down to the most insignificant thing.

Also, the King was allowing him to explain what had happened, something he did not always allow others to do. What concerned him more, though, was what King Talon intended to do with Anin, since his words made it clear that she would not be Queen.

Paine detailed each attack though he did not speak of the Drust's death trap or of the meeting of the Drust and someone wearing the garb of a King's warrior. That was left to tell when he could speak with the King alone.

The King listened intently to Paine and Wrath's accounts and when they finished he stepped close to Paine and Wrath so they could only hear what he had to say. "Only those close to me knew of your mission, Paine. Someone betrays me."

"There is more to tell," Paine whispered and the King gave a barely noticeable nod.

King Talon stepped back and looked to Paine. "Now you will tell me why you and the once future Queen was found sleeping naked together."

Anin gave no thought to her action, she stepped forward. "It was my fault, my King."

Paine shook his head and stepped up beside her. "She speaks nonsense. I did what was necessary to protect her."

Anin turned to Paine. "If I was not so afraid of thunder, you would not be defending yourself to the King."

"My task was to keep you safe, no matter what your fears."

"Enough!" King Talon shouted and looked to Anin. "You are part Lammok. How can you fear thunder?"

Anin bowed her head before she spoke. "I cannot explain it, my King, but thunder frightens me and Paine kept me safe from my own fears."

"Then why were you naked together?"

"A rainstorm soaked us and we slept apart until...the thunder." Anin lowered her head, knowing how it must sound to the King.

King Talon turned to Paine. "You have done well. You have saved me from an unfit Queen. You will be rewarded." He turned to Anin. "As for you, you shall be imprisoned until I determine your fate."

Anin felt darkness descend over her, squeezing the life from her and without thinking she threw herself against Paine and wrapped her arms around him. "Please, do not let them do this to me."

"Would you prefer I have him take your head?" King Talon said with a snarl.

Anin shook her head, then shocked everyone with her actions. She turned and grabbed King Talon's arm. "Please, my King, do not imprison me, I meant no disrespect." She should not touch the King without his permission, but it was the only way to know how he felt toward her.

She released him almost as quickly as she had taken hold of him, dropping back to lean against Paine. Never had she felt such immense power, such potent strength, such sureness in word and deed, and threading through it all was a smoldering passion. And what did he feel about her? She was of no consequence to him.

"Never dare touch me without permission again!" King Talon ordered sharply, then summoned a warrior with a wave of his hand and ordered, "Lock her in one of the prison chambers until I decide what is to be done with her."

Paine shoved Anin behind him away from the warrior who dared not approach the executioner. "Anin has suffered much on her journey here and has done nothing wrong."

"That is for me to decide. Now move aside and let the warrior take her," King Talon ordered.

Paine did not hesitate. "I cannot do that, my King." He was sealing his fate, but it did not matter. Anin would not survive a prison chamber. It was an enclosure without a shred of light and if it should thunder...he could not imagine the fear she would suffer. He could not bear the thought.

King Talon stared at him for several moments, then ordered. "Throw him in there with her."

Fright gripped the warrior's face at having to force the executioner.

Wrath stepped forward. "I will imprison them both, my King."

"No," the King snapped. "You will stay here and speak with me. Paine will give the warrior no trouble. Will you, Paine?"

"As you say, my King," Paine said with a bob of his head.

"Take them," King Talon ordered.

Paine turned and slipped his arm around Anin and walked toward the doors, the warrior trailing behind them.

"What are you about, Talon?" Wrath whispered, addressing him as a close friend, something they had been long before Talon had become King.

The King's eyes followed Paine. "The truth."

~~~

Paine kept his arm around Anin as they walked around to the back of the two story structure, Bog following them. He knew well where the prison chambers were, for he had made use of them many a time. They worked well. They were tightly built huts, not a shred of light entering them and in the cold the small chamber would grow bitter and in the heat the occupant would swelter. Many were more than willing to talk after spending only a few hours in one, though a person was imprisoned no less than three days to ensure he spoke the truth when released.

Anin had spoken the truth to the King and so had he and he supposed it was the truth that had the King imprisoning her. He could not allow himself to be made to look the fool and that worried Paine. King Talon could very well decide to have Anin executed for betraying him and Paine along with her.

Why, after all this time of keeping himself from feeling anything, had he allowed himself to feel for this woman meant to be Queen? He could not explain it and when Anin had thrown herself at him begging for help, he knew he could not abandon her—he would never abandon her.

Anin gripped his hand tightly when she saw the small, confined hut that was the prison chamber.

"I am with you. You have nothing to fear," he whispered to her. She looked up at him with such fright that he tightened his hold on her.

"You will not leave me?" Anin need not ask him, her hand on his arm already giving her the answer. *Never!* One word so powerful, and uttered with such determination, that it helped ease her concerns not only for this moment, but for the future as well. She was eager to hear it spill from his lips and therefore she was disappointed when he spoke.

"I will be there for you when in need."

Anin wondered why he denied the truth to himself.

The warrior opened the narrow door and darkness yawned from the narrow opening.

Paine was not surprised that the warrior did not prod him or Anin with a spear as was usually done to a prisoner. The young warrior was wise enough to know that Bog would have attacked him if he did. Though, Paine would have grabbed it off him and snapped it in half after giving the young warrior a good prod in the middle with the opposite end.

Paine ordered Bog to guard and the wolf sat in front of the hut. Then he moved his arm from around Anin and took her hand. The entrance was too narrow for them to fit through it together. He entered first and drew Anin in after him. The door closed as soon as she was inside and the board came down hard, locking them in.

Anin felt the darkness close in around her like a burial chamber. Her chest quickened and her breathing grew heavy. Paine's hand was instantly at her back, stroking it, and she lowered her head to rest on his hard chest.

"We will do well," he whispered and tugged her closer against him as his hand continued to caress her back. Paine waited until her fear receded some before saying, "This chamber is meant for one with little room to stretch or rest."

Anin raised her head. "There is not room to sit or sleep?"

He was glad to hear that her voice held no tremor. "There is only room for one to sit, so you will have to sit atop me."

"I do not mind. The closer I am to you, the safer I feel."

Having her tucked so close against him, her breasts pressed to his chest, reminded him of how she felt naked in his arms. Her skin was soft and there was not a single body drawing on her body. She was untouched, pure, and he had no right to mark her with his evil ways.

Paine forced his thoughts on other matters, saying, "There will be no food tonight."

"I am not hungry. I am more concerned with how long the King will keep us locked away?"

"Three days is the least anyone has been released from a prison chamber."

"What will happen once we are?"

"That has always been for me to determine, but since I am now a prisoner, I cannot say what fate we will meet."

"What fate did you deliver those who were released?"

"Those imprisoned here deserved the fate they met."

She need not hear the horrible suffering he had inflicted on people or how with one swing of his axe he took their lives.

"I wonder then what fate the King intends for me and you, though I do not think he will lose his executioner."

"The King is a fair man," Paine said, hoping that he would be more than fair in this matter. "It has been a long journey and a difficult day. We should rest."

"Aye, my body grows tired."

"I will sit first, then I will ease you down on top of me." He was struck with a sudden image of her naked,

217

his manhood slipping into her as she came down on him and he grew aroused and annoyed at doing so.

Once he positioned himself as comfortable as possible on the hard ground, his back against the wall, he said, "Turn so my voice is behind you and remove your cloak. We can use it as a blanket. It will get cold in here tonight. Then stretch your one hand out behind you. I will find it."

As she did, she realized how small the space was, her shoulder brushing the opposite wall as she turned after removing her cloak. She stretched her hand out behind her as he told her to do and his hand found hers as he said he would.

"Come down slowly. I will guide you."

She startled when his other hand touched her backside as she lowered herself, though he moved it to her waist quickly.

It took some maneuvering to finally settle as comfortably as the small space would allow. Their legs were bent at their knees with her legs tucked tightly between his and her back rested against his chest. Her bottom fit snugly in his lap, his arousal pressed firmly against her, though she made no mention of it. How could she when it caused tempting stirrings in her?

After she spread her cloak over them, his arms settled around her beneath the soft wool and his hands hugged her arms she had folded over her chest.

They sat quiet, Anin's fear having dissipated, replaced by a stirring that grew as the warmth of their bodies mingled together and she felt his arousal stirring beneath her.

Paine grew annoyed that he could not stop his desire for her from growing. He could easily poke her here and now and be done with it. After all, she was no longer to be Queen. But that would only prove to the King that he had wanted Anin all along. He had to make the King see that he saw to his task of keeping her safe and no more. Maybe then he would return Anin to her family and it would be done. He would never see her again.

Sorrow that he had not felt in many years washed over him. He had never thought to feel it again, never wanted to, it hurt much too much. It was why he never allowed himself to care. It was why he made a good executioner. Why he would continue to be a good executioner.

He forced the sorrow away, burying it deep before it became unbearable as it once did. He would see this done. He would see that the King sent Anin home. He would see her safe and out of his life...no matter how much it hurt.

Chapter Twenty-three

Paine woke to Bog growling. "Are you out there Wrath?"

"Aye, and tell this animal of yours to stop and move aside," Wrath said with an angry tone that intensified Bog's growl.

"Let the fool pass, Bog," Paine ordered.

Anin stretched, arching her body against Paine and wincing from the ache in her limbs.

"Stand before Wrath opens the door," he ordered and grabbed at her waist and hoisted her off him.

Her limbs were stiff from not moving all night and she remained hunched over, having trouble stretching the aches out.

Paine was on his feet with ease and with a hand pressed to her chest and one to her back he eased her up straight just before the door flew open.

"The King commands both your presence," Wrath said.

Anin gathered what courage she could to help meet her fate.

Though the sky was heavy with clouds, Anin squinted when she stepped out of the hut, the pale light difficult to look upon, at first, after complete darkness.

Paine shielded his eyes after stepping outside, his hand falling away after a few moments. He knew the consequences of spending time in the prison chamber, though they were far worse after spending three days in one. He looked to Bog waiting patiently for a command

and signaled him to do as he pleased, knowing the wolf needed time to roam.

The short walk to the feasting house helped dissipate the aches in Anin's limbs, though only made her worry grow. If the King no longer wanted her as his Queen, what would he do with her?

Anin remained close to Paine when they entered the feasting house and she saw King Talon waiting for them in front of the long table. He appeared even more intimidating than yesterday, garbed in black, his arms crossed and resting on his chest.

"Take her," King Talon ordered with a nod at Anin and two of his personal guard stepped forward.

Paine stepped in front of her. "Tell me you intend her no harm."

"You dare question me?" the King snapped angrily.

"I do," Paine said without hesitation. "Anin is a kind woman and does not deserve harm."

King Talon dropped his crossed arms away from his chest and stepped forward. "That is for me to decide."

Anin would not see Paine suffer for defending her. She stepped around him. "I will go with the warriors." She turned to Paine, sensing he was about to say something and laid her hand on his arm. "I will be fine. See that you are as well." She could feel her words console him some, but she had not eased his worry. "Truly, I will be fine." She turned and went with the two warriors before Paine said or did something that would only make the matter worse.

"Wrath tells me you saw some Drust meet with one of my warriors and that a Drust death trap has been found near Pictland. Tell me about it and I may be lenient with you and Anin."

Paine detailed what he had seen and what had happened, though he did not mention that he had kept Anin tethered to him.

"You could see nothing of the man's face who betrays me?" the King asked.

"He kept himself well concealed, but that is not all I have to tell you. Anin and I came upon a Wyse settlement and I requested their chieftain meet with you." He went on to explain the many things he had learned about the Wyse Tribe and about his brief stay there.

"You may have just saved Anin's life," King Talon said.

If he told the King the suspicions he had about Anin, he wondered what would happen. Would he use her to his benefit? He certainly would not wed her if it turned out that Anin was from the Wyse Tribe, for their firstborn would be a daughter and he needed a son. And what of Anin's mum? What would be her fate for lying to the King? It was his duty to speak the truth to the King, but so far it was only a thought on his part. He had no proof to present. Still he was honor bound to inform the King, but what of the consequences for Anin?

"You do not ask about your own life," the King said.

Paine shrugged as if it mattered not to him. "It is for you to decide."

"You have nothing to say for yourself."

"I did what was necessary to keep Anin safe. If it was not for her, we would have never known about the Drust death trap, then in death the Drust may have claimed one of ours."

King Talon tilted his head, his eyes narrowing in question. "How was it that Anin learned of the trap?"

"She fell into the trap." Paine wanted to pull his words back once they slipped out. Now he would have to explain it all to the King and Wrath, and he would never hear the end of it from Wrath.

"How was it that Anin did not get hurt from her fall into the trap?" King Talon asked.

Paine explained, though he had no wont to. "She was tethered to me and I stopped her fall before she suffered any harm."

"Tethered?" Wrath said with a grin. "She gave you such trouble that you had to tether her?"

"She did not obey you?" King Talon asked before Paine could answer.

Wrath answered for him. "Since he had to tether her, I would say she paid no heed to his word."

"The more I hear about this woman, the more I believe you saved me from a dreadful union. I want no wife who will not obey my word or a woman so weak that thunder frightens her."

Anin was far from weak and Paine made that known. "Anin has courage as she showed when she met the Giantess."

"No one meets the Giantess unless she allows it and it is the same with the Wyse Tribe. They choose who they will let enter their villages," King Talon said, settling a stern glance on Paine. "What is so special about Anin that not only the Giantess, but the Wyse Tribe welcomes her?"

Paine caught Wrath's grin and he knew what he thought. Now he would have to tell the King what he had refused to tell Wrath. Paine saw the disappointment on Wrath's face when he said, "I would rather be sure of what I suspect than say and be wrong."

King Talon turned and poured wine from the small jug on the table into a glass vessel, one of many, a foreign merchant had brought for him. He looked back at Paine and took a sip of wine before asking, "Or is it that you do not tell me for fear of what I may do to Anin if it proves I was deceived?"

223

Donna Fletcher

"I believe Anin has been deceived as well, though until I can discover more I cannot say for sure."

"I will give you until mid-day to get the truth from her," King Talon said.

Paine glared at him. "You expect me to torture her?"

"If necessary."

Paine took two quick steps toward the King.

King Talon's hand shot out to stop Paine from taking another step. "So far, Paine, your mission has been more than successful. You delivered Anin safely. You made contact with the Wyse and asked for a meet. You warned that the Drust still war with me. I strongly advise you not to add to that...betrayal. Find out who perpetrated this deception against me and why, and not only will you remain in good stead with me, but I will generously reward you. Now go and see it done."

Paine nodded, knowing if he did not do as the King ordered, someone else would be given the task, and that he could not abide. He also wanted no reward. He only wanted Anin safe from harm.

Wrath followed him out of the feasting house. "Do not challenge the King. He gives you a chance to prove your loyalty. Do not do something foolish."

"You think me foolish?" Paine snapped.

"Aye, you are foolish when you challenge the King." Wrath went to put his hand on Paine's shoulder and Bog snarled in warning. He dropped his hand. "He could have had your head for what you did with Anin."

"We did nothing," Paine snapped and heads turned to stare at the two men.

Wrath pointed to the corner of the feasting house, a more secluded place to talk and Paine followed him there.

Wrath kept his voice low. "I see the way you look at Anin, the fierce way you protect her, even from the

224

King. She has bewitched you. She has robbed you of your senses. Do the task the King has ordered you to do and discover the truth before you lose your head over a woman that may have been sent to destroy the King."

"You are wrong," Paine said, "and I will prove it."

"Good, that is all the King asks of you."

Paine walked away, Bog keeping pace beside him. He had little time to prove Anin innocent and he could not let how he felt about her interfere, not if he wanted to keep her safe. But how did he prove her innocence? The thought troubled him all the way to the dwelling that purposely sat a good distance away from the other dwellings in the King's stronghold. However, the distance still could not keep the horrifying screams from being heard.

Anin would soon realize how truly evil he was and she would care for him no more.

Chapter Twenty-four

Anin wondered where two of the King's personal guards were taking her. When the King had dismissed her, the guards had brought her to a small room where she had been given something to eat and drink. She had eaten little, her thoughts on Paine and what could be happening to him.

They stopped in front of a dwelling, larger than most. One guard pushed the door open and the other shoved her in, the door closing behind her. Her eyes widened at what she saw and she wrinkled her nose at the unpleasant odor that lingered in the air. She wanted to turn and run, but her legs would not move. Besides, the two guards probably stood outside the door to prevent her from leaving.

A fire pit sat in the middle of the room and a long narrow table sat to one side of it. Two lengths of ropes lay at either ends of the table, one end appearing to be fastened to something under the table. On another table were different shaped metal and wood objects and it did not take her long to imagine what they were used for or the suffering they brought. Two leather coverings hung on pegs on the wall not far from the table and several empty buckets sat beneath them.

"These are the tools of my trade."

Anin jumped, but was relieved to see Paine step out of the shadows, though at first glance she felt a twinge of fear. The fire's light flickered across his naked chest, causing his numerous body drawings to appear as if they came to life and moved in a macabre fashion. The look in his green eyes was far different than it had been when last she saw him. There was a coldness to them that almost caused her to shiver. What had happened since they were last together only a short time ago? She had to touch him. She had to find out what had happened.

With strength having returned to her legs, she approached Paine slowly. "Why am I here?"

"The King wants answers."

She kept walking towards him. "He need only ask me."

Paine stood where he was. "The King looks for the truth."

"The truth is all I have to tell." She stopped in front of him and gasped when his hands shot out and clenched at her waist, lifting her to quickly deposit her on the table. She cringed, knowing she sat where suffering and death took place.

His fingers dug in at her waist. "No, you hide something and I want the truth."

Anin was quick to lay a hand on his arm, needing to feel for herself what he felt. The room spun from the barrage of feelings that assaulted her. The emptiness she had felt when she had first touched him was there, warring with the part of him that cared deeply for her. It took a moment for her to understand what had happened to him.

"Anin!"

She shook her head as she fought her way past all his mixed and potent feelings, past the spinning to be able to open her eyes that she had not realized she had closed and look at him. It was all too much what she had felt, what he had felt, and what the King expected of him, and her head fell against his chest.

Paine wanted to hold her tight and protect her, but he had only so much time if he was to see her kept unharmed and to do so, he had to make her think she was no longer safe with him.

227

He grabbed her chin and lifted her head off his chest prepared to squeeze hard and when he looked into her soft blue eyes and saw no fear only caring, he did what he never expected to do...he kissed her.

Anin felt her heart soar. He cared for her much too deeply for the emptiness in him to win the battle. As soon as his hand fell off her chin, she quickly slipped her arms around his neck and savored the hungriness of his kiss. It overwhelmed her and all she wanted to do was get lost in it.

Paine thought of nothing but the taste of her, sweet, warm, and giving. She gave of herself more deeply to him with every kiss. He could only imagine how it would feel when they joined. His thought startled him and made him realize that it was not Anin who was being tortured but himself, for they would never join as one.

He abruptly pulled away from her, shaking his head. Time was drawing near and if he did not have answers, she would suffer for it. He stepped back in front of Anin. "I need you to be honest with me."

"I have been."

"No, you harbor a secret. Do not make me force you to tell me."

"You would never harm me," —she raised her hand when he went to argue— "but the King would and you would defend me. I will not see you harmed. I will tell you, though my mum has repeatedly warned me against telling anyone, but you are not anyone. You are the man who holds my heart and always will." She did not wait for a response, though he did take hold of her hand and that pleased her. She was concerned of what he would do and how he would feel when he learned the secret she had kept for so long.

He squeezed her hand as if reassuring her and she felt a tug to her chest. He had given his heart to her as well, whether he realized it or not and she had nothing to worry about. They were one and nothing would change that.

"It all began when I was young and would follow my brothers into the woods. They did not want me there with them and would run off and leave me on my own. I was too small to catch up with them and I would sit and cry until one of them returned for me and dragged me home, warning me never to follow them again."

"I am going to beat your brothers."

From the angry look on his face, Anin believed he would. "One day, when they had run off without me and I was in desperate need of comfort, I hugged a tree and—" she hesitated.

"Do not be afraid to tell me. It will change nothing between us," he said, though wondered how it would change her.

"The tree whispered comforting words to me and told me I was in no danger, I only needed to reach out to the trees, the foliage, to the animals and they would help me, protect me. I was so excited to tell my mum, but she scolded me and told me it was nonsense and I was not to tell anyone. But the trees continued to whisper to me and I continued to listen.

"Then one of my brothers had an accident. I grew upset upon hearing him cry out in pain and I went to him and placed my hand on his shoulder to comfort him. I suddenly found myself feeling his pain. It tore through me and I cried out, telling him I was so sorry he suffered so badly. My da yelled at my mum to get me away while they tended his wound. While she dragged me away I told her how I could feel my brother's terrible pain and how frightened he was and they had to hurry and help him. She shook me hard and warned me never to say such nonsense again. I did not know what I had done wrong, but when it happened again and she punished me again I knew I had done something terribly wrong. After that I was careful of touching others, but then I met you."

"What difference did I make?"

"You made all the difference. When I touched you, it was as if something opened in me and it grew stronger and stronger each day I spent with you, every time I touched you. It was as though you freed me. That is my secret, all of it."

Paine reluctantly stepped away from her. He could not let her feel what he was feeling, not take a chance of her realizing that there was more to her ability. He needed to talk with her mum. She was the one keeping the true secret.

"I have told you everything. There is nothing more I keep from you," Anin said and hopped off the table. "What happens now? Am I to be punished?"

"You did nothing wrong," Paine said, walking to the door and opening it before Anin could question his actions.

The guards stepped in.

"Take her back to the room where she waited," Paine ordered.

Anin walked over to Paine. "I can only assume you do what you do to protect me so I will not question it...for now."

"I will come for you as soon as I can."

"I am pleased to know that."

Paine left after them, going to the practice arena where he knew the King would be. It was an enclosed area and the only ones permitted to enter were the King's personal guards and those he invited. Paine was allowed in anytime and when he entered he stopped and watched as the King stepped into the sparring circle naked to fight two of his personal guards. It did not matter that it was a chilly day, the air crisp. The King made his guards fight naked in all different weather. He wanted them prepared for anything.

Paine had to laugh. The two guards did not stand a chance against the King. There were none who stood taller than the King and he was stronger than most. He was skilled in all weapons, though his prowess with a sword was unbeatable.

Today they used no weapons, only their hands.

Paine joined Wrath where he stood removed from the other warriors. He was naked as well, his body dripping with sweat. He had already battled the King.

"The King bested you again," Paine said with a grin.

Wrath shook his head. "I thought I had him this time."

"Paine!"

He turned at the King shouting his name.

"Come fight me. I have no worthy opponents today." The King pointed to the two fallen warriors on the ground.

One warrior struggled to his feet and hobbled over to the other warrior to help him up and holding on to each other they stumbled out of the sparring circle.

"Come fight me!" the King shouted and waved Paine over.

It was not a request and Paine stripped off his garments.

Rarely did the King call his executioner to fight him, so all the King's guards gathered to watch in eager anticipation.

Paine approached the King slowly. The King's courage was well know, his body lean and taut with muscle and he possessed strength that far exceeded most men. Paine had seen the King snap a large man's neck with little effort and watched him swing his sword with even less effort and he did so because of his keen mind.

He was wise in the ways of battle strategy and wise in taking stock of his opponent. When his anger raged all fled and when he spoke with wisdom all listened. He was a true King, and Paine was proud to serve him.

Paine entered the sparring circle, all eyes on him. It was not often others saw all his body drawings. And once he began to fight they would stare even more intently, each drawing appearing as if it moved of its own accord. It caught the eye, mesmerized, and distracted.

"Do not hold back, Paine."

"You are the King," Paine reminded.

The King circled Paine as he spoke. "Not at the moment. I am your enemy, for I hold the fate of the woman you care for in my hands."

"And I hold the truth of Anin in my hands."

The King's nostrils flared with annoyance. "I am not your King while we fight."

"You mean like the day we met, before you were King, and I pounded you into the ground?"

The King's dark eyes flared. "I was too far into my cups."

"You would call that a poor excuse."

"I say you talk too much instead of fighting."

Paine nodded, waiting, knowing the King would lunge any moment and when he did...Paine ducked and slipped his arm between the King's legs to lift him high and slam him down on the ground.

Silence fell over the practice area.

The King lay sprawled on his back, his eyes wide, staring up at Paine. "Damn, I misjudged you." He stretched his hand out to Paine.

Paine shook his head. "You never give your opponent a hand."

"I am going to beat your arse," King Talon said, getting to his feet.

Paine shook his head. "You would need your guards to help you do that." Paine was sure that smoke would spew from the King's flaring nostrils. The King lunged at him once again.

This time their body's locked and no one could take their eyes off the two large men tossing each other around like they were nothing more than sacks of grain.

It went on for some time until the King stood panting opposite Paine and said. "Enough! One day I will beat your arse, but today is not that day."

Paine nodded. "I am here to serve you, my King."

King Talon held his arm out to Paine.

Paine reached out and they gripped each other's arm just below their elbows. Cheers went up.

The King stepped closer to Paine. "Your word you will always fight me to win."

"I have beaten you once, I will beat you again."

"One day. One day your arse is mine!" The King turned to his warriors and shouted. "You are dismissed. You know your duties, see to them."

All left but Wrath. He joined the King and Paine on the one long bench outside the circle. It was only when the three were alone that Wrath and Paine sat beside the King as nothing more than friends. It brought back memories of when the three first met and were young warriors fighting to drive the Romans out of their land. But Wrath and Paine always knew that Talon was meant for greater things. They fought beside each other and when Talon became King, they pledged their fealty to him and once again fought by his side in uniting the tribes.

"So tell me what you learned about Anin," King Talon said.

"I believe Anin is from the Wyse Tribe, though I need to confirm her innocence, since Anin is not aware of the deception."

"You believe she is Wyse but does not know it?" the King asked as if not believing it himself.

"After meeting the Wyse I have no doubt. She can feel what others feel with one touch and the forest speaks to her." Paine went on to detail what Anin had told him and Esplin as well. And whether it was out of duty or the need to protect Anin from herself, he let the King know of her curious spirit. "She is inquisitive to a fault, asking far too many questions."

"I have no need of a curious wife and with her strange abilities, she would not make a good mate for me. I would not want her knowing what I was feeling, though feeling what others feel could benefit me." King Talon stood and slipped a cloth around his waist. "Who deceived me?"

Paine stood. "Anin's mum, Blyth of the Girthrig Tribe, though I do not believe it was intentional."

"If she kept something from me when I entered into the agreement with Girthrig for his daughter then she deceived me. I will send for her and you will get the truth from her."

"And Anin," Paine asked.

"She may be of use to me yet. Have her brought to my sleeping chambers, I will talk with her." King Talon turned and walked away.

Wrath grabbed Paine by the arm when he went to follow the King. "Let it be."

"I will not stand by and let him have his way with her," Paine said his fury mounting at the thought.

"If that is what he wishes, that is what he will do. She was to be his Queen."

"So now she becomes one of the long line of women he pokes throughout the day?"

"Again that is his choice and if he finds no satisfaction with her, then he may just give her to you."

"Give her to me!" Paine seethed.

234

"She is no more than chattel to him. Let it be before he punishes not only you, but Anin as well."

"If he does this, it punishes us both."

Wrath rested his hand on Paine's shoulder.

"Perhaps that is the punishment he intended all along."

Chapter Twenty-five

Anin followed the two warriors through the large
dwelling, wondering once again where they were taking
her. Paine had told her he would come for her, so they
would not be taking her to him. When they climbed the
wood stairs to the second floor, she grew concerned. She
had surmised this was the King's private chambers. Why
was she being brought here?

There appeared to be two rooms, once at the tops of
the stairs, one to the left and one to the right, both with
closed doors. The warriors took her to the right and
tapped at the door.

Anin recognized the King's voice as soon as he bid
them to enter. The guards, however, did not enter. One
opened the door and stepped aside and the other gave her
a gentle nudge, letting her know she was to enter. The
door shut behind her after she took a few steps in.

A sense of unease ran through her as soon as she
saw that she was in the King's sleeping chamber. The
sleeping pallet was raised and looked large enough for
three people. It was well dressed with coverings. Several
pegs lined one wall, various garments hanging from
them and beneath sat a long, narrow bench, folded
garments on top. The fire pit sat in the middle of the
room and cast welcoming warmth throughout. King
Talon stood by a table with two short benches, beneath
it, not far from the fire pit. His features were strong and
sharp, and he held himself erect as only a King could.
His long dark hair was braided at the sides and left to
hang free. He wore a tunic that was spilt down the center
and fell to just above his ankles. A braided leather tie

wound around his waist holding the tunic closed and Anin was glad it did, since it was the only thing he wore.

King Talon wasted no time in asking, "Why was I not told of your abilities?"

"Why does it matter?" Anin cringed, realizing too late she questioned the King.

He approached her slowly.

She wisely lowered her head and said, "Forgive me, my King. I am prone to curiosity and asking far too many questions."

"So I have been told. What makes you so curious, Anin?"

She raised her head. "I do not know, though my mum would be quick to say that my head is much too crowded with thoughts. Do you not wonder the why of things sometimes like why are some people good and others evil?"

"At least you can tell the good from the evil with one touch." The King extended his hand. "Tell me, Anin, am I good or evil?"

That was a question, if answered wrongly, could prove harmful for her.

"Do you fear touching me, Anin?"

His voice was a soft whisper that embraced her much too intimately and though she laid no hand on him, she sensed his passion sparking. Fear prickled her skin and she wondered why had she been brought to his private chambers?

"Touch me, Anin."

Her skin prickled again at his strong command, though it was only a mere whisper. She forced herself not to tremble as she reached out and laid her hand on his arm. It hit her so hard that she gasped. The smoldering passion she had felt running through him when she had first touched him had taken control and consumed him, and it was born only of need. He cared not for who he joined with. He cared only for satisfying his insatiable need. The woman who would be Queen would know endless mating with him, but never, ever would he give his heart to her

She dropped her hand off him and once again spoke before she gave thought to her words. "I could never mate with you. There is no tenderness, no caring. You wish only to satisfy your need. I wish for more."

"Did you find more with my executioner?" he accused.

She raised her chin with false bravado. "I lost my heart to Paine, but we did nothing wrong. Paine would never betray his King."

"Did Paine lose his heart to you? And do not bother to tell me you do not know. You touched him. You know."

Anin had no choice but to answer, but then the King had been aware of how Paine felt the moment he refused to let her be locked away alone. She chose to respond with a single nod. She was glad the King turned and walked away from her.

"So the future Queen and my executioner lost their hearts to each other," he said, turning to face her once again. "Whatever shall I do with the both of you?"

Anin understood he expected no response. The choice was his to make.

"Come here," he ordered with the snap of his hand.

Anin preferred to keep her distance from him, but she could not deny the King. She went to stand in front of him, though not too close.

He bridged the gap between them in one easy stride and lowered his face to hers.

Anin's breath caught, so fearful was she that he would kiss her. She wanted only Paine's lips on hers. Though, his breath was warm and not unpleasant, she cringed when he brought his lips closer to hers.

"Go sit on the bench!"

Anin's eyes shot open and she raced around him to do as told.

King Talon went and stood by the fire pit, staring at the flames as if in thought.

Anin sat in silence, waiting.

~~~

"Drink up, your mission is done and there is no one who needs torturing," Wrath said, pushing a vessel filled with wine toward him.

Paine ignored the drink and regretted joining Wrath in the feasting house. The King's decision to have Anin brought to his sleeping chambers had disturbed Paine and his concern for her was growing worse. "We both know why the King summoned Anin to his sleeping chamber. He will have his way with her."

"Do not think on it," Wrath ordered. "Besides, the King never forces himself on any woman. He does not have to. They willingly submit."

"Not Anin."

"Then you have no need for concern. He will speak with her and then release her," —Wrath grinned— "unless she finds him too potent to resist."

Not once had Paine seen a woman deny the King and never had he seen him take a woman against her will. Every one of them was eager to mate with the King, though none could match his appetite for mating.

Wrath went to speak and Paine was quick to warn, "Say one more thing and I promise you will not be able to speak for a whole moon cycle."

Paine was glad Wrath wisely remained silent. He was aware that Wrath had no intentions of leaving his side, fearful that Paine would do something foolish. He was not prone to displays of foolishness. He did what he was told and never questioned...not until Anin.

He had grown used to protecting her, keeping her safe from harm. How did he simply stop or was it because he had grown to care for her far too much? That he could do nothing about Anin being alone with the King in his sleeping chambers had his insides twisting and turning. He fought to keep himself on the bench when he wanted to jump up and rush upstairs and rip Anin away from King Talon. But what good would it do either of them. The King would see him punished and Anin would have no one to keep her safe.

He rolled his shoulders, trying to chase the ache that centered between them.

"The King will enjoy himself this night," a warrior said to the other warrior walking beside him as they passed the table

"And well he should with such a beautiful woman," the other warrior added.

Paine glanced up and saw that it was the two warriors who had guarded Anin.

He clenched his hands into fists so tight his knuckles turned white.

"Paine, you will only make it worse," Wrath cautioned.

"Worse? You think it can get any worse than it already has?"

"You know the King would not hold her against her will."

"Aye, I know that, but I also know Anin would do anything to ensure—"

"Her safety," Wrath finished. "She will do fine."

Paine shook his head. "Not her safety...*my* safety. And that I cannot allow her to do."

Wrath grabbed his arm when Paine went to stand. "Think about what you do. Unless it is dire circumstances, no one disturbs the King when he is occupied in his sleeping chambers."

"This is dire circumstances."

"It is foolishness."

"Then I am a fool," Paine said and yanked his arm from Wrath's grip and stood just as frightful shouts were heard from upstairs, followed by rapid pounding on the floor. Paine and Wrath did not hesitate, they ran for the stairs.

~~~

King Talon had yet to move from where he stood by the fire pit or speak. Anin wondered if he remembered that she was there, he stood so still. She kept watch on him, not knowing what to expect, but intending to make it clear that she had no desire to mate with him. If he was as fair a man as Paine had said, then he would leave her be.

The fire crackled and spit and she watched as several sparks flew out of the pit and caught the bottom edge of the King's long tunic and flamed to life.

Anin screamed, jumped, grabbed a long garment off one of the pegs and ran to the King. She fell on her knees at his feet, smothering the flames with the garment.

King Talon was quick to shed his tunic and looked down at Anin pounding the life out of the last few stubborn, small flames with her fist.

"Are you harmed," she asked, bringing her head up and her eyes rounding as her glance landed on his manhood.

At that moment, Paine and Wrath burst through the door.

Fury raged through Paine, seeing King Talon naked and Anin on her knees in front of him. He went straight for Anin, grabbed her by the arm and pulled her to her feet.

"Release her!" King Talon demanded harshly.

Fearing Paine would not obey the King, Anin yanked her arm free.

"Your hand, Anin," King Talon demanded.

Paine's fury mounted and he was about to reach for Anin again when he saw the back of her hand as she held it out to the King. It was swollen red.

"Wrath," the King called out. "Get a servant to clean this mess."

"Are you harmed, my King?" Wrath asked.

"Anin's quick action saw that I suffered no harm. Now go send the servant here."

"Should I get the healer," Wrath asked

"No, Paine will take Anin to Bethia when we are done here," King Talon said and walked over to the pegs on the wall as Wrath took his leave.

Paine would tend Anin's wound himself, though he would not tell the King that. He took quick steps to Anin as the King reached for his long leather tunic and belted it at his waist.

Anin spoke before he could, resting her uninjured hand on his chest. "I am fine, though I am glad you are here." His feelings rushed over her. He was angry he had not been there to protect her, upset that she had been hurt, and furious with—

King Talon interrupted her thought with his command. "Tell me what my executioner is feeling," King Talon said.

Paine turned to face the King. "I can tell you myself."

"I do not want your words. I want hers." King Talon looked to Anin.

Anin surprised both men and herself when she stepped closer to Paine, slipped her arm around his and

242

said, "It is not right of me to voice his feelings. He will have to tell you himself."

"I command *you* to tell me," the King snapped.

"I will—"

"Hold your tongue or lose it!" King Talon ordered Paine and pointed to Anin. "You will tell me."

A servant hesitated at the open door, his eyes wide with fright.

"See to cleaning this mess," King Talon ordered and walked out the door.

Paine slipped his arm around Anin's back and eased her to the door to follow the King. They passed by the steps to enter the only other room on the second floor, the King's private chamber.

Anin hesitated to enter and Paine gave her a nudge. It was not a large room and a good-sized table and bench occupied most of it. Several chests sat about, some stacked three high. The small fire pit barely had a flame and Anin shivered from the chill.

Paine felt it and drew her closer against his side.

The King shouted for the servant and when he appeared, he ordered the man to tend the fire pit. In no time, flames sprouted and cast a glow around the room, warmth began to follow. The servant hurried out, shutting the door behind him.

King Talon pointed to Anin. "You will answer me."

Paine gave her waist a slight squeeze. "Tell him."

With Paine's permission, Anin did not hesitate. "He is upset that I am hurt and that he was not there to protect me."

"And he feels nothing towards me?"

"He felt anger, but—"

Again the King interrupted and looked to Paine. "Only anger? I thought I saw fury in your eyes when you entered the room."

Paine did not deny it. "You did, my King."

"But the anger was not for you, my King," Anin said.

King Talon looked questioningly at Paine.

Paine knew the King would have his answer, but he hesitated.

"If there was one thing I could count on with you, Paine, is that you always spoke the truth to me."

"I always will, my King."

Again the King waited for an answer, his eyes intent on Paine.

"Anin would do whatever it took to protect me, to keep anything harmful from happening to me and I was furious I could not do the same for her."

"It is good that you will always seek to protect and keep Anin safe, for that will be your task from this day on," the King ordered. "Anin will not make a fitting Queen, but her abilities will serve me well. You will see no harm comes to her—ever."

"You have my word, my King, that I will protect her with my life," Paine assured him.

"I have no doubt you will."

Anin did not like that her fate was once again not hers to choose, but at least she would not lose Paine.

"Take Anin's hand," King Talon ordered.

Paine took hold of her uninjured hand.

The King walked to stand in front them and placed his hand over theirs. "I join you two as one from this moment on. No one can break this union. No one can see it undone. I seal it forever."

Chapter Twenty-six

Anin smiled, her heart soaring. The King had joined them in marriage. She and Paine now belonged to each other and nothing could change that. "I am most grateful, my King."

"You will serve me well, Anin," the King said. "I will call on you when necessary."

She nodded, thinking Paine was right, the King was a fair man.

"Have you nothing to say, Paine?" the King asked a glint in his eyes and a slight smirk on his face.

"What life will Anin have being joined to the executioner?" Paine asked annoyed he had been forced on Anin.

"Whatever life you choose to give her." The King waved them off. "Now go and have Bethia see to your wife's hand, then go make many bairns." The King looked to Paine. "My word is law. This is done."

Paine nodded and took the stairs down to the feasting hall, ignoring the stares of every one there as hand in hand he and Anin made their way through it. Once outside, he stopped. Dusk was fast turning to darkness and a sharp chill came along with it.

"You are upset the King joined us," Anin said.

"Is there nothing I will be able to keep from you?" he snapped, releasing her hand and taking a step away from her.

Anin felt an ache in her chest. She had thought only of how deeply he cared for her. She had never given thought to how her ability might be a hindrance to that caring. "I should have listened to my mum and not let anyone know of my ability." She shook her head. "My curse, she called it, and she was right."

He wanted to reach out and take her in his arms and tell her it was no curse, it was her birthright. But until they heard the truth from her mum, it would not be fair of him to say anything. Paine grabbed for her hand and she yelped. He silently cursed himself for having grabbed her injured hand by mistake.

"Come, I will tend your hand." He held his hand out to her.

Anin did not reach for it. "Do you want me as your wife?"

"It matters not what I want. We have been joined by the King and nothing can change that."

"It matters to me as does the truth."

"I am pleased the King joined us and I am not pleased, and I do not know how to make sense of that to you."

"It is a good start." She took his hand and they walked in silence to his dwelling.

Anin was not surprised to see that his dwelling was removed from the others and pleased that it was not near where tortures took place. Two drying racks with hides stretched out on them sat to one side of the dwelling and a fairly large planting area, all but a few plants harvested, sat to the other side. Not far from the drying racks was an outside fire pit and a thick tree trunk cut at both ends looked to serve as some type of work table. A bench sat under the one large tree and another bench sat against the wall to the left of the door and that was where Bog lay sleeping, his eyes drifting open to see them approach, then closing once again. There were fresh patches of thatch on the roof in preparation of the coming cold as well as fresh patches to the walls.

The inside was as well cared for as was the outside. There were barely any flames in the fire pit which was the way it should be if no one was there, less chance of sparks escaping and setting the place ablaze. A good-sized, raised sleeping pallet sat to one side of the room and a table with two benches on the other side. It was like many other dwellings, but this one was different. This was her home now. She would spend her life here with Paine, raise their children here, care for her family here and the thought brought great relief and great pleasure to her.

"Sit and I will tend your hand," Paine said, pulling out a bench from beneath the table.

Anin sat and watched as he tenderly wiped her hand clean and just as tenderly pressed along the back of it.

"I feared you had burnt it, but it is swollen and sore from the pounding you gave it."

"Why do you fight against how you feel about me?"

He released her hand gently and stepped away from Anin. "You deserve more than being forced to join with the executioner."

"I may not have been asked if I wished to join with you, but I was not forced. I was thrilled when the King joined us. It is what I want...I want you. I want you without question. There is nothing you can say that will make me feel any differently. We were meant to be together."

"You are so sure?"

"Nothing will change how I feel about you."

Paine was not so sure of that.

Bog growled, alerting them to someone's approach.

"You are needed, Paine," Wrath called out.

Paine shut his eyes and shook his head for a moment. There was only one thing that would have Wrath interrupting him on this night. "Let him pass," Paine commanded and Bog stopped growling, though he followed Wrath into the dwelling.

Wrath did not bother to explain, he simply said, "A Drust has been caught and brought here."

Paine turned to Anin. "You will wait here for me. I will see that food is sent to you."

"There is no place for me to go nor do I want to go anywhere. I will wait here for you."

Paine turned and hurried out of the dwelling, Wrath right behind him.

"Word is spreading that the King's executioner has a wife. So why deny what is now yours?" Wrath asked

"Ask me that when I am done torturing the prisoner and blood soaks these hands."

~~~

Anin watched from the open door as the two men walked away, disappearing into the darkness and Bog ran off in the woods to hunt. Flicking torches in the distance caught her attention and she waited to see two warriors carrying them, leading the way for the King. He was going to watch his enemy be tortured.

With a shiver, Anin quickly entered the dwelling and shut the door, leaning against it. It was not long before a knock sounded and a woman's voice called out that she had food for Anin.

Anin opened the door and a young woman stood there with a basket in hand. She was taller than Anin and her lovely features captured the eye as did her dark hair that was long and looked completely untamable. She wore the plain garments of a servant, though her tunic was cinched tightly at her narrow waist with a leather belt.

"I am Atas. I have brought food and drink for you."

She breezed past Anin, though she had not bid the servant to enter.

Atas placed the basket on the table and turned to look at Anin. "I came myself, though it is not a chore of mine to do so. I serve only the King, but I wanted to meet you and tell you how grateful I am to you for saving King Talon from being badly burned. It would be a true tragedy for a man as potent as he is to be maimed in any way."

"I am glad to have been of help."

Atas stepped closer to Anin. "Now that the King has joined you and the executioner, there will be no need for you to be in his sleeping chambers again." She turned to the door.

Anin knew a warning when she heard one and she reached out and took hold of Atas' arm.

The woman's head snapped around, her chin going up as she said, "No one touches what belongs to the King," —she wrinkled her nose— "least of all the executioner's wife." She marched out the door highly annoyed.

Anin should not have touched her with intentions to see what she felt, but there was an uncomfortable presence about the woman and she had to know what it was that disturbed her so. Atas was a foolish woman. She thought herself better than others because she felt that she satisfied the King's insatiable appetite so often that he not only favored her, but cared for her as well. Anin knew the King cared for no woman. One day Atas would learn how wrong she had been.

Anin went to the table and emptied the basket, smiling at the warm bread and chunks of meat and crock of mead and a vessel of wine. Seeing the food, she realized how hungry she was and she sat down to eat her share, saving the remainder for Paine.

She enjoyed the food and favored the taste of the wine until she heard the first agonizing scream. The second followed soon after and the third unbearable scream had her dropping what food she held in her hand to cover her ears.

The tormenting screams were as bad as the mighty thunder that frightened her. They tore through her, ripping at her as if they were tearing her body apart. She jumped to her feet, sending the bench tumbling over, cringing at another scream that seemed to echo around the dwelling.

Suddenly the screaming stopped and Anin stood, her breathing heavy, her body tense.

Please. Please. Let there be no more.

Her breathing began to calm while worry for Paine took hold. She understood now why he had felt empty, devoid of anything, when she had first touched him. He could never make someone suffer so horribly if he allowed himself to feel. Her heart ached for him.

She stumbled back when an anguished cry pierced the dwelling. She slapped her hands against her ears, trying to drown it out, but it grew louder and louder until she thought it would consume her whole.

Unable to take it a moment longer, she ran out of the dwelling, following the torturing screams. She ran as fast as she could. She had to stop the suffering, her suffering, the Drust's suffering, Paine's suffering. It could not go on. She could not bear it.

She ran so fast that the two guards, a short distance from the door, did not see her until it was too late. She ran past them, throwing the door open.

"Stop!" she screamed once inside. "You must stop!" She looked around for one man and when she spotted him, she ran to him. "Please, my King, please stop this now. I can get what you look for with one touch."

A hand suddenly grabbed her arm.

"Let her be," the King ordered and turned to the two guards who had followed her in. "Leave us and let no one enter."

Paine spoke as soon as the two guards closed the door behind them. "I do not want her here."

Anin turned to her husband, fearful he would challenge the King. There was more concern than anger in his green eyes and it touched her heart. "Please, Paine. His screams tear me apart. I cannot bear them."

"It is not his decision, it is mine," King Talon said. "Anin will touch the prisoner and tell me what she learns."

"I will stay by her side," Paine said as if the King had no choice in the matter.

"With my sanction," King Talon snapped.

Anin responded before her husband could say anymore. "We are grateful, my King."

"I will have a word with you, wife, when we are alone," Paine whispered as he guided her by the arm over to where the prisoner was strapped to the table.

Anin barely heard him, her eyes rounding at the man on the table. He was naked and bloody with wounds and burns all over his body. She did not have to touch him to feel his fear. It was there for all to see.

She pulled her arm free of Paine's grasp and laid a gentle hand on the Drust warrior's chest, trying to avoid his wounds. She gasped and quickly squeezed her eyes closed tight. Fear like none she ever felt before reached out and grabbed hold of her and she had to fight to get through it. Deep shame surfaced, once through the fear, for not having enough strength not to scream when tortured. Hatred hit her hard and strong. Hatred for all he felt that had been taken from him and his tribesmen. Hatred and distrust for the King and what he continued to take from them, pride for being one of four chosen to scout the area and discover where the sentinels are located around the King's stronghold. He held hope for the time his tribesmen would arrive here and conquer the King. The last feeling, faint, but there, was his longing and deep caring for his wife and two bairns and no regret for the sacrifice he made for them and his tribe.

She thought it done when she felt something he was trying to keep locked away. She scrunched her brow as she fought to go deeper and though she was barely able to feel it, she got something, and she shivered.

She opened her eyes and met his and felt his confusion. She moved her hand off his chest to pat his shoulder, trying in some small way to comfort him, for she somehow knew he would never see his wife and bairns again. She stumbled slightly as she moved away from him, her legs feeling weak.

Paine hurried his arm around her to steady her. "Never again," he whispered when her body dropped back to rest against him. He kept her steady on her feet as they walked to stand in front of the King.

"Tell me," the King ordered.

"There is great fear for what he suffers and deep shame that he does not suffer the torture more courageously. He holds deep hatred for what has been taken from him and his tribesmen and hatred and distrust for you in failing to keep your word and provide for them until they could once again stand a proud tribe."

Anin saw the way his brow rose ever so slightly as if surprised by that. She continued. "He is proud for having been one of four chosen to scout the area around your stronghold and he is eager to see his tribesmen arrive and conquer you. He holds no regret for the sacrifice he has made for others and," — she shivered again— "though he has never met him, he is grateful to the Pict who betrays you and will lead the battle against you when the time comes."

"Not a word is to be spoken of what went on here tonight," the King ordered and turned to Anin. "You will benefit me more than I realized. "With you and Paine working together, I will get all I need from a prisoner."

Anin felt her insides churn at the thought. She shook her head at the King. "Never again could I be part of such suffering."

King Talon scowled at her. "You are already part of suffering. You are joined with the executioner."

Anin turned to Paine, realizing how her words must have hurt him.

His green eyes held no warmth, no caring as he ordered, "Return to our dwelling now!"

Chapter Twenty-seven

Anin paced around the fire pit endlessly, waiting for Paine to return. She had scrubbed her hands of blood in the rain barrel on the side of the dwelling before entering, glad to be rid of it and the reminder of what she had felt. What upset her most though was that she had foolishly spoken without thought to her words and had hurt her husband. She had not meant to and when she had seen the coldness in his eyes, she knew she had hurt him badly.

Her heart wrenched with how she must have made him feel. She was no different from others who treated the executioner poorly. His task was burdensome yet necessary. It was not his fault that she could not bear the screams.

She shook her head. She truly did wish she could rid herself of this curse. It had brought her nothing but heartache.

The door opened and Paine walked in. His stern face and naked chest glistened from a fresh washing. He walked straight for Anin and the anger that flashed in his green eyes had her running around the fire pit away from him.

He caught her as she reached the door and shoved her against it, pinning her there with his hands planted against the door to either side of her head.

"Did I not order you to remain here and did you not tell me that you would wait here?"

Anin cringed, having done just that.

"Do you realize what you have done?" Paine did not expect a response. He continued speaking. "You have shown the King the depths of your abilities and he will make use of you whenever he wishes. As far as not wanting any part of suffering, I warned you suffering and death were my constant companions. Now they are yours. And my hands?" He held one in front of her face. "They may look clean but they are forever stained with blood. So now, Anin, tell me you are pleased to be my wife."

She wanted to reach out and touch, but part of her was fearful of what she would feel.

"Are you afraid to touch me, Anin, and find out what I feel? Have you yet to realize how truly cruel I can be? Do you want to find out?" Again he did not wait for a response. He grabbed her chin and brought his lips down roughly on hers.

There was no tenderness or kindness in his kiss and his fingers bit at her chin. She instinctively grabbed at his arm to pull it away. His feelings jolted her. His anger was not at her, but at himself that she had been forced into his world of misery and pain. But what she felt most was the strength and depth of how much he cared for her, how his heart belonged to her and only her. So much so, that he had been willing to let her go rather than have her be part of the executioner's life.

She winced as she felt the wound on her lip split open again and the blood run into her mouth and onto her chin.

Paine tore his mouth away from her, cursing himself and winced when he saw what he had done. He left her side, grabbed a cloth from the table, and hurried back to her, dabbing at the blood.

She stopped him when he went to speak and pressed her cheek to his and whispered in his ear, "*Tuahna.*"

He felt a catch to his heart and though he wanted to say it to her as well, he felt himself unworthy to do so.

He eased her away from him. "Come and let me tend your lip and we will talk."

She shook her head, stepped around him, and slipped off her garments to stand naked in front of him. "Make me your wife."

He stood breathless at the sight of her pale, untouched skin, not a single body drawing on it. Her ample breasts sat high and firm, her waist slender, her hips curved full, and the dark triangle of hair hiding where he wanted desperately to plant his seed.

It did not take him long to shed the little he wore and walk naked over to her. He gently pressed the cloth to her wound once again, the bleeding almost stopped. "Since last we kissed, I have ached to kiss you and not only your lips."

Anin looked at him questioningly.

He threw the cloth aside and said, "The lips are not the only place meant to be kissed."

He kissed her high on the cheek and her eyes fluttered along with her insides, then he kissed the rest of the way down her cheek. When his lips touched her neck, he began to nibble there and nip gently with his teeth. A shiver ran through her and a soft moan escaped her lips.

His loins tighten when he felt her shudder and he proceeded to kiss and nip down along her shoulder.

Another soft moan slipped from her lips and when his lips drifted over her breast, she felt herself grow wet between her legs.

He kissed her nipple, then teased it with his tongue and enjoyed how it grew hard with each lick and nip. Then he took the hard nub in his mouth and rolled his tongue around it before he gently suckled on it.

Anin's moan grew a little louder and her whole body grew taut as he crouched down in front of her to place kisses along her stomach, his hand slipping behind her to stroke her backside as he did.

She let out a small yelp and another when he brought his hand back around to slip between her legs and spread them apart.

His fingers spread her soft triangle of hair away from the small nub that pulsed wildly and he settled a kiss on it before his tongue began to lick and tease.

A tingle rushed through her and she almost gasped from the pleasure it continued to spread through every part of her. Her body never felt so alive and she reveled in the pleasurable feeling.

She cried out in protest when he scooped her up and laid her on the sleeping pallet, but it turned to an endless moan shortly afterwards when his tongue returned to pleasure her. She had never thought mating could feel so wonderful. Though, she discovered soon, it could be even more wonderful as she felt her desire begin to build and build until she thought she would burst and she cried out to Paine.

He moved over her, his knee spreading her legs apart as he settled between them. He could wait no longer himself, his need for her pulsing his manhood until he thought he would explode, spilling his seed before he could slip inside her.

She arched against him as he brought his manhood to rest between her legs, causing him to slip slightly into her and once he did, he could not stop. He reached for her hands, locking his fingers with hers as he stretched them above her head and pushed all the way into her.

Anin let out a sharp gasp and felt herself settle around the thick size of him and began to sway her hips against him as she closed her fingers around his even tighter. She cried out, her pleasure soaring and she realized then that it was not only her desire she felt, but his as well and she thought she would burst with joy.

Paine joined her slow pace at first and then began to thrust faster and harder until she matched his eager pace.

Anin could not stop her moans from growing louder and louder, the deeper Paine sunk himself into her. Whatever was building in her was going to burst soon. She could feel it growing ever stronger.

"Paine," his name spilled from her lips on a moan and she bucked against him hard

He knew she was on the edge and he sent her tumbling over, following along with her.

Anin groaned and it grew louder as she felt as if every part of her burst with a fulfilling pleasure over and over again, and she squeezed her legs tight to hold onto every last tingle and ripple that ran through her.

Paine groaned as he poured into her and when he felt her squeeze him tight, he burst like he never did before. He threw his head back and moaned with satisfaction. He collapsed on top of her, though rolled off her quickly, knowing the size of him would be too much for her to bear and took her in his arms to settle her against him as he rolled onto his back.

It took a few moments for Anin to catch her breath but when she did she looked up at him with a smile. "I did not know mating could be so enjoyable. I thought it was done much like the animals, though I do recall my mum her sisters saying they were pleased their mates did not rut like animals."

Paine laughed. "There are those that rut and those that explore. I like to explore."

"You have explored?" she asked, feeling a bit annoyed that he had done so with other women.

"Not near as much as I intend to explore with you."

Her smile grew. "I would like that."

His look turned serious. "It will not be easy."

"Exploring?"

He shook his head. "No, being the executioner's wife."

She laughed. "It will not be easy being my husband when others learn what my touch can do. So I would say we make a good pair."

Her laughter and words brought a smile to his face. "Perhaps we do."

It was her turn to be serious. "I am sorry, Paine."

"For what? Our first mating, with many, many, many more to follow, pleased me beyond reason. You have nothing to be sorry for."

"It is not that," she said unable to keep from smiling at his response, though her smile vanished quickly. "I am sorry for not remaining here." She shook her head. "I could not stand the warrior's anguished cries. I felt as if they were tearing me apart."

He wished he could return to the Wyse village with her and have her talk with Esplin. Perhaps there was a way Esplin could help her better understand her abilities. But until this matter with the Drust was settled, they could go nowhere. And until her mum arrived to explain things, he could say nothing.

"I was desperate to stop it and desperate to be with you. I do not like being separated from you. I feel a part of me is missing when we are not together."

"I feel the same," he admitted and hugged her close, "but do not worry. I do not intend to let you far from my sight." That she gave no response disturbed him. "What troubles you, Anin?"

She rested her hand on his chest, pleased to feel such contentment in him and a bit of worry over her. "I cannot help but wonder if perhaps I was cursed and if so who cursed me. I asked my mum when once she called it a curse and she warned me never to ask again. That some things were better left unknown. My curiosity will not allow me to let it be. I want to find out and make sense of it and know for sure that I will not pass it on to any sons or daughters I may have."

I would not worry about that now, perhaps in time, it will make itself known."

"At least my mum will be pleased that I did not wed the King," —she grinned at him— "though I do not know how pleased she will be that I wed the executioner."

"It only matters if we are pleased with our union."

Anin tried to stifle a yawn, but it escaped.

"Sleep, you are tired."

"And safe, I feel truly safe in your arms." Anin yawned again and shivered.

Paine reached for a blanket behind his head and spread it over them both. He slipped his arm beneath and stroked her arm, watching as her eyes drifted closed. He watched her sleep, his wife, here in his arms. He still could not believe that the King had joined them, that they were one and would remain so. He never thought Anin would be his and now he could not see a time without her.

He was concerned what would happen when her mum and da arrived. What would Anin do when she learned the truth? Or could he possibly be wrong? Was there a chance Anin was not from the Wyse tribe? Could it be nothing more than a curse as her mum had called it?

He did not believe so, though whatever the explanation, Wyse Tribe or curse, made no difference. Anin belonged to him now and he would let nothing or no one take her away from him.

He settled comfortably against her and fell asleep, more content than he had been in a long time.

~~~

Anin smiled softly when she woke to her husband curled around her. Not sure how long she had slept, she listened and hearing only silence and knew morn had yet to arrive. Also, the flames in the fire pit were still fairly high, not that she needed their heat with her husband's body keeping her nice and warm. Of course the blanket helped as well.

She reached for the blanket where it lay on his arm to pull up over his shoulder and stopped, the body drawings there catching her eye. She could not resist tracing her finger along the intricate drawings, each one flowing into the next as if ever continuous. She wondered what they represented.

All body drawings were specific to each tribe and were distinct in their meanings. Her finger stilled. She did not know her husband's tribe. Thinking on it, she did not know much about her husband. She continued tracing her finger, following a drawing across his shoulder and up along his neck.

She turned her eyes on his face and was pleased to see he was awake. With questions nagging her and once again tracing along his neck, she asked "Tell me about them."

No one knew of his body drawings, they were meant for him and him alone, though perhaps not anymore.

"They tell a story."

"I would be pleased to hear the story." She was more than pleased, she was eager to hear all he had to tell her.

It had been some time since he had spoken about it, leaving the painful memories buried deep, perhaps it was time to speak of it now. Before he could give it too much thought, he said, "I come from the Nomad Tribe."

Anin gasped. "I am so sorry, Paine." She knew the tale well, though had not heard it from anyone who had lived through it, but then only a small few had survived.

"We were a small tribe and we wandered, never settling long in one place. It was our way and we enjoyed it. We were skilled in many crafts; metals works, wood carvings, adornments, and weapons. We kept to ourselves, disturbed no one, and warred against none, though we were well versed in weapons. The tribes traded with us and gave us no trouble."

His words painted a clearer picture of him. His wandering was why he knew the land so well and his tribes knowledge of blades and weapons was why he was so adept with his battle-axe.

"My da was a skilled weapon maker, my mum our story keeper, telling tales of our ancestors each night around the fire. My sister was several years younger than me and was learning our stories so that one day she would take my mum's place and be our story keeper."

Anin felt a piercing pain to her chest and realized her hand lay on his arm. She left it there as he continued, wanting to feel along with him.

"I had gone out hunting for the tribe. I was skilled with most weapons from the time I was young and I was the best hunter in the tribe, so I often went alone. I was usually gone two sunrises and would return with enough meat to feed our tribe for several sunrises. That was why I was not there when my tribe was attacked." He grew silent.

His anger, pain, and sorrow overwhelmed her as he relived the horrible memory. She kept her hand resting on his arm, hoping that her touch would remind him that he was no longer alone. He had her now.

"Two other tribesmen survived, though one not for long. The other was an elder woman, Della, who had been off gathering berries and plants. When she heard

262

the screams, she hurried back to our camp, but when she saw our tribe being slaughtered, she hid. She knew she had to survive so there would be someone to tell me what had happened to our tribe." He paused again.

Anin remained silent and waited. It would be his choice to continue or not.

He shut his eyes as he spoke. "It was a foreign tribe from the north, a vicious lot that brutalized and butchered and left everything smoldering in their wake even some of the bodies." He opened his eyes, though did not look at Anin. "The young lad, who had survived along with Della and I, died shortly after we left the camp. Della and I made our way further south and when we came upon an abandoned dwelling, she insisted we stay there. She told me she did not have much time left and before she died she wanted to make sure that the stories of our tribe survived and so they do—on me."

Her heart suffered for his tremendous loss and she was amazed at the strength and courage he had taken to continue on after all he had lost. She ran her hand along his arm. "All of this tells the stories of your tribe?"

"All that my mum told and her mum before her and her mum before her. I carry the stories of my tribe with pride and one day I will tell them to my children so that my tribe will always live on."

"I would very much like to hear them and learn them myself, so that I can be sure to share them over and over again with our children."

Paine ran a gentle finger down her soft cheek. "You deserve—"

She gave him a quick kiss. "I got what I deserved...*you*!"

"The execu—"

She kissed him again. "The man who I gave my heart—"

His quick kiss silenced her. "Foolishly gave your heart to and the man who is most grateful that you did." He rolled over slowly, easing her onto her back, his leg slipping between her two.

She held onto his arm, smiling as she felt his need for her take hold deep inside him and felt him grow hard against her. It made her growing need for him soar. She went to speak and he kissed her silent once more.

He moved his mouth off her lips to kiss along her cheek to her ear, and whisper, "Time to explore." Paine captured her response with his lips and no more words were spoken as they explored together.

Chapter Twenty-eight

Paine walked to the feasting house, worried for Anin. Knowing Bethia would greet Anin warmly, he had taken her to meet the healer. And as he expected, Bethia greeted her generously. He could not say the same for those people they passed on the way to Bethia's dwelling. Every greeting Anin called out was met with a turned head or downcast eyes. He had grown accustomed to being treated such, but Anin was not, though he was proud that she continued to greet everyone with a smile regardless of how they turned away from her.

Give them time, she had told him and while he did not agree with her hopefulness, he would not deny her it. Of course, it probably did not help that Bog remained at her side, but he would have it no other way. If he could not be with her to make certain she remained safe, then Bog would. Besides, the wolf had taken a liking to her, especially after this morn when he came across her sitting on the ground, Bog practically in her lap as she looked closely at his paw.

"There, I have found it," she had said proudly and held up a tiny stone for Bog to see. "You will do well now."

He smiled at the memory. It was not only him and Bog anymore. Now they had Anin and their family would grow. They would have a daughter first if Anin proved to be from the Wyse Tribe. His smile grew at the thought of a small lass just like Anin and he would protect his daughter as fiercely as he protected her mum.

"That is quite a smile you wear. I take it your wife pleases you?" Wrath said with a chortle as he fell into step beside Paine.

"Very much," Paine said his smile softening.

"At least you two have time to enjoy each other, since there is no telling what will happen when her mum and da arrive."

"Their arrival matters not to me. The King has joined us and nothing can separate Anin from me." He had lost far too much once. He would not allow that to happen again.

Paine entered the feasting house, his smile gone.

A few steps in, he and Wrath turned to the left and entered through the open door of the Council Chambers. Wrath acknowledged two of the King's personal guards who stood to either side of the door. The room held a long table with benches on either side and a single bench at one end. A fire pit sat in the middle of the room and narrow tables sat against the other walls. On the tables were different projects, on a smaller scale and in various stages of construction, created by the King.

Paine admired the King's many skills, especially the ability to create things others thought impossible or nonsense. He had helped the King work on many of the small scale dwellings since the day he had pointed out why one of the structures would not hold as the King had planned. He was most proud of the feasting house with not only a second floor, but the two rooms that extended off to the sides. It had taken much work and many changes to secure the strength of the dwelling, but they had done it and it was an example of the King's brilliance.

Paine was not part of the High Council, though he was summoned to a meeting when necessary, so he took a stance behind Wrath as the warrior took a seat at the table.

The High Council was comprised of seven. Gelhard was High Counselor, the most important person on the counsel next to the King. Wrath was the commander of the King's Personal Guard and often confidant of the King, to the annoyance of the others. Midrent was the Tariff Collector and charged with collecting a portion of what each tribe owed the King. Ebit was the Crop Master charged with the field workers. Bodu was the Master Constructer charged with building. Tarn was the Warrior Commander charged with all of the King's troops and the King was the seventh to make up the High Counsel. His decisions were law.

All stood when King Talon entered the room and did not sit until he took his place at the head of the table.

"I will hear from Ebit first," the King ordered.

Ebit stood. He was not a man you would expect to be in charge of anything. He was short and thin and his hands trembled at times, but Paine had learned early on that the King knew people well and placed them where they would benefit the tribe the most.

Ebit was far wiser than others when it came to planting an abundant and successful crop and dealing with those who worked the fields. His report was brief as usual, finishing with, "The last of the crop is being harvested and with the tariffs collected we are well prepared for the earth to sleep and regain strength."

"You do well, Ebit," the King praised and looked to Bodu.

Bodu stood as Ebit sat. Bodu was a man of strength and it showed in his large size. He was a stern taskmaster but could often be found drinking mead and telling tales at night with the men who served him.

His report was brief as well. "The cold will be upon us soon enough and since we finished the new storehouse in less time than planned, I have the men helping the people make repairs to their dwellings before the cold sets in."

"Well done," The King said.

"Midrent," the King said and the man stood. "Have the Drust improved their conditions or do we still continue to supply them with needed food?"

Midrent shook his head. "They continue to do poorly, my King, though I do not understand why. We have replaced their old animals that could birth no more with young ones that should be doing well. Their land is another matter. It still does not flourish as it once did, so we continue to supply what they need. I put together a large stock that should see them through the land's rest and sent it to them. I wanted to be sure they got it before the cold settles in."

"Who reports on the Drust to you?" the King asked.

"Whoever Tarn assigns the task to," Midrent answered with a glance to Tarn.

"Anything else to report?" King Talon asked, keeping his eyes on Midrent.

The man detailed a few problems here and there, and the King advised as to how they were to be handled and then dismissed Midrent, Ebit, and Bodu.

"Sit, Paine," the King ordered after the three men left the room.

Paine took the bench next to Wrath.

King Talon looked from his High Counselor to his Warrior Commander. "You both were informed that a Drust was found, tortured, and died here last night. More are in the vicinity and more will come and war will once again bloody our land. I want this stopped before it can start. There is a traitor among us and I want him found so that Paine may take his head."

~~~

Anin liked Bethia. She wore a smile, on a face that was worn more from the trails of life than years. Her gray hair barely reached her shoulders and she kept it tucked behind her ears. She was taller, by a good head, than Anin and much too thin. Anin did not have to touch her to know she had suffered much in her life.

"I am so pleased, Paine has wed. He is a good man," Bethia said as she crushed dried plant leaves on a smooth rock with a smaller, smooth rock.

Anin sat with Bethia on the ground outside the woman's dwelling. "I keep telling him that he is a good man, but he refuses to believe me. I am glad someone else feels the same. Though, I wish others felt the same. No one will even acknowledge him with a simple nod."

"It comes with his chore, pay it no heed."

That was difficult for Anin to do. While it might not bother Paine, she worried what harm it would bring when they had children. Would they be ignored because their father was the executioner?

Bethia distracted her from her disturbing thoughts by asking her about her family. The two women were soon laughing at Anin's tales about growing up with four brothers and being the daughter of a Lammok warrior.

"Forgive me for intruding," a young woman, cradling a baby, said from a few steps away.

"Simi," Bethia greeted with a smile, though when she saw the worried look on the young woman's face, she quickly got to her feet. "What is wrong?"

"Wren is still not well," she said her dark eyes flaring with fear.

"Let me have a look," Bethia said softly and Simi gently handed the fussing bairn out to her.

"He does not sleep well or eat well and cries often."

From the tired look of the mum and how thin she was, it appeared to Anin that the young woman was suffering from the same as the bairn.

Bethia looked the babe over, touching him here and there. "He seems a fit lad."

"He fusses all the time and takes from my breast hungrily at times and other times barely suckles, and he wakes often crying."

"Let us talk," Bethia said and turned to Anin, handing her the bairn before walking a distance away with Simi.

Anin was only too happy to care for the bairn and she cradled him in the crook of her arm and spoke soothingly to him. He continued to fuss and let out a cry now and then. Anin quickly laid her hand to his chest to see if she could discover what was causing his discomfort.

With the bairn only having been born a few moon cycles ago, Anin did not have to wade through various feelings to discover what bothered the child. She cringed when she felt his hunger. From what she felt, there would be no soothing him until he ate and as soon as Bethia and Simi joined her, she quickly said, "He is hungry."

Simi stared at her. "He just fed. That cannot be and how do you know that?"

Anin had been so concerned for the child that she had not given thought to how her words would be received, though she was quick to cover her stumble. "He suckled my finger eagerly." She placed her finger at his tiny mouth and he sucked on it frantically.

"I believe it would be wise if another mum helped you to feed Wren," Bethia said and reached out to give the bairn's tiny hand a light squeeze. "You may not be producing enough milk for this hungry, little fellow."

"You think that is all it is?" Simi said her face brightening.

"I believe so," Bethia assured her. "It happens sometimes and there are always mums willing to share their abundance of milk. Haddie recently mentioned that her breasts are left heavy, her little lass not as hungry as her other children when born. I am sure she will be only too glad to help you."

Simi reached for her son, eager to have him in her arms. "I will go see her now. She went to turn away, then stopped and smiled at Anin. "I am grateful for your help. If you should need something, I will be only too glad to oblige."

Bethia spoke up. "Anin could use a friend. She wed Paine yesterday."

Simi took a step back. "Bless you for being so brave, having the executioner forced on you."

Anin smiled. "Paine was not forced on me. I gladly wed him. I care deeply for him and I am proud to be his mate. He is a good man."

Simi stared at her, looking bewildered.

"You should hurry," Anin said, "Wren is hungry."

Simi nodded and appeared glad to hurry off.

"Are you sure you do not have the gift of healing?" Bethia asked, returning to sit on the ground to continue her task. "You seemed to understand the bairn's problem by simply holding him."

"I am no healer," Anin said, "and it is time I take my leave and explore the place that is now my home."

"Do visit me often," Bethia said and Anin assured her she would.

Bog left the spot by Bethia's dwelling where he had sat waiting for Anin and joined her, though instead of exploring the village, she returned home. Bog stretched out in front of her when she sat on the bench not far from the door, her thoughts troubling.

She felt like a prisoner, though no shackles bound her, her abilities or curse, whatever it might be, had made her one. First, her mum had forbidden her to speak of it and now the King had forbidden her to speak of it.

Be who you are.

It was easy for the Giantess to say that, she was feared, whereas Anin feared anyone learning of her secret. But was her secret her mum had once called a curse, no curse at all? What if it was part of her as she had come to believe? Could that be what the Giantess meant? But if her ability was made known how would others treat her? Would they avoid her like they do Paine? Would they believe her evil?

Why? Why must she be different?

~~~

Paine sat silent as the others spoke, watching each one, listening to what they had to say.

"Anyone could have taken one of my warrior's hooded-cloaks and then returned it," Tarn said as they discussed what was known about the traitor.

"You mean *my* warriors," King Talon said, turning a scowl on Tarn.

"Forgive me, my King," Tarn said hastily and looked to Paine. "You can tell us nothing more?"

"That was all I saw."

"It could be anyone," Gelhard said and turned to Tarn. "Have any trackers been sent out recently?"

"The trackers are good men and loyal to the King," Tarn said annoyed. "What of your personal guard, Gelhard."

"You dare accuse one of my men or is it me who you truly accuse?" Gelhard challenged.

"Enough!" the King said, bringing his fist down on the table and looked to Tarn. "You will take men out and search for the other Drust that are here. Make certain you capture them all, but bring one back alive so that Paine can question him."

"As you wish, my King," Tarn said with a respectful nod.

"Go see to it now," the King ordered and just before he reached the door the King called out to him. "Do not fail me, Tarn."

Tarn turned and nodded. "I will see it done, my King."

King Talon turned to Gelhard once the door closed. "You know everything that goes on here. Have you heard anything about the supplies we have been sending to the Drust not reaching them?"

Gelhard appeared stunned. "I have heard no such thing. If that is true, then it is being kept very much a secret."

"A secret is being kept from you?" the King said in a tone that questioned strongly, though he gave Gelhard no chance to respond. "To achieve such a feat more than one person has to be involved in this? It would take several men to see the supplies we send disappear. And it is difficult to keep secrets when more than one person is involved. Others know about this. Find out who they are and bring that information to me."

The King's word set Paine to thinking. The King was right about secrets. The more people who knew about a secret, the less likely there was a chance of it being kept a secret for too long. If he was right about Anin being part of the Wyse Tribe and it had been kept a secret since she was born, then her mum had to be the only one who knew about it. But how had it all come about?

"As you wish, my King," Gelhard said, "but I would consider that this has something to do with the rumblings that you have wed twice and still have not produced a son, no child at all. There are those who fear Pict rule will end, possibly cease to exist if you do not do your duty and produce a son."

"It has nothing to do with me having a son. It is those who never wanted the tribes to unify that continue efforts to unseat me. They will see our land and people thrown into chaos again, then the tribes in the south will march forth and claim victory over us and that foolishness is what will bring Pict rule to an end." His fist came down on the table again. "I will not allow that to happen."

Paine knew the King as a man of his word. He would do what needed to be done to see that the Picts continued to rule.

"Have the dal Gabran approached you about trading with the Lammok Tribe directly?" the King asked Gelhard.

"The dal Gabran knows direct trade with the tribes is forbidden. All trade takes place at the three gatherings throughout the twelve moon cycles. I have received no such request, nor would I grant it."

The King nodded at Paine.

"I came across a small group of dal Gabran who claim they were given permission to search our land for a warrior of theirs who had consent from the King to trade directly with the Lammok, as they once did, and had not returned. I also came upon that same troop slaughtered by the Drust, though one dal Gabran warrior survived and looked to be in a hurry to return home."

Gelhard looked bewildered. "What is the dal Gabran doing here and what do they want with the Lammok if that was truly their intended destination?"

"More questions that need immediate answers," the King said.

Gelhard's brow knitted. "You did not share this with Tarn."

"It will be known only among us here until I say otherwise," The King ordered and the three men nodded.

Wrath spoke, "If the one dal Gabran warrior met no more Drust and survived his return journey to his tribe, he will inform the chieftain to what happened here. The dal Gabran will be looking for revenge once they discover their warriors have been slaughtered."

Gelhard shook his head. "The dal Gabran had no permission to be on Pict land. They will need to explain what they were doing here, though they are known to war so we should be prepared."

"I will not see another war erupt. More is lost than ever gained in war," the King said. "I want the Drust problem put to rest before the dal Gabran can become a problem. No good can come with enemies at both ends of us." He turned to Gelhard. "Let me know if you hear any word from the dal Gabran."

"I will, my King," Gelhard said, then cleared his throat before continuing. "There is another matter that must be discussed."

"I know what you will say, Gelhard, but you did a poor job of finding a fitting woman to be Queen the last three times. How do I trust you again to find me a suitable woman who will bear me sons?"

"I give you my word, my King, that I will not fail you again. I will find a woman who will make the perfect Queen."

"And one that will bear me many sons, for I intend to make certain Pict blood runs in all throughout the land long after me and my sons are dead. Picts will then always live on."

Gelhard nodded and left, leaving Paine and Wrath with the King.

"Do you think Anin would know anything of the Lammok meeting with the dal Gabran?" the King asked Paine.

"I do not believe so. She was as surprised as I was to see the dal Gabran and she does not know their language."

"Speak with her and see what she knows of trade between the Lammok and the dal Gabran," the King instructed and turned to Wrath. "Find out if there is any unrest among my warriors, but let no one know what you do."

Paine and Wrath went to leave and do the King's bidding when Paine turned upon hearing the King shout out his name.

"I expect to hear that Anin is with child soon—a son—who will be as loyal a friend to my future sons as you are to me."

Wrath laughed and slapped Paine on the back. "He will probably have all daughters."

"Be gone with you then and work on a son, since none of my sons will join with a woman whose mum had only daughters," the King said and dismissed them with a wave of his hand and a rare laugh.

Paine parted from Wrath and went to find Anin, thinking on what Wrath had said. He probably would have more daughters with Anin than sons, but that did not bother him. They would be strong like their mum and he would see they were skilled in weapons. Thinking on having bairns made him realize how much he missed Anin, though they had not been parted for long. Even so, he felt a strong need to have her in his arms. He hurried his steps and was disappointed when he found Anin was no longer visiting with Bethia.

"I think Anin would make a good healer," Bethia said. "She discovered what was ailing a small bairn after a few moments of cradling him in her arms. After that, she was going to explore the village, though I think she may have returned to your dwelling. The people have not been very accepting of her. Or perhaps it was that wolf of yours that deterred them from approaching her, since he never leaves her side."

This was what had worried Paine once joined with Anin. That she would be shunned and treated pitifully, though the worse part was that he could do nothing about it. He could not force the people to be kind to her.

He approached his dwelling and saw no signs of Anin or Bog. He entered the dwelling, expecting to find them there only to find it empty. He stepped outside and cast a glance around. The isolation from the other dwellings never bothered him. He much preferred it that way, though he could see how Anin might find it lonely with her having such a curious nature.

He wondered where she had gone off to and was glad that Bog was with her. That was until Bog trotted around the corner of the dwelling and Anin did not follow behind him.

Chapter Twenty-nine

"You left Anin's side?" Paine said with a snap of anger.

Bog stared at him a moment then turned and walked around the corner of the dwelling. Paine followed and was relieved to see Anin, her back to him, squatting down as she tended to Bog's shelter. It did not surprise him when she spoke to the wolf, since she had often done so on their journey here.

Paine watched as Bog went and sat and leaned his furry body against Anin. He was letting Paine know that Anin was part of their pack. He was stunned when Anin wrapped her arm around the wolf and pressed the side of her face to his and Bog did not protest.

"I have cleaned out what the wind had dragged in, though with the chill getting stronger in the air, it would be best for you to sleep inside the dwelling soon."

Paine scowled. That she had little recourse than to speak with the wolf since no one else would talk with her, made him hurt more for her than angered him.

"Let us go inside and tend the fire pit so it is warm when Paine comes home," she said to the wolf and stood and turned. As soon as she saw Paine standing there, a smile burst across her face and she hurried to him.

Paine held his arms wide and, once in them, closed them around her tightly. Her lips reached for his, eager for a kiss. It was a soft, gentle kiss, though he felt a hunger for more in it.

"I have missed you," she said as soon as her lips left his.

"And I you." He had missed her much more than he wanted to admit. "I need to speak with you about—"

She pressed her finger against his lips. "Later." She stretched up on her toes to press her cheek to his and whispered, "*Tuahna.*"

Her warm breath tickled his ear and the cherished word that expressed how deeply she cared for him sent a rush of desire racing through him that aroused him quickly. He lifted her off her feet with one arm around her waist and hurried her inside the dwelling, glad Bog did not follow. He cozied up in his freshly cleaned shelter.

He yanked her up against him to capture her lips in a hasty, hungry kiss, then just as hastily said, "My need is too great to go slow with you."

"I am glad, for I feel I will burst before you can slip inside me."

Paine tossed her gently on the sleeping pallet and pushed up her tunic, Anin eagerly helped, lifting her bottom. He yanked his tunic up, took hold of her legs to place over his shoulders, then grabbed her bottom and pulled her forward to enter her swiftly.

Anin's quick gasp turned just as quickly to pleasurable moans and grew as Paine pounded against her. She looked at her husband, his head tilted back slightly, his brow knitted, and his jaw set tight and knew each thrust was building his own passion as strongly as her own. And she wanted desperately to feel his passion join with hers.

"Paine!" she cried out, stretching her arms out to him, begging him to come to her so that she could wrap her arms around him.

He felt the frantic need of her body, saw the fiery passion in her eyes, her pleading hands reach out to him and he slipped her legs off his shoulders and dropped down over her. He positioned his hands on either side of her head, holding himself just above her as he thrust into her again and again.

She could not get her arms around him, so she grabbed onto his taut arms and cried out when his passion hit her, ran through her and connected with her own. Her body responded, demanding from him as much as he was demanding from her. After a moment, they were no longer separate, they were one in every way.

She did not need to hear his rough groan to know he was close to bursting. She felt him soar along with her, felt them step to the edge, and together plunge quickly, bursting into divine pleasure that shot through their bodies over and over until they were both left spent.

Paine shuddered as the last of his release faded, then he rolled off Anin, taking her with him as he went to rest against him.

Anin never felt so content and she sent a silent blessing to the spirits for gracing her with such a good and wonderful husband. She rested her hand on his chest and was pleased to feel that he felt the same, and a soft sigh escaped her lips.

Paine took her hand on his chest and locked his fingers with hers. "Tell me something, Anin, do you feel what I am feeling when we join together?"

She looked up at him and smiled. "I feel it all and it is the most wonderful thing I have ever experienced." Her smile vanished. "Are you angry that I feel everything you feel when I touch you?"

"I am not angry at you and I do not mind that you touch me in that way when we join. I envy you. I wish I could feel what you were feeling as we joined."

"Endless pleasure and a release that is...magical," she was quick to tell him.

"I am glad I please you so thoroughly, but I am concerned about you always touching me and feeling what I feel."

"I wish there was a way I could control it, but I cannot stop it. I have never been able to stop it from happening. It is why I touched few people through the years. My mum thought I pushed it away, never to bother me again. I let her believe that so I would not have to hear about my curse, how bad it was, and how I should not surrender to it." She ran a finger slowly across his lips. "At least with you, there is no hiding, no condemnation no—secret. I want no secrets between us. Not now. Not ever."

He had to tell her. He could not keep what he had learned about the Wyse Tribe from her any longer, though he would not tell her what he suspected. Hopefully, she would come to the conclusion on her own.

"If there are times you prefer me not to touch you..." Anin could not bring herself to finish, the thought of not being able to touch him freely caused her heart to ache.

"No, Anin. You are free to touch me whenever it pleases you and it would please me if you touched me often. I asked because I worry about you feeling my anger, my concern, and my heart when it hurts for you."

"I do not only want to share your good feelings, but your sad and hurtful feelings as well, so that I can be there for you and help you through them. I spent too many years alone with my feelings, fearful of telling my mum or da and be scolded me for my nonsense."

He slipped one finger under her chin and lifted it. "Never will you be alone in your thoughts or feelings again. I do not care if you chatter endlessly about them. I will listen."

She laughed softly. "You might regret you said that."

"I will not regret it. I speak the truth to you." His own words reminded him what he wanted to tell her, needed to tell her...was time to tell her.

"What is it that you wanted to speak to me about?"

One kiss and a whisper and he had forgotten all about what the King wanted to know from Anin. He turned on his side so they lay face to face, draping his arm over the curve of her waist. "What do you know of the Lammok Tribe's dealings with the dal Gabran Tribe?"

The question surprised her, though she answered it easily enough. "The only thing I know about them is that my mum's tribe traded with them regularly before the tribes unified."

"You were never present when the tribes traded?"

"At the last gathering, I watched as my mum's two sisters traded with them. Why do you ask?"

"It would seem the dal Gabran we met were not truthful with us. They were never given permission to search for one of their warriors they claimed had not returned after being granted permission to trade with the Lammok."

"The Lammok are loyal to King Talon and would never go against his edicts. The Lammok respect strength and courage and hold the King in high regard for having an abundance of both," Anin said concerned that the King would think her tribe disloyal.

"Worry not. Your tribe has served the King well. It is more the dal Gabran he has concerns with." He felt a shiver run through her and not sure if it was from relief or a chill that was settling over the room, since the fire had dwindled, Paine pulled the blanket over them.

"I know nothing of them and as you know I do not speak their language, so I could not participate in the trading."

Paine suddenly flew over his wife as the door burst open, ready to protect her.

Wrath hurried in. "Tarn caught three Drust and one has broken free of his ties and hides somewhere in the stronghold."

A horn sounded at that moment, warning of danger. Anin shivered, having heard the sound in her own village and knowing that some of the women and bairns would be running for shelter while other women joined the men in grabbing their weapons, ready to fight. Her mum would be ready to fight alongside Anin's da and so would her brothers. She would be left to seek shelter alone in their dwelling.

Paine looked to his wife. "Do not leave this shelter. I will leave Bog outside the door."

Anin nodded, wishing she was as brave as her mum and as able with a weapon as her mum, then she could join Paine when danger presented itself. Instead, she was soon pacing around the fire pit, waiting for her husband to return safe and unharmed.

~~~

"You let a Drust escape within the stronghold?" the King said his strides rapid as he approached Tarn with his sword gripped in his hand and his personal guard keeping stride with him as he entered the feasting hall. His hand went up when Tarn went to speak. "I will hear no excuses. I will speak to you when this matter is settled, though if one person is harmed because of your failure, you will suffer for it. Tell me the other two Drust you captured have been secured."

"They are well secured and heavily guarded as they await the executioner," Tarn confirmed.

"They better be," King Talon snapped and looked around at the other High Council members who had hurried to the hall at the sound of the horn. "You know what to do. Sweep through each of your sections with your men and find the Drust before he can do any damage."

The men hurried off. Wrath remained by the King as did the King's guard.

The King turned to Paine. "Your wife can help us get what we need faster than the tools of your trade can. Is she at your dwelling or gone with the other women to take shelter?"

"She is at the dwelling with Bog guarding her," Paine said.

"We can stop for her along the way," the King said and they all followed him.

~~~

With the dwelling sitting off on its own, farther away from others, Anin heard nothing but silence. It only served to worry her more. She stopped suddenly when she heard Bog growl.

The wolf was warning someone away.

She listened as his growl grew, then jumped when she heard him cry out in pain. He growled again and once again cried out. He was being harmed in an effort to draw him away from the dwelling. The wolf would not leave her unprotected. He would not charge the person trying to harm him.

A thud to the dwelling made her realize that someone was throwing rocks at Bog and the rocks would not stop until the wolf was so badly injured, he could protect no longer. Anin would not let that happen. Her dagger and lack of skill in using it would do her little good, but if she could charge the attacker, Bog would follow her.

Instinct had her alerting her husband with a frantic thought. *Paine, help! Help!*

She hurried to the door, threw it open, and ran out screaming as loud as she could.

~~~

Paine stopped abruptly as Anin's plea for help echoed in his head. "Anin is in trouble." And as he went to run, her scream split through the air like a mighty roar of thunder. He took off, the others following.

~~~

Bog did as she thought he would—he ran straight for the Drust warrior along with her. The warrior did not hesitate, he ran at them. Bog lunged at him, his teeth sinking into the Drust's arm, but not before his other arm grabbed Anin around the neck.

The three went down on the ground hard. Anin grabbed at the Drust's arm that squeezed at her neck tighter and tighter, but try as she might, she could not budge it. Bog let go of the arm he had and circled around to sink his teeth into the Drust's shoulder. The warrior screamed, but still would not let go of Anin.

She not only gasped for breath, but at his feelings and thoughts that rushed through her. He wanted her dead and did not care if he died with her. His task was to kill her. She could not survive. No woman of the Wyse Tribe could be allowed to wed the King or serve the King. It would ruin everything if she did.

Woman of the Wyse Tribe was her last thought before she fell into darkness.

Chapter Thirty

Anger and fear raced through Paine when he saw the Drust squeezing the life out of Anin. He ran to her, yanked the Drust's arm off his wife, and pulled her limp body into his arms. The Drust was near to death, blood pouring from his arm and shoulder wounds.

"Enough," Paine ordered Bog and the wolf released the warrior.

Paine left the dying Drust to the King and Wrath, carrying Anin inside the dwelling to gently place on the sleeping pallet. He patted her face repeatedly. "Open your eyes, Anin, Open them! You are safe. Open your eyes *now!*" He got no response. "Listen to me, wife, I will not let you go. You are mine now and you will not leave me." Again he got no response. The darkness that had taken hold of her would not let her go, but then either would Paine. He leaned down and with gentle strength whispered in her ear, "*Tuahna. Tuahna. Tuahna, Anin.*"

He felt her body stir against him and looked to see her eyes flutter and he continued whispering, drawing her out of the darkness and back to him.

Her eyes finally opened and a slight smile touched her lips.

"*Tuahna,*" he said before kissing her lips lightly, wanting her to see and hear him say it and not have her think it a dream.

Anin rested her hand against his cheek. "We are one."

He placed his hand on top of hers. "Always."

The door flew open and the King walked in followed by Wrath and a growling Bog, who immediately went to Paine's side.

Paine stood, but laid a hand to Anin's chest before he did, letting her know she was to remain where she was.

Anin was glad she did not have to stand, her strength still limp, though she turned on her side, reached out, and rubbed the wolf's head and whispered, "You saved me, Bog, and I am grateful to call you friend."

"What did you learn from the Drust?" the King demanded of Anin.

Anin stared at him a moment before recalling what had happened to her and when she did, she felt the shock of it all over again and a shudder ran through her.

"You learned something. Tell me!" King Talon ordered.

Paine reached down and helped his wife to sit up. While he would have preferred to tell the King she had suffered enough and needed time to rest, he knew how important it was to learn what they could as soon as possible.

Anin held onto her husband's arm as she spoke. "The Drust warrior was intent on seeing me dead."

"Do you know why?" the King asked.

"He feared that all would be ruined if I was allowed to wed or serve you."

"He knew of your abilities? How could that be?" Wrath asked.

"That I do not know," Anin said.

"You will serve me right now," the King demanded. "You will touch the other two Drust and see if they can tell us more." The King raised his hand as Paine went to speak. "Anin has suffered an ordeal, but more will suffer and far worse if we do not find out what the Drust have planned."

As Anin went to slip off the bed, Paine's arm went to her waist and with little effort helped her to her feet. "I would be only too glad to serve you, my King."

"You are a wise woman, Anin." The King turned and walked out the door, a sign that all should follow.

His words froze Anin, the King's words recalling to mind what the Drust had said. *No woman of the Wyse Tribe will be allowed to serve the King.* The Drust had believed she was from the Wyse Tribe. Why? Whatever would make him think that?

"I will be by your side as will Bog," Paine said, having felt her resistance to move when his hand had gently urged her forward. "Besides, you are stronger and more courageous than you allow yourself to believe." He felt the stiffness leave her body and he quickly hurried her out the door before the King lost his patience, something he had a difficult time keeping.

As they kept pace with the King, Anin thought more on her encounter with the Drust warrior. Something had been different about it and it did not take long for her to realize what it was. It had not been only his feelings she had felt, but his thoughts as well. It was as if the two were one. But how had that come to be?

She had no more time to think on it. They stopped and Anin saw two Drust warriors tied to stakes much like Dunnard had been tied. Though, unlike Dunnard who had showed fear, false as it was, the Drust showed none.

Anin stepped forward, Paine right beside her and Bog at her other side, before the King ordered her to do so. She was eager to touch both warriors and see what she could learn from them, and to see if their thoughts opened to her as the other warrior's had done.

It did not take long to determine that both warriors felt as the first warrior had...anger at the King for failing to keep his word, honor to be chosen to scout the area around the stronghold, hope that the battle to come would be victorious for the Drust.

Anin stepped away and Paine took her hand and walked with her to the King.

"You appear confused," the King said when she stopped in front of him.

"It is odd, my King. It would seem that these two and the first Drust caught are on the same mission to scout and report, but not so the other one. His mission was clear. He was to see me dead, no matter what it took."

"It would seem they were on two different missions," the King said.

"I believe they were," Anin agreed and turned to look at the two Drust, then turned once again to the King. "They are good men. They do not deserve to die. Perhaps if you speak with them, you and they will learn the truth of this situation."

"That is for me to decide," the King said.

"Then please decide wisely, my King."

Paine saw annoyance, but also admiration for Anin speaking as she felt, though respectfully. Perhaps his wife was finally finding the courage she always possessed, but doubt and fear had held prisoner.

"Wrath, bring the two to the Council Chamber," the King ordered and walked off, his personal guard following close behind him. He stopped abruptly and looked to Paine. "There is something your wife does not share with me. Find out what it is or I will?"

Anin stared after the King, her insides feeling as if someone was squeezing them. She was not sure what the King was referring to. It could be only one of two things. That the Drust had mistaken her for a woman of the

Wyse Tribe or that she now could sense thoughts as well as what someone felt.

Anin watched as Atas approached the King with a sway in her generous hips and a smile that invited more than simple kisses only to be rebuffed by him with a dismissive wave of his hand. She lowered her head and took hasty steps away from him, but beneath her submissive response, Anin could see that Atas was angry.

"Atas holds herself in more esteem than the King does," Anin said.

"How do you know of her?" Paine asked, tugging at her hand for her to walk along with him.

"She brought food under the guise of a message she wished to deliver. Her message was clear. The King belonged to her and no other woman. I was to keep my distance from him."

"That is odd. Atas knows full well that the King would not join with a woman who belongs to another man and that she is not the only woman the he joins with daily."

Anin turned wide eyes on her husband. "How many women does he join with daily?"

"That is no concern of ours."

A gentle wind snatched up her soft laughter and sent it twirling in the air. "I do not ask out of concern, I ask out of curiosity."

"It is not something you need to know and it will do you no good to try and distract me from finding out if you hide something from the King."

Anin turned silent.

Paine let his wife linger in her silence, though he knew it was more in her thoughts that she lingered. When they reached their dwelling, he did not take her inside, he sat with her on the bench near the door.

"There is trust between us, so why do you hesitate to share something with me?"

Anin shrugged and continued her silence, not sure what to say.

"Would you want me to keep things from you?"

"Do you?" Anin asked surprised at her question and his hesitation was his response. "You keep something from me?"

"I have wanted to speak to you about it. It is only a thought, I have nothing to say it is so. I could be wrong."

"Tell me," Anin urged.

"When we were at the Wyse tribe, I spoke with Esplin. She told me a little about the tribe. The Wyse have occupied the land far longer than any would believe. Through the years the Wyse became sensitive to the land and to touch. One touch and the Wyse feel what others feel." Paine saw Anin's mouth drop open slightly and her eyes turn wide. "You are like the Wyse. One touch and you know what others feel. It made me wonder since you are not anything like your mum's tribe the Lammok that perhaps you truly come from the Wyse Tribe."

This time she did not remain silent by choice. Her husband's words had robbed her of her speech.

Paine continued. "The day I spoke with your mum to find out your whereabouts, I knew she would reveal nothing. She would die to protect you. I knew then that it was much more than you simply wedding the King that she wanted to protect you from."

Anin looked down at the ground, shaking her head slowly. Could this be possible? Could she be a Wyse woman? If so, that would mean her mum was not truly her mum. And what of her da? Was he not her da?

"It is only a thought," Paine reminded. "Your mum would be the one to know the truth."

Anin looked to Paine. "She would not be the only one."

"What do you mean?"

"What I did not tell the King is the reason the Drust wanted me dead...no woman of the Wyse Tribe would be allowed to serve the King."

"If it is true and the Drust knew it, then—"

"Others know as well," Anin finished and gripped her husband's hand tightly. "How do others know of me and I know nothing of who I am?"

"We will find out. The King has ordered your mum and da to Pictland."

"The King knows of this?"

"I had to tell him of my suspicions."

"Before you told me?" she yanked her hand away from his.

"I could not keep it from the King."

"But you could keep it from me?" She stood and went to walk away.

Paine's hand shot out, grabbing her arm.

"Let me go!" Anin demanded.

"No!" Paine said as he got to his feet. "You will listen to me. I know you are angry with me."

She shook her head. "It is not anger I feel for you. You hurt me by keeping this from me and confiding in the King before speaking with me."

"I had good reason."

"No, you have poor excuses."

He yanked her up against him. "I make no excuses nor do I have any regrets for my decisions. I did what I thought best."

"Best for who?" she challenged.

He brought his lips down until they almost touched hers. "For us."

She glared at him bewildered.

He kissed her lightly. "Listen well, wife, for I have much to say. Everything changed when I met you. Your smile, your endless chatter, your kind nature, and that you did not fear me—the executioner—stirred things in me I thought I had buried forever. The more you made me feel, the more I began to care for you. I fought against it, knowing no good could come of it. It was that day in the pool of water when you begged me to kiss you and I could not resist that I knew I could never let you go. Never let you wed the King. I continued to fight the thought, for I knew it could bring harm to us both. But then I had already brought harm to us by sleeping beside you, swimming naked with you, kissing you, and falling asleep with you naked in my arms. The King would learn of it all and I did not care any longer. When I learned the Wyse women possessed your skill and you could possibly be one of them, I knew the King would not harm you and he would definitely not wed you. I needed to know that you were safe from wedding the King and safe from punishment from the King before I spoke to you about it. You and you alone were foremost in my thoughts and everything I did was to keep you safe. And it matters not if you are Lammok or Wyse, since now you belong to me."

Anin threw her arms around his neck and kissed him.

Paine's arms went around her and held her tight, never intending to let her go, and her heated kiss let him know that she felt the same.

Anin tugged him toward the door and he lifted her off the ground with one arm and with his mouth not leaving hers, shoved the door open with his shoulder and shoved her against it to close it. Their mouths never parted, their kiss demanding more.

Paine was about to lift her and carry her to their sleeping pallet when he heard his name shouted. He moved Anin away from the door and ordered, "Do not move."

She smiled and peered around the door when he stepped outside. It was one of the King's personal guards and she wondered if the message had to do with the Drust. She saw that Bog sat next to the door, his eyes and slight snarl focused on the guard, which was why the guard stood a distance away.

It was not long before the guard walked off and her husband turned and hurried toward her. Something was wrong.

Anin stepped around the door and took quick steps to him.

"I must go to the King."

"What is wrong?"

"A troop of dal Gabran warriors come from the south. They will reach the stronghold on the morrow." He reached out, his arm circling her waist.

"Tell me," she said, feeling there was more.

"Your mum and da reach the stronghold on the morrow as well."

Chapter Thirty-one

Paine listened as the King and the High Council spoke of the situation, though his thoughts kept drifting to Anin. He had not wanted to leave her after telling her of her mum and da's near arrival, but he had no choice.

He was brought back to the meeting by the loud bickering of the council members. Some of the council wanted the King to strike at the dal Gabran before they got any closer to the stronghold. Others argued that the troop had not hidden their presence, but rode openly toward the stronghold. A ruse, the others were quick to predict and so it went on.

The King listened to all before making a decision, though Paine knew King Talon well enough to know his decision had been made before anyone had spoken. His quick response in many situations had been what made him victorious in battle. Some were happy with it and others were not, but the King's word was final.

The King announced a message would be sent to the dal Gabran demanding their reason for being here in Pictland unannounced. Scouts would be sent to track them. Some discussion followed, though in the end the King's edict stood and Tarn left annoyed that Wrath would decide on the warriors who would deliver the message and the scouts who would track the dal Gabran.

The King ordered Paine to stay and Wrath to return after he saw to sending the warriors off on their mission before it turned dark.

Atas entered the room after Wrath left and Paine saw the surprise and disappointment in her eyes to find the King was not alone.

"Do you need anything, my King?" she asked.

"No, go and wait my summons," the King ordered.

"With pleasure, my King," she said.

"Did you find out what your wife failed to tell me?" the King asked as Atas closed the door behind her.

"The Drust believe Anin is a woman of the Wyse Tribe and that she cannot live to serve the King."

The King looked puzzled. "How would they know for sure she was a Wyse woman?"

"I do not know, but I believe we will have answers when her mum and da arrive on the morrow."

"With Anin's abilities I might have been wiser to wed her."

"It was wiser you did not."

"Why? Would you have battled me for her?" the King asked.

"If I had to I would and I would make certain I won, but that is not why. You see all Wyse women birth a daughter first and birth more daughters than sons."

"Then you saved me from joining with a woman that would not have suited me at all. So, you think you would have won in a fight against me for her."

"I would do anything to make and keep Anin mine."

Wrath entered the room and talk turned to the dal Gabran once again, then to the Drust.

"The Drust warriors were surprised when I sat them at this table, gave them food and drink and told them what the other Drust warrior's mission had been," King Talon said. "They knew nothing of it. They were to scout as Anin said and nothing more. I also learned that it has been some time since they last received supplies from me and with little food they feared their tribe would not survive the cold that comes soon."

"Someone wants them to believe you are not an honorable King," Paine said.

"The traitor is using the Drust, trying to turn them against me and force a battle between us. I think this person intends to see me dead and the Drust as well, claiming the throne for himself."

"Do you think the arrival of the dal Gabran is in any way connected to the Drust?" Wrath asked.

"The Drust made no mention of them, but that means little if a secret alliance has been formed between them. We will find out soon enough," the King said and looked to Wrath. "The warriors are ready?"

"They know what to do," Wrath assured him.

Paine was glad when the King stood, signaling the meeting was at an end. He was eager to return to Anin. Paine left Wrath in the feasting hall as he watched the two guards at the council chambers doors follow the King to the second floor. It was not something they usually did, but with the present problems, Wrath had ordered guards to stand ready at the King's door.

Paine hurried off, though once outside he stopped abruptly a few steps passed the end of the feasting house. He thought he heard footfalls and saw movement in the shadows. Hearing and seeing nothing, he walked on. He turned at the storehouse and stopped, then as quietly as possible peered past the corner and waited.

It was not long before someone stepped out of the shadows. It was Tarn, the King's Warrior Commander. He looked quickly about then hurried away.

Paine wondered what he was doing lurking in the shadows and was about to turn and leave when another person stepped out of the shadows. Paine was surprised to see that it was Atas. What was the unlikely pair up to? He was sure the King would want to know as well. He would tell him on the morrow.

Paine smiled at his hasty steps. After late meetings with the King, he never rushed to his dwelling, but then he never had reason to. Now he had Anin. The thought had him quickening his pace.

Bog lay in front of the door, though he sprang to his feet when he saw Paine approach. Before he reached the door, Bog turned and headed to his shelter.

"Bog," Paine said and went to the wolf as he turned. "You did well, my friend. You protected what is ours." He gave the wolf a quick rub behind the ear and before Bog turned away he rubbed his face against Paine's leg.

Bog went to his shelter and Paine to his dwelling.

He was disappointed to see that Anin was asleep, though not surprised. The day had not been easy for her and she could use the rest. He stared at his sleeping wife as he shed his garments. He never planned to wed, never thought a woman would want him, and never did he think any woman would care deeply for him, and certainly not one as beautiful and kind as Anin.

He slipped beneath the covers and curled himself around her, and she turned in his arms to snuggle against him, her head resting on his chest.

"I will never let you go," he whispered and kissed the top of her head.

Anin raised her head, her eyes drifting open. "I will have your word on that."

Paine smiled. "You have my word and my heart. You have all of me."

Anin smiled and stretched her head up to kiss him.

Paine lifted her so their lips would meet and he savored her sweet kiss, fighting his need for more. She was tired from her ordeal. She needed to rest. She needed to sleep.

"I need *you*," she whispered.

He moved her gently onto her back and eased his body over hers. She was warm and soft and he was hard and aching. He nuzzled her neck, her skin sweet tasting. His head snapped up when he felt her capture him in her hand and tug gently. He groaned as she continued to tug. "I will spill in your hand if you continue to do that."

She stopped. "I want you inside me. I cannot wait. I need you now or I will burst whether you are inside me or not."

He did not wait. He spread her legs further apart with his knee and slipped into her with ease, his pleasure that she was so ready to receive him exciting him even more. He set a quick pace and she joined him, her passionate sighs pleasing to his ears.

Anin felt herself drowning in a pool of pleasure. Never had she felt with such intensity and it continued to build with each thrust of her hips against her husband. She wanted him as deep inside her as he could go, so they could share the power and the pleasure that joining as one could only bring.

Paine groaned and Anin felt him ready to release. She threw her hips against him, forcing her own release along with his, crying out as she felt them burst together and his seed spill into her. She hugged him tight never wanting this moment to end, never wanting to let him go.

When the last shudder left their bodies, Paine rolled off her and before he could slip his arm beneath her to ease her close, Anin snuggled against him.

She rested her head on his chest and smiled listening as the mighty thumping of his heart slowed. She draped her arm across his middle and sighed contentedly. "You do so please me, husband. I believe I will keep you."

She felt his rumble of laughter before she heard it.

"You have no choice, for I will never let you go."

She laughed. "It pleases me to hear that."

"You always please me, Anin."

She looked up at him with a smile, though a yawn quickly stole it away.

"You are tired, sleep."

"I am too curious to sleep. Tell me of your meeting with the King. Do we go to war?" she shivered at the thought.

"No, the King is too wise to be drawn into a trap, but he also will be prepared if a battle is necessary. He will wait and see what the dal Gabran has to say and they will be followed and watched. He also took your advice and spoke with the two Drust. He offered them food and drinks and discovered much as did the Drust warriors. They were surprised to learn that the other Drust warrior's mission was to see you dead and uncertain of the King's word on it. If anything, the King has placed doubt in their minds. They will talk more, but at least it is a start."

"What will he do with them?"

"Their fate will have to wait until the King deals with the dal Gabran, but they presently have no worry that the King will do them harm."

"What of the one who betrays the King? Is he not a threat to the traitor?"

"The King has seen to that."

"But what of—"

Paine kissed her silent. "Sleep. We will talk more on the morrow.

Anin went to protest, but a yawn stole her words and while curiosity had questions tumbling around in her head and ready to slip from her lips, her need for sleep proved stronger.

It was not long before Paine followed her into sleep, though it was concern for his wife that was on his thoughts. He wondered what her mum would say, but then if Blyth of the Girthrig Tribe was not Anin's true mum...who was?

~~~

Anin pressed her hand to her middle as she had done many times since she woke, wishing she could reach in and calm the flutters there. She was concerned with seeing her mum, though if it was true and she was of the Wyse Tribe then her mum was not truly her mum. Anin was curious and eager to learn the truth and she hoped the truth would not diminish the love she had for her mum.

She had combed and plaited her long dark hair shortly after she woke and had scrubbed her face with the rainwater in the barrel outside. She did her best to freshen her garment and she so wished that she had a decent cloak to wear, the one that had been given to her was almost threadbare. If anything, she would like to look presentable upon seeing her mum and da.

The door opened and Anin smiled upon seeing her husband. Her heart soared every time she laid eyes on him and it brought her such joy to touch him and feel how he cared for her and how content he was. The emptiness she had felt in him when they had first met was gone, not a dark spot left. He had changed and soon it would be too difficult for him to remain the executioner.

"What have you there?" she asked, seeing a cloth draped over his arm.

"A gift from the King for you," Paine said and walked over to her.

"I got the best gift I could have ever gotten from the King when he joined us, but there is another gift, though not from the King, that would please me."

Paine stopped close in front of her. "And what is that, wife?"

"Your baby inside me."

Paine leaned down and gave her a quick kiss. "I will work on that most diligently." He took a step back and slipped the cloth off his arm and around her shoulders.

"It is a hooded cloak and a most beautiful one," Anin said thrilled with the softness of the dark blue cloth.

"It is a small show of the King's appreciation."

"I am most grateful, especially with the cold not far off."

Paine slipped his arms beneath the cloak, circling her waist. "I will always keep you warm." He bent his head to kiss her when the horn blared through the village, halting their kiss.

"Who arrives first?" Anin asked, taking strong hold of her husband's arm.

"It matters not. The King wants you to be present in the feasting hall for both arrivals. Do not worry, I will not leave your side."

Anin nodded. The dal Gabran mattered not to her. It was her mum and da's arrival that held concern for her.

"We must go," Paine said and Anin nodded again and took hold of her husband's hand as they left the dwelling.

"What of Bog?" Anin asked, turning her head in search of the wolf.

"He has not had time in the woods of late. He will return later."

Anin wished she could have gone with the wolf. She missed the solace of the woods and the way the trees would whisper to her. The woods had always helped her clear her head of too much thought. She would need to visit soon, for her head was much too full.

Paine kept his wife close, a crowd having gathered to see the dal Gabran enter. The stronghold was heavily guarded inside the walls as well as outside and the size of the dal Gabran troop that entered was no match for the King's horde of warriors.

He eased Anin to the side away from the crowd, having seen something he had not expected to see.

"What is it?" Anin asked, feeling her husband's sudden distress.

"Do you know who that is that rides behind the two large warriors on horses?"

Anin stared at the man. He sat his stallion with authority, his wide shoulders drawn back and his head held high. Even though he was draped in furs, one could see he was a man of good size. While his features were not fine, they were pleasing and the many lines on his face spoke of an aged man as did his long dark hair that held much gray.

Anin shook her head.

"He is Comgall, King of the dal Gabran."

"Why would King Comgall come here to Pictland?"

"A good question. We will find out soon enough." Paine hurried Anin along and into the feasting house before the dal Gabran reached it.

King Talon stood in front of the long table and his personal guard and warriors lined the side walls. The King waved Paine and Anin to him when they entered.

"You will stay to the side with Anin if I should need her," the King ordered.

"I will not see her placed in harm's way," Paine said.

"Either will I," the King snapped, "which is why you will remain by her side at all times."

"Aye, my King," Paine said and kept tight hold of Anin's hand.

Anin stepped closer to her husband when the King of the dal Gabran entered the feasting hall. He was a large man, not only in size but in presence as well. It seemed as if he took up the whole room, though when King Talon stepped forward, Comgall appeared small in his presence.

"Why are you here in Pictland and why did you not send a message of your arrival?" King Talon demanded.

Anin was surprised when King Talon spoke in his own language and even more surprised when Comgall answered him in the same.

"For fear your stubborn nature would refuse to welcome me," Comgall said in a voice so deep it filled the room.

"So you admit you fear me?" King Talon challenged.

Comgall's face grew red. "I fear nothing and I am not here to argue with you or war with you."

"Then why are you here?"

"To claim my daughter!"

Chapter Thirty-two

Comgall, King of the dal Gabran walked over to Anin. "You are my daughter and you will come with me."

Paine pushed his wife behind him. "Anin is my wife and she stays with me."

Comgall turned an angry scowl on the King. "You will give me my daughter or I will go to war with you."

King Talon walked over to Comgall. "You do not come into my home and demand anything. Anin is the daughter of Cathbad and Blyth of the Girthrig Tribe. Can you prove differently?"

Comgall pointed a finger at Anin. "Her mum knows the truth. Let your executioner get it from her."

That had Anin hurrying around her husband. "No, no one will hurt my mum."

"Blyth of the Girthrig Tribe is not your mum."

"Then who is?" Anin demanded.

"I will speak to my daughter before I speak to anyone else."

All eyes turned to see Anin's mum walk forward, her husband Cathbad at her side. Both came to a halt in front of King Talon.

"You will speak here and now," King Talon ordered.

"I will not," Blyth said. "I will speak to my daughter alone or I will not speak."

Cathbad shook his head. "Blyth, obey the King."

Blyth shook her head and tears filled her eyes. "Forgive me, my King, but I must speak to my daughter alone first."

Anin rushed forward before Paine could stop her. "A word, my King?"

King Talon nodded and walked to a corner of the hall, raising his hand as he did to stop Paine from following.

If it had been anyone else, Paine would have followed, but he would not disrespect his King. And he was still close enough to protect his wife if necessary.

"My King, for the short time I have been here I have served you as you wished and will continue to serve you along with my husband. But I beg of you to allow me this private time with my mum. I wish to hear what she has to say to me before it is said in front of others."

"I will grant you this favor, Anin, if you give me your word you will be truthful with me in what your mum tells you and that you will touch her to make certain she speaks the truth."

"You have my word, my King."

"Then it is done. Go to your husband."

Paine stepped forward when his wife rushed to him and took hold of her, tucking her tight against him.

"You can speak with your daughter first," King Talon announced when he stood in front of everyone again.

"You let a woman dictate to you?" Comgall said with brewing anger.

"You let the mother of your child escape you along with your child?" King Talon retaliated.

"That does not concern you. You will give me my daughter," Comgall shouted.

King Talon stepped forward abruptly. "Make one more demand in my home and I will see you and your men slaughtered, then I will ride to dal Gabran land and claim it my own. Now hold your tongue until I say otherwise."

"The truth will be heard after I speak with my daughter," Blyth said, stepping forward and holding her hand out to Anin.

Comgall looked ready to shout and another quick step forward from King Talon silenced him.

The King looked to Paine. "Take the two women to the High Chambers room and guard the door."

Pain nodded, though he needed no order to do so. He would not stray far from his wife. He took a stance outside the closed door once Anin and her mum entered and Wrath came and took a silent stance beside him. Both their presence assuring no one would venture past them.

Mother and daughter sat next to each other at the long table and Blyth reached out and took Anin's hand. "Forgive me, my daughter, and please understand what I did, I did with your true mother's blessings."

Anin squeezed her mum's hand and waited, wishing she would wake and find this nothing more than a dream.

"I was on my way home alone from visiting my sisters, though your da had not wanted me to go being so close to the time you were to birth. But I had no worries. I had already birthed four sons without a problem, one more would not prove difficult.

"I was not far from home when my pains came on suddenly. I thought I could make it the rest of the way, but fate thought differently. A terrible thunderstorm struck. The slashing rain would not let me take another step and so I sought shelter in a dwelling I came upon. To my surprise, I found a woman getting ready to give birth. We helped each other as best we could and I delivered before her," —Blyth paused, a tear in her eye— "my daughter did not breathe one breath. I had no time to mourn. The woman was about to give birth and she was having difficulty. She birthed a daughter and

307

had only enough breath to tell me to keep her as my own and when the time came her tribe would claim her.

Blyth squeezed Anin's hand tight. "Fate had given me the daughter I had lost and the moment I took you in my arms I knew you belonged to me. I worried every day that someone would arrive and claim you. When your strange abilities surfaced, I grew even more fearful so I warned you against them. And when the King chose you to be his Queen, I feared the truth of your origin would finally come to light and it could do you more harm than good.

"You have my heart, Anin, you had it the moment your mum asked with her dying breath that I take you and keep you safe and I gave her my word I would. You were my daughter from that day on and you always will be."

Blyth spread her arms out and Anin fell into them, throwing her arms around her, and not because the King ordered her to touch her, but because her mum wanted to embrace her, hold her tight, and give her of her heart completely.

Tears welled up in Anin's eyes. Not only did she feel how deeply her mum cared for her, but she also felt her mum's worry and suffering through the years that someone would take the daughter she loved away from her. She also felt the deep sorrow she felt for the woman who had given birth to Anin and how strong her conviction was to keep Anin safe for her true mum.

Blyth sat back and continued. "I placed my daughter's lifeless body in your mum's arms, wrapped them in a blanket and left them for her husband to find, since she had told me he would come for her. She told me nothing of your father and I was glad of that. Your da knew nothing of my secret. He believed you his daughter and he still claims you are his daughter though he now knows the truth. I confessed all to him on our way here. Now I fear what my secret will do to you and possibly others."

"I trust my true mum knew what she was doing when she had you take me. Now the rest is for fate to decide."

Blyth shook her head. "No, it is for King Talon to decide what your fate will be." She looked away a moment, then turned back to Anin. "There is something else your mum told me, though she made me give my word I would say nothing and only tell you when the time proved right...you are of the Wyse Tribe. Your mum was a Wyse woman."

Anin shut her eyes a moment relieved to finally know the truth of who she was and oddly enough she heard the Giantess in her head.

Be who you are.

She had never been able to be who she was, since she had never truly known who she was, but now she did and she did not have to think herself different or strange anymore or fear what she was capable of doing. She could finally be...a Wyse woman.

Anin hugged her mum. "I am grateful you were brave enough to save me and grateful my mum was brave enough to give me to you."

"You have my heart, Anin, and you always will."

"And you have my as well, Mum."

Mother and daughter hugged and with hands gripped tight they left the room, Paine and Wrath following them into the feasting hall.

"Tell the truth now," Comgall demanded, glaring at Blyth. "Tell them all how you took my daughter and left the woman I gave my heart to, to die, leaving your dead daughter in her arms," Comgall accused.

"Let her speak," King Talon ordered.

Blyth, with Anin by her side, repeated the story she had told Anin, though said nothing of Anin being of the Wyse Tribe.

The King gave a glance to Anin and she gave a slight nod, letting him know it was all true.

Comgall disagreed. "Eviot would have never let you take our child. She knew I was searching for her. She knew I would find her."

"But you did not find her in time and she would not see your child die and for some reason she feared others finding your daughter, for she made sure I gave my word to keep her safe, and I swore I would give my life to do so," Blyth said.

Comgall shut his eyes and shook his head, his hands fisting at his sides.

"Eviot was your kept woman?" King Talon asked. "Your enemies searched for her?"

Comgall nodded as he opened his eyes and kept his chin high. "When I found Eviot in that dwelling, she and the baby wrapped together, I thought my enemies had gotten to her and killed them both. But my enemies would have never left them as I found them. They would have slaughtered them. Something was amiss, but it would not be until years later when those on my council attended one of the trading gatherings you began with your reign that he saw Anin," —Comgall looked to Anin— "the exact image of her mum that I began to wonder what had happened at that dwelling. When I sent a man to speak to the Lammok to find out who the lass was, and he did not return, my suspicions grew. I traveled here while a small troop of my warriors were dispatched to find out what they could and only one returned with news that my troop did not survive an attack by the Drust and the one I searched for was on her way to Pictland with the King's executioner. I was on your land without permission, without your protection, so I cannot lay blame on you for the loss of my warriors. But I came to claim my daughter, and claim her I will. You had no right joining her with your executioner. Only I, her father, can say who she can wed and I forbid a union between her and the executioner."

"You will not take my wife from me," Paine warned.

"That is for your King to decide, not you," Comgall said.

"We will speak in private," King Talon ordered and his personal guard followed alongside him as he walked to the High Council chambers, Comgall and his guard trailing behind.

Paine did not like the King going off to discuss the fate of his wife without him being present, but there was little he could do about it. But no one, absolutely no one was taking his wife away from him. He would take everyone's head before he would let that happen.

"You are wed to the executioner?" her mum said as if not believing what she had heard.

"I am," Anin confirmed, "and I am pleased and happy to call him my husband."

"You chose him?" her mum asked, glancing at Paine as if she still did not quite believe it.

"I did and he has my heart. We are one," Anin said with the conviction of one not to be swayed.

Her mum looked from one to the other several times before saying, "If he is your choice, then nothing more matters. It is what I wanted for you, to choose for yourself as Lammok women do."

"Perhaps it is what you wanted," Cathbad said, "but it will be the King who has the final say."

"I do not care what the Kings says. I will not be taken from Paine," Anin said and stepped closer to her husband.

"Worry not, no one will take you from me," Paine said and slipped his arm around her to pull her tight against him as if daring anyone to pry her from him. Yet he did wonder what the King would do to keep at least a tentative peace with the dal Gabran.

Food and drink were brought to the tables and most sat to eat, though some guards both Picts and dal Gabran remained standing, watchful of all that went on.

Anin had no wont to eat, concerned too much with her fate. Her insides tightened when she heard the door to the High Council chambers open and the King and Comgall entered the feasting hall.

The King stopped a moment to speak briefly with Wrath, then he proceed along with Comgall to stand in front of the long table.

Anin held tight to her husband's hand, her chest pounding.

"Anin, come here," the King called out.

Paine stepped forward with Anin to stand in front of the King.

"I order you to go with your father, Comgall of the dal Gabran Tribe."

Anin shook her head and turned to Paine just as Wrath and his warriors descended on him, ripping at his hand that held hers. "No! No! I will not go!"

Paine cursed himself for leaving his battle-axe by the table and squeezed Anin's hand until he thought he would break it.

Comgall shouted and his guards descended on Anin.

"No! No!" Anin's screams echoed through the feasting hall.

Suddenly her mum was by her. Even though weapons had been taken from her upon entering the stronghold, it did not matter. She used her fists, knocking warriors to the ground. Her da also joined in ripping warriors off Anin.

Paine roared like a mighty animal and threw off the men who were trying to hold him and tried to get a firmer hold of Anin, but more warriors descended on him.

Tears began to cloud Anin's eyes. She felt the fierce pain that stabbed at her husband at the thought of her being ripped away from him and it tore at her heart. She fought with all her might not to let go of him, not to let the warriors tear them apart. But it proved useless. More warriors piled on Paine until they took him to the ground and her hand slipped from his grasp.

Her mum and da had been yanked away from her and one large warrior held her firm around the waist as she kicked and fought to break free. She looked to the King. "How could you? He called you friend."

"I do what I must," the King said and looked to Comgall. "Take her."

The warrior hoisted her off the floor and as he carried her away, she screamed out, "Paine! Paine!"

Paine could not move, too many warriors were piled on top of him, holding him down, his arms spread. The pain in his chest at hearing his wife scream out to him for help and him unable to reach her was far worse than any torture he could inflict.

"I will come get you, Anin! I give you my word, I will come for you!"

Chapter Thirty-three

Pain sat in the High Council chamber trussed like a prisoner waiting execution. He dropped his head back against the wall behind him and tried to calm his rage. He needed to think clearly, needed to find a way to free of the rope that bound him tightly and go after Anin. After that they would run and go where they would be safe, but where would that be with King Talon bowing to Comgall's demand.

He shook his head. Never would he have thought that Talon would do such a thing to him, but it was not Talon, his friend, who had made the decision, but the King. It came to him suddenly like a whisper in his ear. He would go with Anin to the Wyse Tribe. They would be safe there.

Death would be the only thing that would stop him from going after Anin and he would not see that happen. He would do what was necessary to see he was freed, and he and Bog would go hunt for Anin.

Stay strong, Anin, stay strong. I will come for you.

~~~

Her husband's words repeated over and over in her head. He would come for her. He had given his word he would come for her. Nothing would stop him. But what if they crossed the border of Pictland? It would be that much more difficult for him to rescue her once they left Pictland. Somehow, she had to delay their journey.

She was placed in front of Comgall on a horse with her wrists tethered and she had not looked upon him since leaving the Pict stronghold nor had she said a word to him. At the moment, she felt nothing but hate for the man.

"Your mum was a good woman. I often wondered how it was she cared for me as much as she did. I forbid her to go visit her tribe with her being with child. There were my enemies to worry about. I also think I feared she would never return to me. I learned early on with your mum that she did as she pleased and while it often annoyed me, I also admired her strength."

Anin turned to look at him. "If you cared for my mum so much, why treat your daughter so cruelly?"

"I will not see my daughter wed to a savage Pict and certainly not to an executioner whose whole body is marred with drawings."

"Paine is no savage. He is a good man and we have given our hearts to each other. I will care for him always and no other but him."

"You will forget him in time."

"Did you forget and stop caring about my mum?"

"That was not the same."

"How was it not? All tribes beyond your border are Picts and that would include my mum's tribe."

"It was the reason I could never wed your mum."

"Then what of me? I am a Pict. Your people will never accept me."

"You may be a Pict, but you are also of the Wyse Tribe and will serve me well."

"Is that what my mum did, serve you? Did you ever truly care for her?" Anin asked angrily.

"Your mum was the only woman I ever gave my heart to."

"That is a lie. If you truly cared so much for my mum, you could never cause the daughter she gave you such horrible pain and sorrow."

"I do what is best for you."

"You do what is best for *you* like most others who rule."

"King Talon is a wise man and did what was necessary."

Anin turned her head away from him to show she would speak no more to him. The first chance she got, she would run. Paine would find her, and then they would run together. They would go someplace where no one could find them. They would go to her tribe...the Wyse Tribe.

They camped at dusk and Anin asked that her hands be freed, needing private time.

"If you run I will find you and you will be kept tethered after that until you accept your fate," Comgall warned.

Anin nodded and while it might appear she yielded, by no means did she.

Her wrists were freed and she walked into the woods with two warriors following. It was not long before the trees began to whisper to her, offering her comfort. Light was fading quickly when she told the two warriors she would be but a few steps away and after warning her not to go far, they let her walk off.

After only a few steps, darkness settled in and the warriors called out to her.

"I am here. I will finish soon," she said for them to hear.

Would she get far in the dark? Would they find her before she could get far enough away? Could she find a place to hide?

"Wait for your husband."

Anin turned, startled by the soft voice and even more startled to see Esplin standing a short distance away from her.

Esplin stepped closer to Anin and kept her voice low. "I have little time to speak with you, but there will come a time when we will talk at length."

There was so much Anin wanted to say, to ask that she found herself unable to say anything.

"There was good reason your mum gave you to Blyth. She knew the woman would care and think of you as her own. She also knew that you needed to live among the other tribes so that one day you would lead the Wyse Tribe with knowledge of the outsiders and wisdom."

"Lead?" Anin shook her head. "I am no leader."

Esplin smiled. "You are a leader and the daughter you carry will be as well."

Anin's hand flew to her middle. "I have been wed only days. How could you know?"

"You will know yourself soon enough. You know more than you allow yourself to believe. You are already growing in the ways of the Wyse and I will help you learn more, though it all will come with ease to you. It is part of you and you need only to embrace who you are."

"Who am I?" Anin asked.

"You are the daughter of Eviot of the Wyse Tribe, granddaughter of Esplin, leader of the Wyse Tribe, and one day you will lead the Wyse Tribe when my time is done."

Anin once again was speechless, though realized why she had felt the way she did the day she had hugged Esplin. The same blood ran through them. They were family.

"You must stay with your father and wait for Paine. He will come for you. Paine is a good man. He cares for you more deeply than I have ever felt a man care for a woman. He gives you far more than his heart. I told him some about the Wyse, you will teach him the rest. You both will live a long life and do well together."

"But the King—"

"The King does not rule the Wyse people nor will he or future Kings ever rule us. We were here long before they came and will be here long after they are gone. Now go and return to your father and wait."

"I have so many questions. I will see you again...soon, Grandmother?"

"You will see me soon and I am never far from you. You need only reach out to me." Esplin stepped forward and wrapped Anin in her arms.

Anin held tightly to her and the depth of caring that poured from the woman into Anin was astounding and brought tears to Anin's eyes.

Esplin eased her away. "You must go, but know this, Anin. King Talon is a true friend to Paine."

"Are you done?" one of the warriors shouted.

Anin turned her head to call out. "I will be right there." When she turned back again Esplin was gone.

"Grandmother," she whispered and it was then she realized that she had spoken in a different tongue with her grandmother. It was the language she had spoken when in the forest of the Giantess, the one she had not known she had spoken. It was the ancient tongue of the Wyse and the Giantess had recognized it and had known she was a Wyse woman.

She would do as her grandmother said. She would wait for Paine. She wiped the tears from her eyes and walked to where the warriors waited.

Once back at camp, her father approached her. "You were wise not to run. I had my warriors circle the area where you were. You would not have gotten far."

Anin wondered how no one had seen Esplin. That was one of many question she had for her grandmother when they met again.

"There is no reason for me to run. My husband comes for me. I will wait for him."

"You think Paine, one man, will conquer my whole troop?" Comgall asked with a laugh.

Anin smiled. "He does not have to conquer your whole troop. He needs to conquer only one man—you."

~~~

Paine pushed his back hard against the wall so he could help himself get to his feet when he heard footfalls approaching the door.

The King walked in first, though a snarling Bog hurried around from behind him and straight to Paine. Wrath followed in, shutting the door behind him.

Bog took a stance in front of Paine, his front legs spread and his snarl strong.

"That wolf of yours is a clever one," the King said. "He snuck his way into the feasting house and waited in the shadows, then jumped out when we opened the door to push his way in here."

"Sit, Bog," Paine ordered and the wolf sat in front of him, a low snarl remaining. "As clever as the King? You would not let the wolf in here if you did not want him here."

"One thing I can say about you, Paine, you were never a fool."

"Either are you, though of course I could not see that until my anger abated. Then I realized you would have never turned Anin over to Comgall with the intentions that she remain with him, not when she is so valuable to you. But more importantly, I believe as my friend, you would not take my wife from me."

"I thought you would figure that out once you calmed down, though I needed your anger for the plan to work," the King said and turned to Wrath. "Get those ropes off him."

Wrath stepped forward and Bog jumped at him, snarling.

"Enough, Bog!" Paine snapped and the wolf gave one last growl at Wrath before he moved aside.

Wrath undid the ties. "It took twenty warriors to hold you down."

"You should be grateful I did not have my axe or they would have lost their limbs and some their lives." Paine threw off the last of the ties and looked to the King.

"I made an agreement with Comgall. I would hold you only for so long, then I would unleash you. If you were successful in rescuing your wife, then Anin would remain here in Pictland and he would never demand her return again. If you failed, Anin was his to keep."

"I will not fail."

"I never thought you would or I would not have struck the bargain with him. As you told me, you would have fought me for Anin, so I knew this would be an easy task for you. I also agreed that no warriors would join you on this quest. It was for you and you alone to do."

"Good, for I and I alone will rescue my wife."

"Go and bring Anin home and be done with it, while I see to settling things with the Drust and find out who it is that betrays me."

Paine recalled seeing Atas and Tarn sneaking out of the shadows after a High Council meeting and was quick to tell the King.

"Interesting," the King said. "Hurry and bring Anin home. I believe I will have need of her to settle this problem once and for all."

"Come, Bog, we hunt!" Paine said and walked to the door, the wolf at his side.

Chapter Thirty-four

A roll of thunder woke Anin just as morn began to break and she was surprised she felt no fear, but then a shiver ran through her and she suddenly understood. The thunder was warning her. Something was not right. She looked around and did not see the sentinels that had stood guard around the camp. They were gone. She caught the sound of several rustling branches and as she jumped to her feet, she let out a scream.

The sleeping warriors jolted awake and had their weapons in hand as Drust warriors burst out of the surrounding woods.

"Anin!" her father shouted and fought his way toward her.

As several Drust warriors ran straight for her, she caught the movement of a dark cloak, slipping past a tree. It was the cloak of the King's warriors. Someone had led the Drust to them.

Anin had nothing to protect herself with, so she turned and ran.

"Drop!"

Anin's heart soared with relief at her husband's familiar command and she obeyed, falling to the ground without hesitation. He vaulted over her, swinging his battle-axe. Bog followed, his long, lean body leaping over her and straight at the Drust.

"Stay down!" Paine ordered as he took two Drust down with ease.

Anin saw her father take down a Drust and fight off another one as he ran toward her to join Paine in protecting her. She felt helpless lying there doing nothing, but she had no weapon and it would be of no use to her since she was no warrior. It was good she finally understood why and now she would learn a different way of protecting herself.

The battle ended quickly with many Drust lying dead and many dal Gabran warriors wounded and few dead.

Paine was quick to yank his wife up off the ground and tuck her close to his side, his bloody battle-axe tight in his hand if anyone dared to try and take Anin from him.

"I am unharmed," Anin said, knowing the question to how she fared was about to spill from her husband's lips.

Comgall went to grab Anin's arm.

"Touch her and you will lose your hand," Paine warned and Bog jumped in front of Anin, baring his teeth. "Anin belongs to me and I keep what is mine."

"My agreement with King Talon was that if you rescued her, I would pursue my daughter no longer. I wanted to know you cared enough to come after her."

"I care enough that I will kill the remainder of your men and you if anyone tries to stop me from taking my wife."

"After seeing you in battle, I believe you could easily do so. But I will have a moment with my daughter before you take your leave with her."

Paine hesitated in letting Anin go. His concern eased and he did not stop her after she laid a hand on her father, then nodded to him. She confirmed her da spoke the truth.

Comgall and Anin took a few steps away, Bog following along with them and bracing himself against Anin's leg.

"It is good that you not only have the protection of the executioner, but his wolf as well," Comgall said.

"They are my family," Anin said with a smile.

"You are pleased with your husband?"

Anin pressed her hand to her chest. "More than anyone would ever believe."

"I am sorry to say I failed to protect your mum, and there is not a day that goes by that I do not remember that, which made me all the more determined to protect you. Your mum made it very clear that a day would come when I would need to make certain that the man our daughter joined with was the man who would never leave her side, always be there for her, always protect and care for her. I gave my word to your mum that I would see it done, so I struck a bargain with King Talon since he refused to let me take you. I told him we would go to war if he did not agree. When he heard the terms, he laughed at me and told me to be careful. That Paine would take my life without hesitation or regret if I stood in the way of him taking you from me."

Anin smiled, pleased that King Talon had not betrayed his friend. "I had no doubt Paine would come for me."

"I may not agree with your choice of a husband, but your mum would be pleased with him and that he would remain forever by your side. Something I should have done with your mum. I doubt our paths will ever cross again, my daughter. I am pleased to have known you if only for a brief time and proud to see that you are as strong and courageous as your mum."

Anin stepped forward and gave her da a hug. Tears clouded her eyes when she felt his sorrow of not having known her and now having to let her go. She knew they would never meet again and her heart ached at the loss of never having known him or her mum.

Comgall walked with her back to Paine, Bog following close beside her. "I know you will protect her and keep her safe."

"I swear on my life, I will never let harm come to her," Paine said and reached out to take hold of Anin and ease her against him. "With the Drust on a rampage, I would leave Pictland as fast as I could if I were you."

"There is unrest with the Drust?" Comgall asked.

"A small band of troublesome Drust that will be dealt with swiftly," Paine said, not wanting the tribes south to think trouble was brewing within the Pict Kingdom and give them reason to believe they could forge a successful attack against the King.

"As soon as we gather our dead and see to our wounded, we will be on our way. Be well, my daughter," Comgall said and with that he turned away from them and joined his warriors, busy with the wounded.

Paine hurried Anin away into the surrounding woods. A short distance in, he stopped abruptly and pulled Anin into his arms. "I should keep you shackled to me."

"Fate shackles us. No one will ever separate us."

"I wish there was time to," —he kissed her quick— "we need to keep moving. A horse is tethered not far from here. We need to let the King know that you are still being hunted by the Drust."

"You did not speak the truth to Comgall about the Drust," Anin said

"The King would not want him to know that there is unrest among the Pict tribes," Paine said and hurried her along, keeping a quick pace.

"I saw someone wearing the cloak of the King's warriors just as the Drust attacked."

Paine stopped suddenly.

"I know why I am hunted," Anin said. "It is best we hurry to the stronghold and speak with the King."

~~~

It was well passed nightfall by the time Paine and Anin reached the stronghold and they went immediately to find the King. Paine sent Bog to his shelter after telling him he did well. The wolf reluctantly did as Paine commanded.

King Talon walked done the stairs into the feasting hall barefoot with only his long split tunic on, tied loosely at the waist. He was not at all pleased about being disturbed. "You rescued your wife, all is well. Why disturb me? You should be home busy filling your wife with a bairn."

"The Drust attacked the dal Gabran and tried to kill Anin. During the attack she caught sight of someone wearing the cloaked hood of your warriors. Someone led the Drust to the dal Gabran."

King Talon's eyes turned wide with fury. "Comgall?"

"He survived, but some of his men did not, though the Drust lost more warriors. Anin believes she knows why the Drust want her dead."

King Talon looked to Anin.

"It is not the Drust who wish me dead, but the man who has made them believe you have turned against them. He worries that I will learn who he is and of their plans and ruin their chances of taking the throne from you."

"You saw the one who betrays me?"

"No, but I know a way to find out who it is," she said.

"Tell me."

"The one who betrays you would have had to hurry back to the stronghold before the gates closed for the night as Paine and I did."

"That proves nothing, since sentinels drift in late."

"I believe the man, who betrays you, sits on the High Council."

"What makes you think that?"

"The High Council members are the only ones who would know the intimate workings of the council and the stronghold. They know the problems you face in finding a wife and keeping tribes content so that they do not rise up against you. They learn of things outside the stronghold and bring to you what is important. I believe one of your council members found out about me and fearing it would ruin his plans sent the Drust after me."

The King nodded. "The first missing dal Gabran warrior that was never found."

Anin nodded. "I believe he was captured by the Drust and he had no choice but to reveal his mission, find Comgall's daughter...a Wyse woman."

"If what you say is true, it would make sense that the leader of this attempt to take the throne from me is a council member?"

"I do not know if he is the leader, but once we discover who it is, we can find out the rest with one touch."

"I will call the council to the feasting hall, all but Tarn. He is not the traitor. He has been restricted to his dwelling since your departure and will remain there until I determine what to do with him. After you told me, Paine, of seeing him and Atas together, I spoke to them both. Atas wanted information about Anin from Tarn and persuaded him to tell her what he knew by means she is quite adept at, pleasing a man. She is in a prisoner chamber and after being there for a few days, she will be assigned a most unfavorable daily chore. But that is unimportant as to what goes on here. We will see who arrives and who is absent or arrives late. Anin you will wait in the shadows. " The King summoned two of his personal guard and sent them to inform the council members that they were to come immediately to the feasting hall.

Paine found a spot consumed by shadows and left his wife there, after saying, "I will not be far from you."

The members started entering the hall. Ebit, the Crop Master was the first to arrive. He was unsteady on his feet, wiping sleep from his eyes as he approached the King. The King waved him to stand aside and he did.

Wrath entered, his garments appearing as if he hastened into them and looked questioningly at Paine, then cast his eyes around the hall, knowing Paine would not be standing there so calmly if he had failed to bring Anin home. He went and stood alongside Ebit, continuing to search the room with his eyes.

Next came both Midrent, the Tariff Collector, and Gelhard, the King's High Counselor. Gelhard looked annoyed that he had not been the first to arrive and grew even more annoyed when he went to stand beside the King and he waved him aside to join the others. Though, he knew better than to object.

When Gelhard saw Midrent acknowledge Paine with a nod, he reluctantly did the same.

The council stood quiet while waiting for the last member to arrive.

It was some time before Bodu, the Master Builder, hurried into the hall out of breath, his face appearing freshly scrubbed. He bobbed his head to the King and joined the other council members.

The King turned to the council members. "Wrath, go stand with Paine."

Wrath did as ordered.

"A traitor stands among you," the King said an angry rumble in his voice.

They all protested at once.

"Silence!" the King ordered and glared at each one of them. "I will not abide a traitor. Step forward and speak the truth or suffer for it." When none moved, the King called out, "Anin, come here."

Bodu's eyes turned wide when Anin stepped out of the shadows, and he turned and ran. Paine and Wrath chased after him and were near upon him when he stopped, turned, and took the dagger he had already slipped from his sheath and shoved it hard into his chest.

Paine and Wrath grabbed him as he fell to the floor. His last words, "Death to King Talon."

Anin hurried over to him and laid a hand on his shoulder as he struggled for a last breath. She had never felt life draining from someone. It felt as if her own breath was draining from her and she sensed she had to let go, but there was a small spark of light and if she could reach it, she could possible learn something. She reached out for it as her breath faded from her.

She suddenly felt as if someone had blown breath back into her and she gasped and coughed and looked to see that her husband had hold of her hand. He had yanked it off Bodu.

"You will never touch a dying person again," Paine ordered. "You were gasping for breath yourself."

Anin took several deep breathes and smiled, grateful he was there with her. Her smile quickly faded and she grabbed her husband's arm. "Bodu led the Drust to the dal Gabran, but he does not lead the traitorous group that fights to claim the throne from the King—it is Tarn."

Paine stood, pulling Anin to her feet along with him.

The King had his sword in hand and was headed for the door. Wrath and his personal guard were close behind him and Paine followed, ordering Anin to stay close by him.

Flaming torches on tall poles lit paths through the village. The King's personal guard kept pace with him as he walked with determined strides toward Tarn's dwelling. A sudden shout halted their steps and changed their course.

Anin and Paine followed and Anin stared in shock as they came upon a King's warrior who lay dead on the ground not far from the prison chambers and at Tarn, holding a dagger to Atas's throat while several of the King's warriors circled him.

Anin shivered, seeing the fear in Atas's wide eyes.

"Help me, my King," Atas begged, tears beginning to roll down her cheeks.

"Let her go, Tarn, the King ordered. "There is no place for you to run."

"Give me your word I will have a swift death and I will let her go," Atas said.

"You have my word. Paine's blade will see it done quickly."

Tarn nodded. "I am sorry I will not see the day the throne is taken from you."

"That day will never come," the King said. "Now release Atas."

Tarn nodded and looked about to release her when he suddenly rushed forward with her and before flinging her at the King, he ran his blade across her face. Her screams pierced the night as sharply as the blade had pierced her face and she crashed into the King, taking him to the ground with her.

While everyone ran to help him, Tarn launched himself at Anin, screaming, "Die!"

Anin felt herself being shoved back so hard she fell to the ground and for the second time that day her husband leaped over her, swinging his battle-axe, this time giving Tarn what he had asked for—a swift death.

Chapter Thirty-five

Anin curled around her husband when she felt him climb into the sleeping pallet beside her. Paine had hurried her away from the chaotic scene after he took Tarn's head and made her promise to remain in their dwelling. She had no trouble giving her word. She was exhausted from the long day as was Bog who stretched out in front of the door.

She had dropped down on the pallet, her limbs feeling as if they could hold her no more, but she woke a few moments before Paine returned and hurried out of her garments eager to slip into his arms when he joined her.

"All is well?" she asked.

"For now," Paine said. "Atas is being looked after by Bethia. Her wound is severe and will probably leave her badly scarred. Wrath is trying to discourage the King from sending him with the two Drust prisoners and supplies to the Drust village to settle any problems and reaffirm his commitment to help them." Paine gave his body a good stretch before he continued, trying to ease the aches from it. "The King calls for a High Council meeting tomorrow to discuss who will fill the two seats, though he has suggested that my duties as executioner have dwindled with your arrival and that I might serve him better on the council as Master Builder since I have helped him build many of the small buildings he constructs before erecting the actual building."

Anin sat up beside him. "That is wonderful. Death and suffering will surround you no more. You will be free. People will not avoid you. They will speak with you and call you friend and when it is time for us to leave here you can help my people to build fine dwellings."

Paine wrinkled his brow. "What do you mean when we leave here?"

"I had no chance to tell you of my visit with Esplin."

"When did you meet with Esplin?"

"I went into the woods for a private moment with two of my father's warriors not far off, intending to run and meet you on your way to rescue me. Esplin warned me against it and told me to stay with my father until you came for me."

"Wise of her since the Drust was on their way and if they had found you..." Paine grabbed her and kissed her. "Remind me to tell her how grateful I am that she saved my wife's life."

Anin sat up beside him again. "Esplin is my grandmother."

He grinned. "I knew I was drawn to that woman for a reason. She is much like you. Is that why there will come a time you wish to leave here and go live with the Wyse?"

"It is more that it will be my duty to go. You see Esplin is the leader of the Wyse Tribe and I will one day take her place."

Paine stared at her, looking as if he was about to respond then closing his mouth only to open it again until finally he said, "You will be chieftain one day?"

Anin nodded. "As will our daughter."

"Are you..." His hand went to her stomach.

"Esplin says I am and I will know soon enough. You do not mind I will give you a daughter first?"

"I look forward to a little lass who will hug me and know without me saying that she has my heart."

Anin leaned down and kissed him. "We will have a good life together and grow old together."

"That is all that matters to me...that we are together always."

"Never to part," she whispered.

"Always one," he murmured and eased her beneath him to join together as one.

THEN END

To make sure you don't miss Wrath's story...The King's Warrior
and King Talon's story...the King and His Queen, coming soon,
subscribe to my Book Alerts on my website
http://www.donnafletcher.com/

Author's Note

There is little know about the Picts, the *Painted People* as history refers to them, though more is being uncovered through archaeological finds. While I sprinkled some facts that are known or believed to be accurate about the Picts throughout the story most all of what I wrote is from my imagination. Though, it seems with some new finds about the infamous *Painted People*, they are discovering that the Picts were not the savages they first believed them to be, but had more of an established society.

Titles by Donna Fletcher

The Pict King Series
The King's Executioner
The King Warrior (coming soon)
The King and His Queen (coming soon)

Macinnes Sisters Trilogy
The Highlander's Stolen Heart
Highlander's Rebellious Love
Highlander: The Dark Dragon

Highlander Trilogy
Highlander Unchained
Forbidden Highlander
Highlander's Captive

Warrior King Series
Bound To A Warrior
Loved By A Warrior
A Warrior's Promise
Wed To A Highland Warrior

Sinclare Brothers' Series
Return of the Rogue
Under the Highlander's Spell
The Angel & The Highlander
Highlander's Forbidden Bride

For a full listing of Donna's book go to
www.donna@donnafletcher.com

About the Author

Donna Fletcher is a USA Today bestselling author of historical and paranormal romances. Her books are sold worldwide. She started her career selling short stories and winning reader contests. She soon expanded her writing to her love of romance novels and sold her first book SAN FRANCISCO SURRENDER the year she became president of New Jersey Romance Writers.

Drop by Donna's website www.donnafletcher.com where you can learn more about her, get a printable Book List, and read her blog.

Made in United States
Troutdale, OR
11/13/2024

24745012R00206